Praise for
Lynsay Sands

"You can't help but fall in love with Lynsay Sands!"

—Christina Dodd

"Sands spins a funny, laughable tale;
you'll cheer as the drunk and the shrew discover
they are a 'perfect match'."

—Eloisa James on
Taming the Highland Bride

"Sands puts her own spin on the classic
Beauty and the Beast story line . . . while at
the same time delivering all the memorable
characters, red-hot sex, and danger-infused
plotting that her fans love so much."

—*Booklist* on
The Highlander's Promise

By Lynsay Sands

My Favorite Things • A Lady in Disguise
The Wrong Highlander
The Highlander's Promise
Surrender to the Highlander
Falling for the Highlander
The Highlander Takes a Bride
To Marry a Scottish Laird
An English Bride in Scotland
The Husband Hunt • The Heiress • The Countess
The Hellion and the Highlander
Taming the Highland Bride
Devil of the Highlands

Immortal Born • The Trouble With Vampires
Vampires Like It Hot • Twice Bitten
Immortally Yours • Immortal Unchained
Immortal Nights • Runaway Vampire
About a Vampire • The Immortal Who Loved Me
Vampire Most Wanted • One Lucky Vampire
Immortal Ever After • The Lady Is a Vamp
Under a Vampire Moon • The Reluctant Vampire
Hungry For You • Born to Bite
The Renegade Hunter • The Immortal Hunter
The Rogue Hunter • Vampire, Interrupted
Vampires Are Forever • The Accidental Vampire
Bite Me if You Can • A Bite to Remember
Tall, Dark & Hungry • Single White Vampire
Love Bites • A Quick Bite

The Loving Daylights

Lynsay Sands

My Favorite Things

A CHRISTMAS COLLECTION

AVONBOOKS

An Imprint of HarperCollinsPublishers

"All I Want" was originally published in the *Wish List* anthology in 2001 by Dorchester Publishing Company, Inc.
"Three French Hens" was originally published in the *Five Golden Rings* anthology in 1999 by Dorchester Publishing Company, Inc.
"The Fairy Godmother" was originally published in the *Mistletoe & Magic* anthology in 2000 by Dorchester Publishing Company, Inc.

First Avon Books mass market printing: November 2019

Print Edition ISBN: 978-0-06-296133-4
Digital Edition ISBN: 978-0-06-296134-1

Cover design by Patricia Barrow
Cover illustration by Anna Kmet

FIRST EDITION

19 20 21 22 23   QGM   10 9 8 7 6 5 4 3 2 1

Contents

My Favorite Things

All I Want

Prologue

$\mathcal{A}$ doll just like the one in Werster's window. That's what I want for Christmas."

Prudence smiled slightly at her sister's words as the younger girl hugged their mother and kissed her good-night. Charlotte had been making her wishes known for weeks now, and Prudence and her mother had been working very hard at making a similar doll for her for most of that time. The doll itself was finished, though not completely satisfactorily. They were not professionals at the job, but they had done the best they could. Charlotte was a good girl, though; she would love it no matter its imperfections. Especially since they were making tiny little dresses for the doll that matched each of the girl's own gowns. Prudence was positive the child would be pleased.

"Good night, Pru!"

She gave a grunt as her younger sister launched herself at her, hugging her hard before spinning away to rush out of the room. Prudence watched the little whirlwind go with affection, then glanced at her mother, frowning when she saw the unhappiness on her mother's face as she peered out the window.

"What would you like for Christmas, Mother?" she asked after a moment, hoping to distract her from whatever thoughts troubled her. Meg Prescott remained silent, so Prudence moved to her side to peer out and see what distracted her so.

Outside, two men stood on the front stoop arguing with Bentley. The last of their male retainers, the older man served as butler, valet, stablemaster, and anything else that was required. His wife, Alice, was their last female servant. The two did their best to keep the house running as smoothly as possible, but if things did not soon change, even they would have to be released. Prudence watched sadly as the older man doggedly shook his head and finally sent the two men on their way.

"Creditors," she muttered with disgust as she watched them go, though who the disgust was for she couldn't say. She could hardly blame anyone for attempting to get funds owed them. If her father would just—

"All I want for Christmas is for your father to stop his gambling before he sees us in debtors' prison."

Prudence glanced at her mother's strained face. Apparently she had heard the question after all. Her gaze returned to the two men as they went through the front gate and pulled it closed with an angry clang. Creditors were starting to arrive at the door every day now. And there were a lot of them. Her father, of course, was never available. When he was home, he was sleeping off the drink from the night before. When he was awake, he wasn't home but off drinking and gambling them closer to ruin. Bentley had managed to turn away the creditors so far, but soon they would not be brushed off. Debtors' prison was becoming a very real possibility. Why could her father not see what he was doing?

She glanced at her mother again and felt her heart tighten at the weary grief on her face. Things had been bad since Pru's brother, John, had died in a carriage accident. He had belonged to the Four Horsemen's club, where the sons of nobility went to race carriages they really didn't have the skill to drive. He had died when his carriage lost a wheel and he'd been sent flying into a tree and broke his neck. That was when their father, Edward Prescott, had started to drink and gamble. He had taken the loss of his oldest child and only son poorly.

"That is all I want for Christmas," her mother said now. "And I pray to God for it every day."

For a moment Prudence felt sadness weigh her down; then she grimly straightened her shoulders. Her mother was of the old school, where a wife did not question her husband or his behavior. Prudence was of the firm belief that when the husband was destroying his family, someone needed to alert him to the matter. Besides, it had always been her opinion that God helped those who helped themselves. Which left it up to her to see if she could help God wrap this Christmas wish up for her mother.

Chapter One

$\mathcal{P}$rudence accepted the hack driver's assistance to alight, paid him, then turned to stare at the front of Ballard's. The building was clean and stately looking, with windows on every level. It looked like a home. No one seeing it would know that it was a gaming hell where men gambled away their lives and the lives of the family members they were supposed to love.

Prudence blew an irritated breath out as her conscience pricked her. She supposed calling it a gaming hell was not being quite fair. There were no Captain Sharpes here waiting to cheat the gamblers who frequented the establishment. This was, by all accounts, an honest concern. But it was not a private club either. Membership was not necessary to enter. However, it did only cater to better-quality patrons. Proper decorum and a certain caliber of dress were required to enter, as well as the desire to stay and gamble your life away.

Fingers tightening around the handle of her umbrella, Prudence scowled at the building, then glanced to the main door and the three men entering. Two men, she corrected herself. The third appeared to be the doorman. He nodded, held the door for the other two, then closed it and settled in, arms crossed over his barrel-like chest, an intimidating expression on his face.

Prudence felt her heart sink. She very much suspected that the man was not going to let her enter. It might not be a private club, but that didn't mean women were any more welcome. Except as servants, she amended. Prudence had heard that Lord Stockton, the owner, had taken the innovative step of hiring female servants to serve the food and drink that persuaded clients to stay longer and lose more money. But those were the only women welcome inside.

Nay, the man guarding the door would not be eager to allow her entry. To be honest, Pru wasn't enthusiastic about the idea herself. It certainly wouldn't do her reputation any good. Not that there was much to worry about. She, her mother, and her whole family had already been as good as ruined—or would be the moment it was revealed the depths to which her father's gambling had brought them.

It would be only a matter of time, she thought unhappily. The rumors and gossip were already beginning to flow. The difference in the way the *ton* in general responded to the Prescott family was already notable. They were starting to distance themselves, not shunning the family openly yet—

that would wait until the rumors and gossip were proved true—but invitations to balls had all but stopped and no one spoke to them at those they did attend. Pru supposed that was why her mother now prayed that her father would stop before they were in debtors' prison and not before the family was ruined. It was too late for the latter.

Still, it was one thing for her father to see them ruined, quite another for Prudence to throw her reputation away, which was what she was doing with this visit. But this was the only way she could think of to get to see her father. Talking to him at home would have been easier, of course, but Edward Prescott had developed the inconvenient habit of leaving the house the moment he awoke each day, leaving his daughter little opportunity to speak to him. Perhaps that was why he did it.

The hack she had hired to get her here began to pull away, the *clip-clop* of the horses' hooves drawing her from her thoughts.

Standing about staring up at the building like a scared ninny would not get the task done, she reprimanded herself. Action was what was needed! Straightening her shoulders, she forced her chin up and marched forward.

Prudence hadn't really considered how she would get past the doorman zealously guarding Ballard's entrance, but taking him by surprise seemed her best chance. That being the case, she started out walking parallel to the building as if she meant to

walk past it. She moved at a quick clip, as quickly
as the slippery walk allowed. It had been unseason-
ably warm and had rained earlier, which was why
she had her umbrella with her. But the temperature
was dropping now that night had fallen and ice
was forming, making walking treacherous.

She waited till the very last moment; then, when
she was directly in front of the entrance, Prudence
veered sharply to the right and straight for the doors.
She nearly smiled upon seeing that the man was distracted talking to a new arrival and that her path
was clear. Tasting victory, she picked up her speed
and barreled ahead. That speed almost saw her
tumbling backward onto her fanny when the doorman suddenly stepped into her path. He was a solid
wall of human flesh, and Prudence crashed into
him, the air rushing out of her with an "oomph,"
then bounced backward, grabbing frantically for
something, anything, to keep her feet. She ended
up with a handful of his shirtfront clutched in one
hand, the other waving her closed umbrella rather
wildly as she fought to regain her balance.

"Ain't no women allowed."

Prudence grimaced at the growled announcement as she found her footing. Releasing her hold
on the man's shirt, she took a step back, tipping
her head up. Way up. The man was huge. Unnaturally tall, she decided as her neck began to com-
plain at the distance it was being forced backward.

Finally able to focus on his face, she forced her prettiest smile.

"Good evening."

His already smallish eyes went even smaller, signifying unpleasant suspicion in his bulldoggish face. "Evenin'."

"I am sorry to trouble you, sir, and I do realize that ladies are not generally allowed inside. However—"

"Never."

"Never?" she asked warily.

"Ladies ain't *never* allowed. Never *ever*."

"Never ever?" she repeated dully, then scowled. "Aye, but you see, this is a somewhat urgent matter, so if you would—"

"What sort of an urgent matter?"

Prudence paused, her mouth still open and her mind blank. She really should have considered a handy lie with which to answer such a question, she realized with dismay. He began to nod his head knowingly.

"It ain't real urgent, is it?"

"Oh—I—But—" Feeling panic set in as her chances of entrance dwindled, Prudence let her reticule drop to the ground between them. As one would expect, the doorman bent to pick it up. Seeing the opportunity, Prudence, quite without thinking, cracked her umbrella down hard over his big thick head. Much to her alarm, rather than bringing down her intended victim, the umbrella snapped in half.

"Now, what'd ye go and do that for?" the man asked irritably, scowling at her as he straightened.

Prudence stared wide-eyed from him to her broken umbrella, quite overcome with shame and horror. She had never, *ever*, used physical violence in her life. It only served her right that the first time she did, she'd broken her umbrella. Oh, this wasn't working at all! She would never convince her father to quit his gambling and drinking. They would all be in debtors' prison by Christmas, and would probably die there. She pictured her mother there, wasting away, her little sister's youth and beauty fading, her own hopes of a husband and children dying a slow, miserable death and, much to her horror, she felt her eyes brimming with tears.

"Oh, now, don't start crying. That won't work with me."

Prudence heard the panic that belied the man's words, and that only made the tears come faster. When he moved closer and began clumsily patting her, she turned instinctively into his chest and blubbered like a baby.

"Please stop now. I ain't angry with ye. Ye didn't even hurt me none, if that's what you're crying about." When that simply made her cry harder, the doorman began babbling desperately. "Ye can hit me again if ye like. I'll let ye inside, I will. Just stop your crying and—"

Pru's tears died abruptly. Her eyes shining with hope and gratitude, she peered up at him. "You will?"

"Ah, damn." The man sighed unhappily. "You're gonna see me out of a good job, aren't ye?"

"Plunkett! What goes on here?"

Hands whipping quickly behind his back, the doorman stepped away from Prudence and whirled guiltily to face the owner of that commanding voice.

Stephen. Lord Stockton. Prudence recognized the man at once as she turned to see him stepping down from his carriage. Everyone knew Lord Stockton. The dashing man was rather infamous—a member of the nobility who was accepted only reluctantly by the *ton*. If they could, Pru felt sure society would have given him the cut direct and excluded him from the more elite balls and soirees. It wasn't that the man wasn't noble enough; his blood was almost bluer than the king's, and his history could probably be traced farther back. Unfortunately, the man had committed that dreaded sin: he worked for a living! If one could call owning one of the most successful gambling establishments in London working for a living, she thought with irritation. It was his club that made him both undesirable as far as most of society was concerned, but also made it impossible to cut him out. The *ton* could hardly exclude him and risk his calling in the many markers he had on the majority of them.

Prudence watched the man approach and silently cursed her luck. She was sure the doorman—Plunkett, as Stockton had called him—had been about to let her slip inside. She was also quite sure that Stockton's arrival would put an end to that likelihood. The blasted man, she thought now with annoyance. She had been so close!

STEPHEN APPROACHED SLOWLY, his eyes narrowing first on his new doorman, then on the young lady the beefy employee had been mauling just moments before. The woman looked angry, but there was no missing the trace of tears on her face. As for the large man he had hired to replace his previous doorman, Plunkett stood with his hands hidden guiltily behind his back, a culpable expression on his face. He was also avoiding looking at the woman.

Pausing before the large man, Stephen snapped, "Explain yourself, Plunkett."

The doorman's round face squinched up in alarm, his eyes filling with panic. "I—She—You—" His gaze shot wildly from Stephen, to the woman, then to the door of the club before returning to his employer's steely expression. Finally, his shoulders slumped in defeat, he rumbled, "I knew this job was too good to keep."

Much to Stephen's amazement, that seemed to upset the woman even more. A scowl covering her face, she turned on him. "You cannot fire this poor man. He did absolutely nothing wrong."

"He was mauling you just moments ago," Stephen pointed out quietly.

"Nay. He was attempting to comfort me. I had—" She seemed to struggle briefly, her gaze dropping to the mangled item in her hand before she visibly brightened and held it up as if in proof. "My umbrella! I had broken it and was quite distressed. He, kind gentleman that he is, was attempting to offer assistance." A cagey smile came to her face as she turned to the doorman and said, "So, while I thank you for your effort to assist me, it is completely unnecessary. Now, if you gentlemen will excuse me, I should be on my way."

Nodding to each of them, the lady started calmly forward, a pleasant smile on her face that died abruptly when Stephen caught her arm and drew her to a halt.

"My apologies, my lady. But your brief upset appears to have rattled your sense of direction." He turned her firmly away from the door to his club, unsurprised to see the vexation on her face as she found herself facing the street. For a moment he thought she would go about her business, but then she turned determinedly to face him.

"I realize that ladies are not generally allowed inside—"

"Never *ever*," Plunkett rumbled, shaking his head sadly.

The woman bent a brief, irritated glance at the

doorman, then continued, "However, this is a somewhat urgent matter and—"

"What sort of urgent matter?" Stephen asked.

"What sort?" she echoed, looking annoyed.

"Watch out for her umbrella," Plunkett warned in an undertone, drawing Stephen's confused glance.

"Her umbrella?"

The giant nodded solemnly. "If she drops her reticule, watch out for that umbrella."

"I will not drop my reticule," the woman said through her teeth, making the man shrug.

"You did before."

"That was purely accidental," she told him firmly.

"Uh-huh. And I suppose breaking your parasol over my head was an accident, too," the larger man added. The accusation seemed to distress the woman further, and she began to twist the broken parts of her umbrella in agitation.

"It *was* an accident. It slipped." She was a poor liar, Stephen decided, and he nearly let the amusement building inside him escape in a laugh. The woman looked like she would like to hit his doorman again. She also looked vaguely familiar. He spent a moment searching his mind for where he knew her from while his doorman continued his argument with the woman.

"It slipped?" Plunkett said doubtfully. "And cracked in half over my head?"

"That is where it slipped to. It *was* an accident," she insisted. But in the pool of light from the lanterns on either side of the door, her face appeared to be as red as a ripe cherry.

"Uh-huh." Plunkett nodded slowly. "Just like your getting inside is an urgent matter."

"It *is* an urgent matter," she said firmly. Then, looking unhappy, she added, "To me."

Deciding he had heard all he cared to, and that Plunkett could handle the situation well enough on his own, Stephen shook his head and turned to enter his place of business. He had barely taken a step in that direction when the woman grasped his arm and tugged. Her expression, when he glanced impatiently back, was imploring.

"Please, Lord Stockton. I beg you. It really is important."

Stephen hesitated briefly, then, wondering why even as he did so, turned back to face her. "So what is this urgent matter?"

He was more irritated than surprised when she looked hesitant and glanced uncomfortably toward Plunkett, then down at the freezing walk. Stephen opened his mouth to repeat the question, but paused impatiently as a carriage pulled up behind his own, spilling several young dandies out onto the street. As they headed for the entrance to Ballard's, he took the woman's arm and urged her away from the door. "Now, why do you wish to get inside my place of business?"

"I need to speak to my father."

Stephen blinked at her quiet pronouncement.

"Your father is inside and you wish to speak to him?"

She nodded, her expression bleak.

"Why?"

"Why?"

"Why?" Stephen repeated firmly.

"My mother . . ."

When she hesitated again, he prompted, "Has she been injured? Fallen ill?"

The question seemed to startle her and she quickly shook her head. "Nay, she . . ." This time when she paused, he had the distinct impression she was mentally berating herself for not grasping at that excuse. Apparently deciding it was too late, she said, "Nay. As you might know, my brother died last year."

"I am sorry for your loss," Stephen said quietly, peering closely at the woman. Her words assured him that there was a reason she looked familiar. Apparently he *should* know her. Unfortunately he couldn't place her name or title. It was quite hard to tell what she looked like, too, with that prim little hat she wore and the way she kept ducking her head.

"Thank you. But you see, it hit my family hard. My brother was the only male child and it was an accident . . . unexpected, so . . ." She hesitated, head lowered, eyes fixed on the agitated movements of her hands. Then she took a chance. "My father took it poorly. He hasn't really recovered. In fact, he is drinking heavily, you see, and gambling—"

"I am sorry that your father is not dealing well with his loss," Stephen interrupted. He knew who she was now. The part about the accident a year ago and her father dealing with it by drinking and gambling had cleared up the matter. Her father was Lord Prescott, a regular at Ballard's. The moment he recalled the man, he recognized his daughter. This was Lady Prudence Prescott. "But you have yet to explain this urgent matter that—"

"It is all she wants for Christmas!" Prudence blurted over his voice, and Stephen frowned.

"Who?" Stephen asked in bewilderment. What was this lady blabbering about?

"My mother. She has been just as distressed by John's death, but is now troubled further by Father's behavior. He is gambling without restraint. The creditors have begun to visit daily and he is not even aware . . . or if he is, he does not care. He insists on drowning himself in drink and . . ." She paused, taking in what Stephen knew was an uncomfortable and even slightly embarrassed expression on his face at hearing such personal details, then forged ahead determinedly. "Several days ago I asked my mother what she wanted for Christmas. Her reply was 'For your father to stop drinking and gambling our lives away and come back to us before he lands us all in debtors' prison.' And I thought, well, the good Lord helps those who help themselves, and if I could just make him see what he is doing to us all, if I could just make him see . . . But he will not stand still long enough for me to approach him on the matter! He is out the door the moment he awakes. He heads straight here to gamble and . . ."

Her voice faded away and Stephen glanced reluctantly back to her eyes. He really didn't want to know all this about the Prescotts. He really didn't wish to become involved in their problems and had let his gaze wander, his mind searching for a polite way to excuse himself. Now he saw her disheartened expression and felt guilt prick him. The man was gambling his family's lives away while they stood outside in the cold winter air.

"Where is your carriage?" he asked abruptly, then cursed himself for the stupid question when her hands tightened on her broken umbrella and she blushed. He was surprised by the candor of her answer and admired the proud way she raised her head and the dignified voice she used to give it.

"It was sold for the creditors."

Nodding, he glanced toward his carriage, then took her arm and urged her toward it.

"What are you doing, my lord?" the girl asked, sounding more startled than alarmed.

"I am having you taken home." He paused beside his closed conveyance to open the door, then tried to hand her up into it, but she was having none of it. Digging her heels in, she turned on Stephen, her eyebrows drawing together in displeasure.

"I have no wish to go home. I need to speak to my father. He—"

"He is a fully grown man. And he is your father. He knows what he is doing."

"Nay," she said quickly. "That is not so. If he knew the effect his gambling was having—"

"He would give it up and return home to sit by the fire singing Christmas carols as a good man should," Stephen finished wearily, then glanced away from the stricken look on her face. After a moment of silence he peered back, a sympathetic expression on his face. "Nothing you say shall stop him, you know. You cannot change his behavior. He must do that on his own."

"I must at least try."

Stephen's mouth tightened at her determination. There would be no reasoning with her. She was desperate. "Then you shall have to try at home, Lady Prescott. Ballard's is no place for a woman."

"It is no place for a man either," she replied quickly, and he felt his guilt replaced by annoyance.

He was much less sympathetic when he said, "Ladies are not allowed inside Ballard's, and I shall not help you ruin your reputation by making you the exception. Now, in you get."

This time, when he tried to hand her into the carriage, she went. Reluctantly, but she went. He closed the door the moment she was inside, afraid she might change her mind, then asked for her address through the window. She gave her answer in such a low voice that he had to strain to hear it. Nodding, he tipped his hat the slightest bit in respect, then moved to give the address and his orders to his driver. A moment later the carriage was away, and Stephen was left to watch her pale face grow smaller as she peered out the window of the departing carriage.

He was annoyed to find that the image haunted him for the rest of the night as he oversaw his club, mingled, drank, and gambled with his guests.

PRUDENCE SAT ON the expensive upholstery of Lord Stockton's carriage seats, rage pulsing through her like a living thing. She was furious and frustrated, and knew exactly who to blame for it: one Stephen Ballard, Lord Stockton. He was the one who owned the club where her father was tossing his family's lives away. He was the one who wouldn't let her in to speak to her father and perhaps turn him from his destructive path.

"So ladies are not allowed in Ballard's. No exceptions," she said to herself as the carriage rolled to a stop before her home. "Then I suppose I shall have to go as a man."

Chapter Two

Tugging the carriage curtain aside, Prudence swallowed as she saw that they were nearing her destination. She had thought this such a good idea when she came up with it. Confronting her father in the club would have to be successful; Edward Prescott could not walk away and leave his daughter inside. He would not want the scandal. Prudence would finally get the chance to say what needed saying. But the closer the carriage drew to Ballard's, the more she was positive that this was a huge mistake. Terrible folly. And she had to wonder how Ellie could have possibly allowed her to go through with it.

Ellie. Eleanore Kindersley. Pru's tension eased slightly at the thought of her best friend. She had visited the other girl for tea that afternoon and proceeded to rant about her father's behavior, her fears about what it was doing to her family, and her failed attempt to get into Ballard's the night before. The other young woman had listened sympathetically, offering to help Prudence in any way that she could with the matter, and when Pru had revealed her plans to gain entrance to the club that night disguised as a man, Eleanore had applauded the "brilliant" idea and had even volunteered to accompany her. Prudence had quickly refused that offer—unwilling to risk the other girl's reputation—but had accepted the proffered use of her friend's private coach.

Well, it was really Ellie's father's coach, she admitted, hoping that Lord Kindersley would not be too upset at his daughter for lending it out. Eleanore was always doing good and generous things like that. She was a dear friend.

Aye. Eleanore is an excellent friend. But really, she should have dissuaded me from this folly, Prudence thought with regret.

Realizing that she was terribly close to giving up and telling Jamison, the Kindersleys' driver, to take her home, Prudence released the curtain and forced herself to lean back on the plush, cushioned seats to take a deep, calming breath. Unfortunately she didn't feel much better when at last the coach rolled to a stop. Peering out the window to see Plunkett standing, grim-faced and arms crossed, before the door of Ballard's did not help much.

Feeling her courage dwindling further, Prudence pushed the door open and burst out of the carriage, coming up short as the Kindersleys' coachman came to an abrupt halt before her, his expression horrified. Pru heaved an inner sigh, but managed an apologetic smile. Eleanore, of course, would never have bustled out of the carriage before the man could open the door for her. But then Ellie was always a perfect lady. Prudence was not. Perfect ladies did not rush about in men's clothes, chasing their fathers out of gambling establishments in efforts to save their families.

Ah, well, she thought philosophically, *no one is perfect*. Besides, she had more to worry about than behaving like a perfect lady, especially while dressed as a man. With that concern out of the way, she straightened her shoulders, stepped around the disapproving driver, and started forth.

Prudence had barely taken half a dozen steps when her breeches began slipping down her hips. Slowing her step, she jerked at them under cover of the cape she wore. Both items were her father's, as were the shirt, waistcoat, and cravat she wore.

Unfortunately, when Prudence had devised this plan, she had not considered the fact that Edward Prescott was a jolly little man of about twice her width. Neither had she recalled that her mother had given her brother's vestments away to charity after his death. Not that John's clothing would have fit properly either. They, too, would have been large on her—but at least she wouldn't have been swimming in them as she was in her father's clothing.

Prudence had spent a goodly amount of time this evening tucking and pinning the breeches in the back in an effort to make them look more presentable, and she had succeeded for the most part.

Well, they looked passable in the front. Unfortunately it appeared that her handiwork was coming undone. The moment she released the breeches they began to slip again.

Scowling in irritation, she yanked them up once more, this time anchoring them in place with a hand on her hip under the cape. Realizing how foolish she must look walking like that, she tried to add a swagger to her step to appear more manly, but found that the excessive activity made her head bob, sending the top hat she wore shifting forward on her head. It, too, was her father's and was too large for her.

At first, that had seemed something of a blessing, since it allowed her to tuck her long chestnut hair underneath. Now Prudence found it more of a problem. She feared it might slide right off her head, spilling her hair and revealing her gender. With her father's old cane in her right hand, and her left hand needed to twist the breeches on her hip, she was rather at a loss as to what to do. After one frantic moment, she raised the cane she held and used it to push the hat back. Fortunately the action worked; the hat shifted into place and Prudence was able to continue forward. She did so much more cautiously, trying to keep her head steady as she approached Ballard's front door—and Plunkett.

Pru hadn't really plotted this part of her plan. She supposed she had just assumed that the man would open the door and step aside for her to enter. He, apparently, had other thoughts. He merely stood in place, his expression turning mean as he squinted at her approach.

"Pip, pip, cheerio," she tried in her deepest voice, hoping her mounting panic did not show as she attempted to maneuver around the man to get to the door. Her heart sank when he stepped sideways into her path, firmly blocking her entrance.

"You look familiar," he rumbled, making Pru's heart skip a beat.

"Aye, well . . . Undoubtedly that would be because I am a regular at this fine establishment," she forced out, following the lie with the deepest laugh she could muster. Unfortunately, the effort scratched her throat and sent her into a coughing fit.

Eyes rounding in horror, Prudence reached up quickly to anchor her hat in place with the hand that held the cane, nearly braining Plunkett in the process. The doorman managed to avoid the blow with a quick duck and feint that would have done any boxing teacher proud, then scowled at Prudence, who, with both hands occupied, proceeded to cough rudely all over his folded arms.

Apparently deciding that holding her up was not to his benefit, Plunkett promptly opened the door, using the act as a way to step clear of her moist coughing.

"Thank you," Prudence rasped as she rushed forward, eager to get inside before the man changed his mind.

The door closed behind her with a snap, and Prudence had just begun to take a relieved breath when she realized that she had only managed to cross the first hurdle. She was not now in the gaming room; she was in an entryway with a cloakroom off of it. There was another door to get through, and two servants between her and that door.

Squelching the panic that rose in her as the two servants rushed forward, reaching eagerly for her hat and cloak, Prudence let go of her hat long enough to brandish her cane threateningly before her.

"I shall not be here long enough to have need of your services," she said quickly, then rushed between them. Pushing through the door, she raised her hand to moor her hat as she did. It worked.

The first thing to strike Prudence as she burst into the gaming area was the noise. There were well over a hundred men in the large room, and every single one of them appeared to be talking or laughing, each voice just a bit louder than the next in an effort to be heard. It appeared men were much noisier when women weren't around. Or, at least, when *ladies* weren't around, she corrected herself as she noted that what she had heard was true; Ballard's did have female servants. There were several moving through the crowd, carrying trays of drinks and various food items.

Prudence watched one such servant distribute drinks at a nearby table and paused to admire her outfit. The long, deep red skirt and snow white top were really quite fetching. Of course, it was nothing she herself would have dared wear. The skirt was just a touch short of being considered proper. Prudence even caught a glimpse of the girl's ankles as she hurried about. The scoop-necked top was a touch risqué as well, she decided critically, but all in all it was an attractive uniform. Since every woman present wore it, she decided that it had to be a uniform.

The entrance of new arrivals behind her forced Prudence to give up her consideration of the apparel Lord Stockton had chosen for his servants. Moving away from the door, she started through the room, her gaze shifting over the sea of men in search of her father. She had reached the back right corner of the club before spying Lord Prescott deeply involved in a game of cards at a table in the opposite corner. Spotting the pile of money in the center of the round surface, she wondered bitterly how much of it her father had added to the pile. The sum there would go a long way toward paying off their debts should he win, she could not help thinking. But that was the trick. He would not win. *She* would lay odds on *that*.

Determined that, however much he had already gambled away, he would be losing no more, Prudence straightened her shoulders and prepared to confront him. She was about to stride forward when a cry of pain by her side made her hesitate and glance over at a dispute taking place. Nearby, a tall, hawkish man had one of the serving women by the arm and was shaking her rather viciously as he hissed into her face.

Frowning, Pru moved close enough to hear what was being said.

"You stupid, clumsy strumpet!" the man said snarling. "This waistcoat cost more than you will make in a lifetime!"

"I am sorry, my lord. I didn't mean to spill ale on you, but you bumped my arm and—"

"Are you suggesting that it is my fault?" the noble barked, giving the servant a bone-rattling shake that had Pru's teeth aching in sympathy. Putting aside the matter of her father for the moment, she slipped closer to the pair.

"I say there, my good man," she said lightly, doing her best imitation of her father's cajoling voice. "Surely the gel did not mean to—"

Pru's voice ended on an alarmed squeak as she found herself suddenly grabbed by the cravat and jerked nearly off the floor. Feet slipping in her father's overlarge boots, she was suddenly standing on the very tips of her toes and nose-to-nose with the hawk-faced man.

"Did I ask for your opinion?"

Wincing at both the pain he was causing in her neck and the cloud of whiskey fumes that spewed from his mouth, Prudence glanced from him to the serving girl, who had tumbled to the floor as he had abruptly pushed her away. The servant appeared rather relieved to be on the floor, and Prudence couldn't blame her. The wooden surface was looking a fairly comfy place to be at the moment, she thought, then noted the shocked horror now coming over the girl's face.

"A woman!"

Pru's attention jerked back to the hawkish man at that exclamation, only then noting that her head was feeling a touch cooler than it had moments before. Alarm rising up within her, she forgot about the cane she held and reached up instinctively to feel for the hat that should have been on her head, nearly knocking herself senseless in the process. Prudence actually saw stars as pain exploded through her head, but it might have been partially due to the fact that the man had lifted her higher in his surprise and she was now dangling off the floor, her cravat becoming a rather effective hangman's noose.

Struggling for breath, Prudence acted instinctively and brought her cane down square on top of Hawkman's head. Her tormentor released her at once. Sucking in great gasps of air, Pru stumbled backward, just avoiding the retaliatory fist the man sent flying at her face as she tumbled to the floor beside the serving girl. She wasn't terribly surprised that the man had tried to hit her despite knowing she was a woman. After all, he hadn't been treating the serving girl very well. Everyone was surprised, however, when the blow he intended for her landed squarely on the jaw of a large blond man who had apparently stepped forward to intervene. The blow was enough to send the man crashing to the floor, and Prudence bit her lip and winced in sympathy, but was more than grateful that she had not managed to stay on her feet for that shot.

Silence fell in a wave that spread to the far corners of the room as the blond shook his head and regained his feet. Then Hawkman, looking pale and frightened, blurted, "I did not mean to hit you. I was—"

It was as far as he got before the blond man's fist plowed into his face. Prudence almost cheered at the blow. She did hate cowards, and any man who was so vicious to women, then quavered when confronted with a man his own size, was definitely a coward.

She watched with satisfaction as Hawkman stumbled backward, then winced as he crashed into a serving girl who had just come through a nearby door with a tray of beverages. The tray upended, sending the drinks flying over a pair of men; then all hell broke loose. The two men promptly joined the fray and were quickly followed by others— everyone soon striking out at his neighbors. The violence moved in a wave much as the silence had a moment before, rippling out over the crowd until everyone seemed to be involved.

Pru pushed herself up to a sitting position and

gaped at the riot breaking out around her, then scrambled up to rescue her father's second-best top hat from between two combatants' feet. Unfortunately she was too slow, and the hat got slightly dented and compressed. Prudence scowled at the damaged item, then glanced to the side a bit wildly when someone tugged at her arm.

"Come on," the serving woman cried, then promptly shifted to her hands and knees and began to crawl away through the legs surrounding them.

Pru stared after her in amazement for a moment, then, afraid of being left to fend for herself in the midst of the mob, shifted to her hands and knees and scrabbled after her. She started out trying to crawl while holding her father's cane in her hand. That was a painful endeavor, as she found herself grinding her fingers between the hard object and the floor with her weight on it. Leaving the item reluctantly behind, she found it easier going and was able to make much better time, despite having to pause every few feet to yank up her breeches— crawling about left her with no hands to hold them up, and the activity seemed to drag at them.

"Do you not think we would move faster on our feet?" she asked breathlessly, dodging between a couple of flailing legs to catch up with the woman, whose path was blocked by a pair of men rolling on the floor, fists flying.

"Sure, if you don't mind a fist to the face," the servant answered over her shoulder as she changed direction to crawl around the battling pair. The words sounded practical enough to Prudence, but she couldn't help thinking that she might prefer a fist in the face to a boot in it.

Pru had barely had that thought when she got a boot to the stomach as someone tripped over her. It was more a knock than a kick, but was enough to startle an "oomph" out of her and make her decide she would risk the fists. Pausing, she started to draw her knees up to rise, only to find herself assisted to her feet by someone grasping the back of her collar and jerking her upward.

Closing her eyes instinctively, Prudence clutched at her drooping drawers and winced against the blow she felt sure was coming. She was spun on her feet to face her assailant.

"You!"

Opening one eye cautiously, Pru nearly groaned aloud—Lord Stockton. She silently cursed her luck. Then, deciding that bravado was her best option in the situation, she beamed at the man as if he were a dear friend she had run into unexpectedly in the middle of a crushingly overcrowded ballroom.

"Oh! Good evening, my lord! What a pleasant surprise. And how are you this evening?"

Watching the red suffuse his face, darken, then turn to purple as his mouth worked silently, Prudence considered that bravado might have been the wrong choice.

"You!" This time the word was not shocked so

much as a long, drawn-out, frustrated and furious sound. Yes, she had definitely made the wrong choice with bravado. Perhaps throwing herself into his arms with relief and pretending to desire his protection from the mad horde around them would have been a better approach. She almost carried that thought through to action, but was denied the opportunity when a pair of struggling combatants suddenly rammed into her captor, sending him reeling. Prudence actually almost rushed forward to catch him and help him regain his balance, then realized that she would hardly be doing herself any favors and decided that fleeing was the better option.

She whirled away and started to try to fight her way through the crowd, only to quickly understand what the serving girl had meant. Not only were fists flying, but elbows were thrusting, and bodies were banging. It was almost impossible to get through the men on foot. Glancing over her shoulder in a purely panicky action to see that Stockton had regained his balance and was now fighting toward her, Prudence returned to her hands and knees and began to scramble past, around, and even sometimes through the pairs of legs shifting and stumbling around her, sometimes hopping along like a three-limbed dog as she was forced to yank at her damned breeches. Still, she was able to move much more swiftly like this, and she was just congratulating herself on the maneuver when she was collared again, dragged to her feet, then hustled through the crowd.

Stockton had pushed his way through the fighting men much more effectively than she had managed, she admitted unhappily as she was half pushed and half dragged through a door. Finding herself in the kitchens amidst the culinary staff and few servers who had managed to reach the relative safety there, she forced another smile to her face and tried to turn it on Lord Stockton. It was no easy task, with the way he still grasped her by the neck of her cape. She ended up smiling into her collar as she offered a cheerful "My goodness! I am forever in your debt, my lord. I was finding it nearly impossible to make my way through that mob."

She did not think it was a good sign when he merely ground his teeth a little harder than they had already been grinding and jerked her along, ushering her through the kitchens to another door. It turned out to lead to an office. His, she supposed as he pushed her inside and slammed the door.

She glanced briefly over the small, neat room with its sparse furnishings of a standing cupboard and a desk with one chair behind it and one in front, then turned to eye the man standing statue-still before the door. "I—"

"Do not say it!" he interrupted harshly, beginning to pace.

"But you do not even know what I was going to say!" Prudence protested.

"I do not care. Do not say anything. Anything at all," he snapped.

"Oh, now surely—" Her words ended on a startled gasp when he suddenly whirled and strode forward with an expression that did not bode well.

Alarm coursing through her, Prudence lurched back, only to come up against the chair before his desk. She opened her mouth desperately, ready to babble that she was sorry and would remain silent, only to have his mouth close down over hers as he paused before her. Eyes wide open, she stood completely still as his mouth moved over hers, her heart seemingly dead from shock in her chest. Then she felt the first smoky tendrils of passion stir to life within her and she softened under the kiss, only to be left gasping when he suddenly tore his lips away.

She started to lift one hand to her lips, but he had grabbed her by the upper arms and still held her.

"You kissed me," she said in a gasp. His mouth twitched at her startled announcement, then twisted when she added, "Why?"

"To silence you," he answered abruptly.

"Oh." She heard the disappointment in her voice and nearly winced at the softening it caused on Stockton's face, positive he would now feel pity for her. Prudence wasn't left to worry over the possibility long. Despite his claim that he had kissed her to silence her, and the fact that she had finally fallen silent, he suddenly covered her lips again, his mouth moving warm and firm over hers. Pru tried to resist the feelings the kiss stirred in her. Well, all right, perhaps she didn't try very hard. It wasn't more than a moment before she gave in on a soft sigh and let her hands slide up around his neck as she kissed him back.

He had opened his mouth over hers, prodding gently at her lips with his tongue to urge them apart, turning the kiss into a terribly interesting experience for Prudence, when a knock at the door interrupted them. Breaking away, Lord Stockton moved a couple of steps distant and turned to call out for the person to enter.

Pru sucked her lower lip into her mouth, tasting him on it as she watched the door open to reveal Plunkett.

"I put an end to the fighting, my lord, and—" The large man's words died as his gaze slid to Prudence. Seeing the shock on his face, Pru grimaced, knowing that the large man no doubt now recognized her and understood why she had seemed so familiar. But then Stephen frowned and followed the man's gaze, his expression changing to one of consternation. When he quickly stepped in front of her, sheltering her from view, she had the most horrendous idea that—

Glancing down, she cried out in horror. Her father's breeches were lying in a pool around her feet. She had given up her hold on them to put her arms around his neck, and apparently the kiss had been sufficiently distracting that she hadn't noticed when they glided down her legs. Only her father's overly large shirt was left to cover her where the cape was open, and that reached only partway down her thighs.

Her face burning with embarrassment, Prudence bent quickly to pull the trousers back up, not even hearing Stephen's babbling excuse. She pushed past both men and fled as fast as her feet would carry her.

STEPHEN TOOK A step forward, intending to chase after Prudence, then caught himself with a sigh. The poor girl had been thoroughly humiliated. His chasing after her would achieve nothing more than to embarrass her further. Besides, he had already proven that he couldn't be trusted around her. He had been enraged when he had spotted her there in his gaming room, shocked that she would dare enter—dressed as a man no less—and furious that she would risk her reputation so. But all that shock and fury had quickly turned to a different sort of fire the moment he had gotten her alone. And hadn't that been a brilliant idea? He took a moment to berate himself for treating her so cavalierly. At the time, kissing her had seemed an acceptable alternative to the throttling she deserved. Obviously he hadn't been thinking very clearly. No lady deserved to be treated as thoughtlessly as he had just done.

Not that she had fought him off, he thought,

enjoying the memory, then gave himself a shake. The girl was obviously as innocent as a babe. She had probably been overwhelmed by his attention. Hell, he had been overwhelmed himself. But his behavior had been simply unacceptable.

A quiet shuffling drew his attention. Plunkett still stood just inside the door, but his stunned expression at the sight of Prudence with her drawers on the floor had turned to grim disapproval that the man was directing straight at his employer. Stephen felt himself straighten defensively.

"I had nothing to do with her trousers falling down." The words came blurting out without his volition. He really had no need to explain himself to his staff. Still, the words came out, and when Plunkett looked doubtful—as anyone would after seeing the red, swollen, obviously just-kissed state of Prudence's lips—Stephen felt compelled to explain further. "Well, I did kiss her, but . . . it is not as if we have not been introduced. We have met at various balls."

That wasn't strictly true. Stephen had attended several of the same balls as the Prescotts and always noted their daughter's presence. Prudence was a lovely woman. Her beauty was the sort that shone through like a collection of snow white daisies in a mixed arrangement, not screaming for first attention like a red rose with its hidden thorns, but subtly drawing the eye with its soft loveliness. Of course, with his precarious situation in the *ton*, he hadn't ever approached the woman until just recently. It was only when the rumors and gossip had begun to circulate about the state of the Prescott finances, when the rest of the *ton* had begun to draw away, that he had dared ask for a dance or two. He had not wanted to sully her with his reputation.

But with the *ton* acting as they were, it had given him the perfect opportunity. He had approached under the guise of saving her from being a wallflower, something he had done in the past with other shy young ladies. That had been the ruse under which he had made his polite request, and he had found himself drawn to the girl with her soft voice and quick wit. The only reason he hadn't recognized her right away that first night outside his club was because of the darkness, the unexpectedness of her presence there, that silly hat she had been wearing, and the way she had been bundled against the cold.

Aware that Plunkett was still glaring at him like a father who had caught him mauling his daughter, Stephen shifted impatiently. "You say the fighting has ended?"

Plunkett spent another moment looking down his stub of a nose at Stephen, then nodded slowly. "Had to clear out the club to do it, though. The place is empty and the doors locked. Should I open 'em up again?"

Moving behind his desk, Stephen made a face and shook his head. He dropped wearily into his chair. "No. That was enough excitement for one night. Is there much damage?"

"A couple tables broke and a couple of the serving girls got roughed up. Sally took a nasty poke to the eye. It's swollen shut and blackening bad, and I think Belle's got a cracked rib or two."

Stephen scowled. For all the years that he had been in this business, it still startled him to see how a little drink and a game of cards could bring out the worst in these supposed "men of nobility." Some nights he was ashamed to be counted a member of them, and those nights were coming more and more frequently. Stephen had always loathed the weakness that shone through as he watched desperate men gamble away what little they had left in the hopes of making a fortune. But more and more often of late, he was also bearing witness to a cruelty hidden beneath some of those men's suave exteriors. It wearied his soul and made him think that perhaps it was time to get out of this business. He had even looked into several alternative ventures, but had not struck on anything as lucrative yet. Once he did . . .

Shrugging his thoughts away, he turned his attention to the matter at hand. "Take Sally and Belle to be tended; then see them home. Here." Unlocking the drawer of his desk, he retrieved a sack and tossed it to his doorman. "Split this between them and tell them not to come back until they are recovered."

Nodding, the large man turned and left him alone with his thoughts, which promptly returned to the woman he had been kissing only moments before. Damn, she had looked fine in breeches. Even sagging, baggy breeches. But, he thought with a small smile, she had looked even better with them pooled around her ankles.

Chapter Three

Oh, dear."

"'Oh, dear' is right!" Prudence quit her pacing and dropped glumly onto the settee beside Eleanore. The Kindersleys' town house was where Prudence had taken her father's clothes to change into them before attempting her infiltration of Ballard's. After fleeing the scene of her humiliation, she had been forced to return to change back into her gown. She would have preferred to have Jamison take her straight home, where she could weep over her humiliating failure in private, but, dressed as she had been, going home had been impossible. Meg Prescott was not aware of what her daughter was up to. It was her Christmas wish, after all. Besides, she probably wouldn't have approved.

Now that she was here and had revealed the humiliating results of her venture, Prudence found that she did actually feel a touch better. Eleanore's sympathy was a soothing balm.

"What was it like?"

Pru turned a confused gaze to her friend. "What?

Realizing that I was standing there with Father's breeches down around my ankles like some—"

"Nay."

The other woman started to smile, but bit it back quickly, Prudence noticed.

"Nay," she repeated. "I meant the kiss. What was his kiss like?"

Prudence glanced away, her mouth twitching and twisting before she could control it. She wasn't at all surprised to find her friend curious about *that*. They had often talked about the members of the *ton*, discussing the men they found attractive and such. Stephen had been one of them.

He was terribly handsome and debonair. And she and Eleanore were not the only ones who thought so. The older set among the *ton* might have resented having to admit him to society, but the younger ladies were more than happy to have him around, and they often vied for his attention. Eleanore and Prudence had never been among those who vied, but they had certainly noticed the man and would not have said nay had he asked for a dance, or the opportunity to fetch them a refreshment.

It wasn't just that he was attractive, but he had shown his kindness on several occasions. It was well known that he had a tendency to befriend those the *ton* saw as just barely acceptable, and there was never a wallflower so long as he was in attendance. He made a point of being introduced, and of making everyone feel included. Pru and Ellie had both appreciated that. Especially Prudence, who just lately had found herself in need of being rescued from being a wallflower. She rarely attended social functions, but had on one or two occasions under pressure from Eleanore. Unable to afford a new gown, she had been forced to wear last season's fashions. That fact had been recognized at once by all, and the fact that it meant the family's wealth was now failing had been understood. There was nothing the *ton* fled from faster than those whose wealth was dwindling. Prudence had found herself in the uncomfortable position of being avoided by most people as if she had the plague. And absolutely no one had asked her to dance—except for Stephen, once, at each of the events. No, he might not have recalled her upon their meeting, but she had had no problems remembering him.

If she were honest with herself, Prudence would admit that after each affair she had wasted several minutes lying abed at night fantasizing that they had shared more than a dance. She imagined that she had seen a certain something in his eyes as they had moved about the dance floor, and that he would someday sweep into her life and save her from the embarrassing situation her father was dragging them all into. But that had been before she learned that he actually owned the establishment her father favored for his destructive behavior. Oh, she had known that he owned some sort of hall, but she hadn't realized it was one where gambling took place—or that it was the exact one her father spent most of his time at. Prudence had stopped fantasizing about the man the moment she had learned that. Well, all right. So she hadn't stopped fantasizing about him, but she had taken to berating herself most firmly afterward for doing so.

"Well?"

Pru turned her attention back to Eleanore at her friend's impatient prompting and shrugged. "It was a kiss, Eleanore. Just a kiss."

"Uh-huh. Just a kiss that distracted you enough that you did not even notice you were losing your trousers."

Prudence felt her face flush with remembered embarrassment, then shifted impatiently and got up to pace again. "Can we not concentrate on my problem? What am I to do now? Plunkett will not let women in and would not be fooled by my being disguised as a man again. I must find another way to get inside."

"Can you not just confront your father at home, Pru? Surely that would be easier than—"

"Nay. He leaves the moment he arises."

"Catch him on his way out then."

"I have attempted to do so, but he continually evades me. Yesterday I waited outside his door for two hours. I left to visit the privy—for just a minute, mind—and he slipped out while I was gone. I think he must have been watching out his keyhole and waited for me to leave."

"Hmm." They both fell silent as Eleanore pondered this news; then she murmured, "Perhaps you should try a different approach."

"What do you mean?" Prudence stopped her pacing and turned to eye her friend with interest.

"Well, you have said that he drinks first, then gambles?" When she nodded at that, Ellie suggested, "Well, if you could prevent his drinking, he might stop gambling."

Prudence considered that briefly. "Think you that would really work?"

"Well, the one does seem to follow the other. Does it not?"

"Aye."

The other girl shrugged. "So if you stop him from drinking, mayhap the gambling will seem less appealing."

A smile slowly blossomed on Pru's face at her friend's logic. It seemed sound to her. "Eleanore, you are brilliant!" she pronounced at last, making the other girl flush with pleasure. "But how?"

"How?"

"How am I to prevent his drinking? He does most of his imbibing out of the house."

"Oh." Eleanore fretted over the problem briefly, then suddenly got to her feet and hurried from the salon. Prudence watched her go with confusion and even stood, uncertain whether to follow her friend or not. But before she could reach the door, Ellie was rushing back into the room, a book in hand.

"What is that?" Prudence asked.

"One of my mother's books of general advice. It includes a medical dictionary. I thought to see what it advises regarding imbibing intoxicants." Leading Prudence back to the settee, Eleanore settled there, waited until Prudence had arranged herself beside her, then held the book between them and began riffling through the pages, muttering under her breath. "Intoxicants, intoxicants, intoxi—No intoxicants, but they do have intoxication," she said with quiet excitement, and lifted the book closer to her face to read. "'Although literally meaning "poisoning of the blood by alco—"'"

"Skip over that part, Ellie, and find what they suggest to rectify the problem," Prudence urged impatiently.

"Suggestions." Eleanore scanned the long paragraph, reading various words aloud as she went. "'Imagination is excited' . . . 'symptoms' . . . 'delirium—'" She scowled impatiently. "Nay, all they say is that 'in cases of poisoning, vomiting should be induced by a subcutaneous injection of apomorphine.'"

"Apomorphine?"

"An emetic," she explained.

"Oh."

"But your father hardly drinks to the point of poisoning himself."

Prudence snorted. "Nay. Not himself, just our lives." She was silent for a moment, misery making her slump; then her head slowly lifted, scheming obvious on her face.

Eleanore eyed her warily. "I know that look. It usually precedes trouble. Prudence, what are you thinking?"

"Think you that there are such things as oral emetics?"

Ellie slammed the book closed, alarm clear on her face. "Prudence!"

"It is perfect!" she cried excitedly. "A bout or two of drinking that leaves him hanging over the chamber pot ere he gets too sotted might cure him of any desire to drink and thereby end his gambling!"

"Pru!"

"Oh, do not look at me like that, Ellie," she snapped with irritation. "I am desperate. I no more wish to end up in debtors' prison than you would. He will ruin us with his drinking and gambling. He has been doing both steadily since John died. I am sure that if we could but keep him sober for a day or two, he would regain enough of his wits to realize what he is doing to our family."

"But—"

"How would you feel if it were *your* father?"

Eleanore fell silent. Prudence watched several expressions flit across her friend's face until resignation settled there. Placing the book on the settee between them, the girl stood and silently left the room.

Prudence promptly picked up the book she had left behind and leafed through it, looking for *gambling*, *betting*, and *excesses*, but none of those terms was to be found. It seemed such was an ailment of the soul, not the body. Sighing, she had just set the book aside when Eleanore hurried back into the room, a large bottle gripped tightly in her hands.

"What is it?" Prudence asked curiously as her friend handed it to her, her lower lip caught between her teeth.

"Do you recall when Bessy had a sour stomach?"

"Bessy?" Prudence shook her head with confusion. "Your horse?"

Eleanore nodded. "At the time the stablemaster was sure she had eaten something she shouldn't have. He procured this to help her remove it." When Prudence stared at her blankly, she sighed and elucidated. "This concoction encouraged her to bring it back up. It is an emetic."

Prudence's eyes widened incredulously. "You think I should give my father a horse emetic?"

The other girl hesitated, looking uncertain. "Perhaps it is a bad idea."

"Nay!" Prudence stood and moved swiftly out of reach when Ellie tried to grab the bottle back. Crossing the room, she peered at it with fascination. "A horse emetic."

"Prudence, I do not think . . ." Eleanore trailed her across the room anxiously.

"But it is perfect. It should have the same results with Papa, do you not think? How much did your stablemaster give Bessy? And how long before it took effect?"

Ellie grimaced. "A couple of spoonfuls. It took effect immediately, but a man is much smaller than Bessy. I do not think more than a drop or so should be used. I—Oh, Prudence, I do not think it should be used at all. This was a terrible idea. Please just give it to me and let us forget this."

"And shall you visit me in debtors' prison?" Prudence asked quietly, turning to face her friend. Eleanore paused, a struggle taking place on her face, until she gave in with a sigh.

"How will you administer it? For your plan to work, if it is going to work at all," she added dryly, "he must receive it while he is drinking. He does that at the club, for the most part. You just finished regaling me with your last foray into Ballard's. After tonight Plunkett will be on the lookout for you. Disguising yourself as a man will not work."

"Aye," Prudence murmured thoughtfully, then slowly smiled. "Plunkett will never again let me through Ballard's *front* door."

TURNING AWAY FROM the ale barrel, Prudence took a few steps, then paused to scowl down at her chest. Muttering under her breath, she balanced the tray with the single mug of ale in one hand, using the other to tug uselessly at the neckline of the white top she wore. Honestly, it was as indecent as could be, she thought impatiently, and wasted a moment wishing she had worn one of her own gowns. Of course, that was impossible. She had seen for herself that all the girls wore the same costume: the red skirt and rather blousy white top with a scoop neck. But this one seemed extremely scooped to Prudence. Her nipples were nearly showing!

Realizing it was a wasted effort, Prudence gave up tugging at the top. She had had to work hard for the use of the indecent outfit for the night. Well, not the whole night. Pru had assured the girl she would need to take her place for only a matter of moments, just long enough to get a message to the man she loved. That was what she had told the girl. Of course, the truth was that she wanted a way to deliver the emetic to her father, but she could hardly have told Lizzy that. The servant's gratitude for Pru's intervention with the hawk-faced man had stretched far enough for Lizzy to agree to loan her gown to Prudence and let her briefly take her place as a servant inside Ballard's, but she suspected it would not have done so had the girl known Pru's true intentions.

Prudence had salved her conscience about the lie by telling herself that it wasn't a complete falsehood. She *did* love her father, and the emetic *was* a message . . . of sorts.

Deciding it was a sad day indeed when a woman began lying to herself, Prudence moved out of the kitchen, then paused to peer around the club proper. She had waited outside the back entrance of the establishment the night before, doing her best to ignore the fact that she was standing in a dark, stinking alley as she had waited for the place to close and the workers to leave. Most of the women had left in pairs or groups. At last Lizzy had straggled out, all alone and one of the last to leave. When Prudence had recognized her as the serving woman that the hawk-faced man had been manhandling, she had pulled her cloak closer about herself and proceeded to follow. Trying to move silently, and staying in the shadows as much as possible, she had trailed the girl up the alley leading from the back of the building around to the front. She had followed Lizzy along several roads, grateful to know that Eleanore's driver was following her for protection—even more grateful that her friend had insisted she use the coach and the family's discreet driver for the excursion.

Once far enough away from the club that she thought no one from it would witness the exchange, she had approached the girl with a story of true love hampered by disapproving parents and her need to get a message to her lover. Lizzy had been sympathetic, but the girl was also the pragmatic sort and hadn't been willing to risk her job to aid in the escapade. Prudence had been forced to resort to bribery, doing her best not to wince as she had bartered away a necklace of some sentimental as well as monetary value. It had been a gift from her grandmother when she was still alive. But if the plan worked, it would be well worth the sacrifice, she assured herself. And she was determined that it would work. Of course, Ellie was positive that it would not. She felt sure that Prudence would be recognized and escorted from the property. But Prudence was of the opinion that no one paid any attention to servants. Neither Stockton nor her father would give her a second glance—she hoped.

There would be no negative thinking now, she remonstrated herself. So far everything had gone without a hitch. Lizzy had met her as promised, entered Eleanore's borrowed carriage, switched clothes with Prudence, and told her, *Just walk in like ye belong. Grab an ale, so it looks like ye're working, find your lover, give him the message, and get back out here so I can get back to work. And don't get caught. I could lose me job if aught find out about this.*

So Pru had walked in, doing her best to look as if she belonged there, grabbed an empty mug, then slipped back outside, where she had carefully administered a couple of drops of Bessy's tonic to the empty mug from the bottle presently strapped to her thigh. She had worried over that part. The bottle Eleanore had given her had been rather large to cart around unnoticed, so she had had to find a smaller one to place the liquid in. Then she had suffered a quandary about where to keep it. It had to be somewhere within easy access. Tied tightly to her thigh, upside down with two pieces of cloth, had seemed the safest place, which appeared to be working. She had doctored the empty mug, replaced the bottle, and slipped back inside, walking boldly up to the open ale barrel to fill the mug with yeasty brew.

"Well, now, what have we here?"

Prudence had just spotted her father at one of the tables when her view was blocked by a rather large, leering man. Forcing a smile, she tried to step around him, only to find her path blocked and herself maneuvered up against a wall.

"You must be new. I do not recognize you."

Prudence nearly groaned aloud, but caught herself. She truly did not need a half-drunk lout to pester her. "Excuse me, my lord, but I must deliver this drink."

"Ah, now, don't be so unfriendly." The man gave her a smile that Prudence forced herself to return, but then he moved in and reached around to grope her behind in far too familiar a fashion. A squeak of alarm slipping from her lips, Prudence immediately grabbed at his hand.

"I just happen to be in need of a drink myself."

She glanced at him, her mouth open to demand he unhand her, when she realized he had taken the mug from her tray and was lifting it to his lips. "Oh, no! Do not—"

Prudence paused, her mouth agape. The irritating patron had poured the drink down his throat with one gulp.

"Mmmm." He wiped his mouth with the back of his hand and smiled at her. "That was refreshing. Thank you, luv."

Pru snapped her teeth closed with vexation, then snatched the empty mug from him. "You are not welcome. Now I shall have to fetch another." She tried to step around him, but found him immediately in her path again.

"Now, now, none of that, Lord Setterington," a deep voice said quietly nearby. "You know patrons are not allowed to bother the girls."

Recognizing the voice, Prudence stiffened. Lord Stockton. Panic rising within her, she stiffly kept her face forward and moved around the man Stockton had addressed. This time the odious man did not try to prevent her, and Pru was able to rush back to the safety of the kitchens. Once there, she frowned at the sight of how busy the ale barrel was. There were three women awaiting their turns at it.

Unwilling to risk one of the other servants recognizing that she didn't belong, Prudence turned back and cracked the door open to peer out to where Lord Stockton and Lord Setterington were still conversing. The two men seemed rather chummy, which didn't bother Prudence as much as the fact that Setterington didn't appear the least bit affected by the tincture she had put in the ale. She watched for several minutes, turning her head away and moving to the side occasionally as servants entered and left the room. Members of nobility might not deign to notice servants, but servants surely noticed each other. After several minutes she gave up waiting on her unintentional victim to show signs of taking ill, and glanced back to the barrel. There was no one by it. Even the cooking staff was gone. But, then, they had finished their shift and left before she had arrived. Prudence had planned it that way, finding out what time the kitchen staff finished, and arranging to meet Lizzy after that.

Reaching down, she felt along her upper leg for the bottle holding the emetic, then glanced out the door again. Setterington and Stockton were still talking, and no one appeared headed in the direction of the kitchens. It seemed safe to fill the mug again. Letting the door slide closed, she turned and hurried to the ale barrel. She started with the drops first, for fear that someone might interrupt if she did it the other way around.

Setting the mug on the half lid that had been left on the barrel, she quickly rucked up her skirt and slid the bottle out. Letting her skirt fall back into place, she undid the bottle, held the lid between thumb and finger, and slid the other three fingers of that hand through the handle of the mug, lifting it to put in a couple of drops of the potion. She hesitated a moment, then dumped a good splash of the liquid in. The two drops she had put in the other drink were taking too long to work—if they were working at all. Obviously more than that was needed to affect a body properly.

Prudence started to try to put the lid back on the emetic then, but with the mug, lid, and bottle all in hand, it was awkward, and she ended up dropping the lid. Clucking her tongue in disgust, she set both the mug and the small bottle on the barrel and knelt to look for her missing lid. It, of course, was nowhere in sight. Thinking that it must have rolled into the shadows against the wall behind the barrel, Prudence shifted to her hands and knees and crawled around, then swept her hand over the dark floor between barrel and wall.

She heard a deep male voice say something, but didn't really catch what it was, so was wholly unprepared for the sudden slap on her backside. Squealing, she jerked to the side, crashing into the barrel, then straightened on her knees and peered around in time to see one of the male servants swaggering out of the room through the door that led to the alley behind the building.

"Men!" she muttered with agitation, then grasped the lip of the barrel to get back to her feet. Once there, she saw that while the mug was still in place, the bottle of emetic was gone. She glanced around briefly, but it was nowhere on the floor. Either it had rolled into the shadows as the lid had done, or the male servant had absconded with it.

Her gaze slid to the door leading to the alley, and she took a step toward it, then changed her mind. The fellow was probably on a break and thought he had stolen her private stock. He was doubtlessly gulping the sweet-smelling liquid down at that very moment. She hoped it was a big swallow, for one was all he would probably take, and Prudence rather hoped he downed enough of it to end up retching for hours. It served him right for touching her behind!

Smiling to herself at that thought, she dipped the already-doctored mug into the ale barrel, then turned back to the door to the gaming room. Cracking it open, she saw that Stockton and Setterington had moved away. In fact, neither man was in sight.

A sudden excited outburst at the center table drew her attention. One man was laughing happily as he scooped up a rather large pile of money. Everyone else at the table looked decidedly unhappy, though they were doing their best to hide it as they slapped the man on the back in congratulations.

"Here!" the winner suddenly called out to a nearby servant. "A round of ale for everyone in the club to celebrate. On me!"

Pru's eyes widened as every single servant in the club made a sudden exodus toward the kitchen doors. Deciding that it was time to move now or risk being discovered as an impostor, Prudence scampered determinedly out of the kitchens and straight to the table where earlier she had spotted her father playing cards.

Her eyes darted nervously about the room with every step she took, watching warily for Stockton, or for anyone who might intercept her and steal her precious drink as Setterington had done. She was nearly at the table where her father was playing cards when she spotted him. The gray-haired fellow who had been seated at the card table next to her father had apparently left, and Stockton sat there now.

Prudence nearly turned on her heel and fled for the kitchens again, but then she caught herself and forced her feet to continue. Stockton would not notice her, she assured herself firmly. She would keep her face averted, approaching with her front to her father and her back to Stockton. She would slide in, set the drink down, and leave. The man would see only the back of her head, and her father wouldn't even glance at her. Members of nobility *never* looked at servants, or if they did, they rarely saw them. And her father was no exception. *Dear God, please don't let Father be the exception*, she prayed as she turned to slide between the two men, her back to Stockton as she set the drink at her father's elbow. He did not glance up from his cards, at least no further than to notice the drink and cluck his tongue in annoyance.

"I didn't order that," she heard him grumble as she quickly started to slide out from between the two chairs, but she kept on going, hoping that if she left it there, he would drink it anyway.

"Girl!"

"'Tis all right, Prescott," she heard Stockton say. "I shall drink it."

It made Prudence pause. Swinging back in alarm, she saw the establishment's owner pick up the mug and swallow a good quantity of its contents. She didn't say anything—at least nothing comprehensible. Instead there came more of a squawking sound that slid from her lips as he lowered the drink and she saw that more than half of it was gone. It was enough to draw Stockton's gaze to her over the rim of the mug he was again lifting to his lips. Prudence nearly stopped him, but realized that there was really no use. He had already downed enough of it that there was no way he could avoid reacting. Especially since she had put in such a large amount.

Oh, he was not going to be happy about this at all, Prudence thought faintly, and took an unconscious step backward. She was paling and knew it. She could feel the blood drain from her face as the man's eyes narrowed on her. She started to back away faster, wincing when his eyes suddenly widened in recognition. She gave a gulp as he excused himself from the game and started to his feet, and she whirled away, heading for the kitchens at a dead run.

She had reached the kitchens when he caught

up to her. In fact, she had pushed her way past the half-dozen servants around the ale barrel and nearly made it out the back door into the alley, but he caught her hand and drew her to a halt. Prudence whirled, mouth open to demand he release her, but he was already starting for his office, pulling her behind him. Catching sight of the curious servants, she decided not to cause a scene and allowed him to drag her where he would.

Tugging her inside the small, cramped office he had taken her to the last time, he released her abruptly, slammed the door, and leaned his back on it to glare at her. "Why are you back? To work? Surely your family's situation has not deteriorated to the point that you have actually been forced to seek a paid position?"

It was the way he said the word *work* that suddenly calmed Prudence. It sounded sarcastic and bitter on his lips, reminding her of the snubs and insults he had suffered for having to make a living in the world—a torment she would not wish on anyone. Her annoyance at his drinking the potion meant for her father was briefly forgotten and she said gently, "There is nothing wrong with earning your living."

He gave a disbelieving laugh. "Certainly there is. Just ask anyone and they will inform you of it. Every one of them thinks I am beneath them because—"

"I am not everyone," Prudence interrupted,

bringing what she was sure would have been a long rant to an end.

He eyed her speculatively for a moment, then said, "I personally choose my workers. You are not employed here. You also made no attempt to talk to your father, which was the reason you gave for wishing to get inside Ballard's. You did not say a word to him when you had the chance. So, my lady, why are you here?"

"I did not come here this evening to talk to my father," Prudence answered evasively.

He stared at her for another moment, then said, "Perhaps you came here to see me?"

Startled by that suggestion, Prudence was slow to notice that he was moving forward. Backing nervously away, she shook her head. "Nay, I—"

Her words died as he slid his palm gently against her cheek. His voice was husky when he spoke. "Nay?"

Prudence started to shake her head, but paused and swallowed when his other hand trailed lightly down her arm. It was as if one of her fantasies had come to life. Not that she had ever fantasized this situation, but the look in his eyes was quite the same. A little more heated than adoring, perhaps, but . . .

"I am sorry for that unfortunate incident the other night. I would never have allowed Plunkett to enter had I realized—" He cut himself off and grimaced when Prudence suddenly flushed bright pink at the reminder of her humiliation.

"I *am* sorry," he repeated. Then she watched wide-eyed as his lips lowered toward hers. Her breath caught in her throat and her eyes slipped closed as she waited for the soft caress of his mouth on hers . . . and waited. And waited.

He had never taken this long finding her lips in her fantasies. Frowning, she popped her eyes open. His face was a mere few inches away, but it was no longer moving closer. He appeared to be almost frozen, and he had the oddest expression on his face.

"Is there something amiss?" she asked with concern.

Lord Stockton heaved. Recalling that he had downed her father's dosed ale, Prudence watched in horror as Stephen clapped his mouth closed. His cheeks bulged and his eyes were huge in his face as he whirled away. After a brief but frantic glance around, he rushed for the window.

"Oh, dear," she murmured as he threw it open. The next moment he was hanging over the ledge, being ill.

Biting her lip, Prudence shifted on her feet, unsure what to do; then she moved forward and patted his back rather limply. He straightened.

"Feeling better?" she asked hopefully.

He started to nod, then whirled back to hang out the window again.

"I guess not," Prudence muttered, wondering how to help. Were she home and he Charlotte, she would have wiped her younger sister's forehead with damp cloths and murmured soothing sounds. Her gaze moved to the office door, and she had an idea. She left him and hurried out to the kitchens. There had to be water and cloths somewhere. This was a kitchen.

Unfortunately it was a rather large kitchen, and empty again, so that there was no one to direct her to find what she sought. She searched for several minutes before coming up with a cloth clean enough to suit her, then wasted several more looking for water. She was wringing out the damp cloth when she became aware of the assorted sounds coming from the next room.

There came a rather loud screeching of chair legs on the wooden floor and the panicky shuffling of feet, and it drew her to the door. Cracking it open, she peered out curiously. Nearly every single man in the club was on his feet, darting madly about—some rushing this way, some rushing that. Prudence gaped at the madness briefly; then a noise behind her made her turn. Lord Stockton stood leaning weakly against the doorway to his office.

"Are you feeling any better?" Pru asked with concern.

"I thought you left" was his answer, and there was no mistaking his relief that she hadn't. Prudence smiled softly and held up the bit of wadded material in her hand.

"Nay. I thought to find you a damp cloth," she explained, then glanced toward the door as the sounds in the next room changed to guttural noises.

"What the devil is that?"

Prudence stepped aside as Stephen moved to the door and tugged it open. She didn't bother to look out. She had finally deduced what the mad behavior she had been watching was about. The sound she was now listening to was the almost symphonic noise of nearly a hundred men being sick. The club was full of vomiting patrons.

"Dear God!" Stephen said faintly, then shouted, "Stop, man! What the hell is going on?"

"I don't know, milord," someone answered—probably a servant, Prudence decided, since the voice sounded hale and heave-free. "Everyone is tossing their innards out. Bad batch of ale'd be my guess."

"Well, find out, damn it!" Stephen said in what was probably supposed to be a roar, but came out too weak to be considered one. Prudence bit her lip guiltily as she watched him sag against the doorjamb. Then he turned and gestured for her to follow him as he staggered back toward his office.

Pru hesitated, her gaze going to the door to the gaming room, then to the barrel of ale. She understood what had happened, of course. The bottle of emetic had not fallen on the floor or been stolen by the male servant who slapped her behind. It must have fallen *into* the ale, probably knocked there when she crashed against the barrel. *She* was what had happened to Ballard's patrons. Fortunately Lord Stockton didn't appear to be aware of that. He was putting it down to a bad batch of ale. She was relatively safe if she stayed for a bit. Which she wanted to do—purely to be of assistance while he felt so poorly, she assured herself. After all, she was the reason he was sick. She really should do what she could for him.

Having reasoned the matter out thusly, Prudence gave up her position by the door to the gaming room and followed Lord Stockton. He was slumped in the chair behind his desk when she stepped into the office. Moving to his side, she peered down at his closed eyes, then gently began to mop his face with her now warm, but still damp cloth, cooing soothing noises as she did.

His eyes flickered briefly at her touch, but they remained closed, his face slowly relaxing. She was beginning to think he had fallen asleep when he suddenly caught her hand in his. Prudence found herself blushing when his eyes opened and peered into hers.

She tugged her hand free after a moment of silence had passed, then turned away. "I shall fetch you a drink."

"Not from out there."

Pru hesitated at the door and glanced uncertainly back to see him gesture to the cupboard along the wall. "There is whiskey in there."

After a moment, Prudence nodded and moved to the cupboard. Opening the door she found a bottle of whiskey and two glasses inside. She took one and filled it, then carried it carefully back to the desk.

"Thank you." Stephen accepted the glass, took a mouthful of the golden liquid, swished it around, then stood and moved to the window to spit. He did that twice more before allowing himself to swallow the next drink. Then he glanced at Prudence and smiled.

"Thank you." His voice was raspy, but still soft as he raised a hand to caress her cheek. "I appreciate your care."

Prudence felt her face flush. She was not sure herself whether it was with pleasure at his touch, or with embarrassment at being praised when she had been the cause of his ailment. She *did* know she was disappointed when his hand slipped away from her cheek and he turned to pick up his glass again. He had just taken another swig when a knock sounded at the door.

Swallowing, he set the glass back on his desk, then moved around her to shield Prudence from view. "Enter," he called out.

Prudence heard the door open; then a male voice announced, "This was found floating in the ale barrel."

By lifting up on her tiptoes, Pru was able to just see over Stephen's shoulder and glimpse what was held out by the man in the doorway. Her bottle, she saw with a wince. The man added, "It looks a deliberate attempt to poison our patrons."

"What?" There was no mistaking the shock in Stephen's voice. "Why would anyone wish to poison our—"

Prudence backed away as he suddenly spun to glare at her. Forcing a smile, she exclaimed, "I am *sure* whomever it was had no intention of poisoning your patrons. They most likely meant to—"

"To poison one particular patron?" he asked coldly. "Such as your father, perhaps? That mug I drank from was meant for him, after all. You poisoned my ale!"

He moved toward her, his repressed fury evident, and Prudence did the only thing she could think to do; she made a run for it.

"Do not let her get away!" she heard Stephen shout, but at that point the devil himself couldn't have caught her. Propelled by fear, Pru was running so fast she wasn't even sure her feet were touching the floor. She was out the door and racing along the alley to the front of the building in a trice. Jamison, bless his heart, either heard the rapid *tap-tap* of her feet, or saw her approaching. Whatever the case, he was off his seat and had the door open when she got there.

"Get us away from here, Jamison. Quickly!" she

cried as she lunged into the carriage. The door was closed behind her before she even landed on the seat.

"What happened? Ye haven't lost me my job, have ye?" Lizzy cried as the carriage shifted under the weight of Jamison remounting the driver's bench.

Prudence grabbed at the seat and waited until the carriage had lurched forward before answering.

Chapter Four

$\mathcal{P}$oisoning the punch, are we?"

Dropping the dipper in the punch bowl, Prudence whirled to find the owner of that silky voice, eyes wary as she met Lord Stockton's mocking gaze. She hadn't seen the man since the night of the little accident at his club. Well, all right, the night she had poisoned his patrons. Which had been two nights ago. Pru had considered sending him a letter of apology explaining the situation, but had decided against it, thinking that such an apology really should be given in person. But here was her chance, and she wished she had sent him a letter. Or that she had refused to allow Eleanore to talk her into coming tonight. Forcing Prudence to attend her mother's ball had been Ellie's attempt to cheer her friend and distract her from the Prescott family's mounting bills.

Prudence was neither distracted nor cheered. She was terribly conscious of the fact that she was wearing a borrowed gown, and nothing could make her forget the subtle snubs she was receiving, or the fact that no one had asked her to dance.

"You have yet to answer my question," Stephen said, drawing her attention back to him. "Are you poisoning the punch? I ask only because I should like to know if you are out to torment *all* of the *ton* for your father's misdeeds, or are concentrating solely on ruining *me*."

Catching the startled glances being cast at them and the way people around the punch bowl were suddenly setting down their empty glasses, Prudence forced a stiff chuckle. "Oh, my lord, you are such a wit. But you should not jest like that or people might truly believe that I would do such a thing."

"The ones who suffered so foully at my club the other night, thanks to your poisoning, would have no trouble believing—"

Prudence cut him off by grabbing his arm, jerking him away from the table of refreshments and toward the balcony doors. She had no delusions about her strength. The only reason she managed to drag him out of the ballroom was because he let her. Since it suited her needs at the moment, she could only be grateful for his docility.

Prudence pulled him outside, shivered as the winter chill struck her skin, then led him along the wall of glass doors until they reached those leading into Lord Kindersley's office. Ellie's father didn't like anyone in there, but it was too cold to stay outside, and she needed privacy for this confrontation.

"So, what plans have you for tonight?" Stephen

asked as she entered the gloomy room and turned to face him. "You have already both started a riot and poisoned a large crowd. Perhaps you intend to start a fire to roast all of—"

"Please stop," Prudence said wearily. She was not surprised by his irritation, but with all the troubles plaguing her, did not have the energy to fend it off. "I did not intend to start that riot. I was attempting to protect one of your serving women from a rather nasty client of yours."

"I know." Stockton's mouth was a bit tight, but some of the tension had left his body.

Prudence felt some relief at that. She was even happier to see the last of that tension leave him as she explained, "Neither did I intend to poison your patrons. The bottle of emetic must have fallen into the barrel while I was searching about for the lid on the floor. I did not realize that it had or I would have warned someone . . . probably," she added, because she wasn't at all sure she would have. She had been so determined to see her father out of Ballard's. She still was, for that matter.

"Emetic?" He grimaced with distaste at the realization of what had forced him to hang out his office window. "I take it the emetic was meant for your father?"

"Aye. Ellie suggested that perhaps getting him to refrain from imbibing would put an end to his gambling as well. It seemed plausible, so . . ." She shrugged.

"Ellie? Eleanore Kindersley?"

"Aye." She brightened slightly. "Do you know her?"

"She is the daughter of our host," he pointed out gently. "And I do know that she is your friend."

"Oh." Prudence accepted the information, then, recalling a suggestion Eleanore had made earlier that day, managed a pleasant smile and raised her hand. "Well, I vow here and now, my lord, that you need no longer fear my disrupting the workings of Ballard's. I will not attempt to gain entrance again."

"Hmmm." He considered her doubtfully. "Never again, eh?"

"Never *ever*," Prudence teased lightly, mimicking Plunkett's deep voice, and felt optimism rise within her when a reluctant smile began to pull at the corners of his mouth. Then he forced it away, a scowl coming in its place.

"You do realize that you have caused me a good deal of trouble?"

"I am sorry for that."

"That may be, but my clientele has taken a dip."

She peered repentantly down at her feet and waited, relieved when at last he sighed.

"Well, I am sure business will pick up again soon enough. And I realize that you did not mean the harm you caused. At least not on the scale you managed. Besides, I tried a similar trick or two on my own father when he was gambling us to ruin. But I feel I should tell you that such tricks will not work. Your energy would be better spent picketing to get the laws changed and all gambling establishments closed dow—"

"Your father?" Prudence interrupted him.

His mouth turned down in displeasure and he moved away. Realizing that it was likely a sensitive issue, Prudence gave him a moment to compose his thoughts and glanced around the darkened room. The remains of a dying fire smoldered in the fireplace. That was the only light. Obviously guests were not intended to be here, and she felt slightly guilty. She knew Lord Kindersley was so jealous of his privacy that he did not even allow servants in here to clean. Had Ellie not told her that, the layer of dust and many cobwebs would have. Thinking of spiders and shuddering, she followed Stephen to a large statue in the corner of the room. It was in the Greek style, a seven-foot woman in a toga reaching toward the sky, her arms turning into the branches of a tree over their heads. Deciding that Lord Kindersley had atrocious taste, Prudence turned her attention to Stephen as he brushed at a spiderweb spun between two of the marble branches and finally spoke.

"My father did the same thing your father is now doing. He drove us to the edge of ruin with his gambling. He did not drink, however. Just gambled. And he did not start suddenly, as a tonic to distract himself from the death of his son and heir; he was always a gambler—but the longer he did it, the worse it got. I used to—" He paused abruptly, and Prudence moved a step closer, laying her hand gently over his now fisted one in a silent effort to soothe him. He glanced down with surprise; then his expression softened and his hand opened under hers, moving to gently clasp it.

"How did you convince him to stop?" Prudence asked after a moment of silence.

A harsh laugh burst from his lips, and his fingers tightened around hers. She didn't think he realized that he was crushing her hand, but she hesitated to draw his attention to the fact, because she desperately wanted to hear the answer to her question. If he had managed to make his father stop, perhaps she could save her father the same way.

Those hopes were shattered when he said, "He stopped himself. He gambled everything away but the Stockton estate. He could not touch that. So he came home that night, after gambling the last of everything else away, and shot himself."

Prudence flinched at his cold admission, horrified. She had a sudden vision of her father taking one of her grandfather's old dueling pistols and—

"Do not look like that. I should not have told you. I am sorry."

Prudence focused on his troubled expression, only then becoming aware of his hand on her cheek. "I—"

He smothered whatever she would have said by covering her mouth with his lips. Prudence stayed still for a moment under the assault—a variety of unexpected responses rushing through her—then kissed him back. She told herself that she was doing so just because she was eager to erase the image of his father's death from her mind, but she knew she was lying to herself. She had wanted him to kiss her again ever since that first time in his office. Perhaps she had wanted him to kiss her even before that. She had fantasized about him sweeping her up at some ball and rescuing her from her troubled life since that first time he had saved her from being a complete wallflower. Since the first time she had seen him, really. He was terribly handsome, and his basic kindness showed through his dissolute air. That, she was sure, was only a defense against the cold cuts society directed his way. She had always seen him as some sort of martyr, for she had never seen anything truly wrong with the fact that he chose to run a gambling establishment . . . well, until she had seen how the vice affected her family.

"Oh, Pru," he breathed against her cheek.

Surprised by his familiarity, but warmed by it, Prudence moaned as his lips trailed down her throat, leaving a blistering trail. She leaned in to him, her hands sliding over his shoulders, then into his hair. It felt so good to be held like this. To let go of the constant tension of her worries and let passion carry her away. For a few moments, to just feel. His hands clasped her breasts through her gown, squeezing gently, and for a moment it felt as if all the air had left her lungs. She was left gasping and arching, little sounds of excitement slipping through her lips, until he muffled them again with his mouth. He kissed her almost violently, and slid a knee between her legs, drawing the material of her borrowed gown with it.

Borrowed gown. Eleanore's gown. Eleanore's advice. As quickly as that, Prudence's troubles crashed back down around her, abruptly dampening her ardor. Recalling what she had intended to do, she clenched her fingers in his hair and tugged urgently at it, trying to pull him away. "Wait. Wait, my lord, I—"

His soft chuckle made her hesitate and peer at him uncertainly as he eased their embrace enough for her to slip her arms between them.

"I think you can call me Stephen now, my lady." His voice was husky with passion as he peered down at her through the dim light. "I believe we are beyond formality."

Prudence offered him a strained smile. "Aye. Well." Reluctant to escape his embrace, she began to play with the front of his shirt, keeping him near, yet far enough away that he couldn't kiss her again and muddle her thinking. "I . . ."

His eyebrows rose at her hesitation. "Aye?"

"I wished to ask you . . ." She got further that time before faltering, then forced herself to continue. "To ask if you would please refuse him admission?"

She said the last with her eyes shut, horrified at how the request sounded. It had not seemed a bad suggestion when Eleanore had made it. *If you cannot keep him from going to Ballard's, the owner can. Mayhap if you ask nicely, Lord Stockton would do that for you*, she had said. Of course, Prudence supposed her friend hadn't imagined Prudence being in his arms when she made the request. Stephen certainly didn't appear as if he was reacting well. His arms tightened around her, his face becoming expressionless. She could feel his emotional withdrawal from her like a physical tearing.

"I see. Well, I imagine it could be arranged. It depends."

Prudence swallowed at the unpleasant undertone to his voice. "Depends on what?"

"How much more of this might I get should I do so?"

Her first reaction was a backward jerk of her head, as if he had slapped her. It couldn't have hurt her more had he actually done so. But her second reaction was chagrin. What could she expect him to think? She had certainly done everything else she could to save her family, much of it likely illegal. Unquestionably it was all improper behavior for a well-bred young lady of the *ton*. And she had also never made any attempt to hide her desperation. She shouldn't be surprised that he had jumped to such a conclusion.

"My allowing you to kiss me has nothing to do with this," she said with quiet dignity. "As a point of fact, I brought a halt to the kiss because I was becoming rather . . . er . . . distracted and feared forgetting to make the request at all." She could feel her face burning with embarrassment as she made the admission, and was grateful for the concealing darkness.

Stephen considered her through the gloom, then said, "So you like my kisses? This is not some new scheme? This is not some way to pay me back because your father loses money in my establishment?"

Prudence frowned, trying to find an argument in her mind to prove that she enjoyed Lord Stockton's kisses, then brightened. "Surely you can tell if a woman is enjoying your kiss? Does it not show?"

"Aye. Unfortunately I was rather distracted with my own enjoyment and did not—" His words broke off on a surprised gasp when Prudence suddenly stepped closer, reached up on tiptoe, and pressed her lips against his.

He did nothing at first to make the kiss easier for her, but as she felt the tension in his arms ease, his hands began to move over her back and his lips moved with true passion. Prudence let a little sigh slip out as her mouth opened under his, her toes curling in her slippers as she arched into him, putting all she had into the kiss. Following his lead, she ran her own hands over his back, enjoying the solid feel of him beneath her fingers. She gasped and lifted further up on her toes when his hands slid up over her rib cage to cup her breasts; then he broke away and trailed his lips over her cheek.

"I believe you," he said softly after several heated moments.

"Aye." Prudence kissed his ear eagerly when it came within reach.

"We should stop, else I cannot promise—"

"Nay." Prudence moaned, biting his chin at the very suggestion.

"Nay?"

"Aye."

A chuckle rumbled from his mouth, reverberating against her throat and making her squeeze her legs together in excitement. "Aye or nay?" he asked, sounding both amused and concerned.

"Oh." She opened her eyes reluctantly, then stilled as a shadow moved into the periphery of her vision. It wasn't a very large shadow, really, a darker blotch in the darkness that surrounded them, but it was moving. Dropping, actually, straight for Stephen's unsuspecting head. A spider! Lowering itself on its silken thread! Knowing she was overreacting, but helpless to do otherwise, she jerked in his arms and opened her mouth to warn him, but suddenly the arachnid dropped the last of the way at lightning speed. Prudence instinctively lifted the fan that had been dangling from her wrist all evening and brought it down atop the spider . . . and on top of Stephen's head.

"What the—" Releasing her at once, Lord Stockton covered the crown of his head and stepped back.

"A spider," Prudence blurted, trailing after him as he moved warily away. "Really, my lord. It dropped out of the marble tree and landed on your head. I was just—" She gestured with her fan, her expression brightening as she spotted the dark blob that had been the spider on the light-colored fan Ellie had given her.

"See! I got it." She thrust the fan out toward him and Stephen stumbled and fell onto a couch to avoid it. "Really, there was a spider on your head."

"*Pru?*"

Prudence let the fan drop and swung around at that concerned call. Ellie was walking along the balcony, rubbing her arms and peering uncertainly out into the darkness of the snow-covered gardens.

"Prudence, are you there? Father said he saw you come out here."

"Damn," she said softly and turned back to Stephen. Seeing the way the man was eyeing her as he got back to his feet, she threw her hands up in disgust. The fan, again dangling from her wrist, swung out, neatly clipping him between the legs. Prudence gasped in horror and started toward him as he bent over with a gasp. "Are you—"

"I am fine!" He held up a hand in self-defense, shuffling back away from her. "Just go. Go."

"But—"

"Pru!"

Shaking her head in frustration, she turned and hurried outside to find Ellie.

"You'd better get a look at this, milord."

Stephen glanced up from the books he was balancing to find Plunkett in the open door of his office. The doorman's face looked even more bulldoggish than usual, wrinkled up in concern as it was. "What is it?"

"There's a bunch of women out front."

Frowning at the vague announcement, Stephen stood and followed the man through the kitchens and out into the gaming room. His expression tightened at the sight of the few patrons seated about the room. Business had dwindled more and more with each of Prudence Prescott's antics. There had been a slight dip in the number of clients the night after the riot she'd caused, and the numbers had cut in half after her poisoning. Now there was no more than a handful of men in the place. The damned woman had cost him quite a bit of money. If she were here right now, he would probably wring her lovely neck. Or kiss her senseless. Strangely, he rather thought he might enjoy the second option more. As infuriating as her antics had been—and painful, he added as an afterthought—he spent more time imagining licentious pursuits with her than punishments. And the little episode in

Kindersley's office, before he had taken the fan to the groin, had managed only to inflame his imaginings. The young woman truly intrigued him, despite her tendency to cause havoc wherever she went.

Stephen pushed his thoughts aside when Plunkett stopped in front of him. Glancing up, he saw that they had reached the front entrance. His doorman swung the door open and stepped outside, holding it for him to follow. Stephen did and gawked at the scene before him.

"What the hell?" he asked, gaping at a horde of picketing women.

"Hmmm," Plunkett rumbled. "They've been here for the last hour, and it's affecting business. A lot of the women out there are wives or daughters of regulars. It's scaring the men off. Carriages pull up, then pull away just as quickly when the women move toward them."

Stephen didn't really need an explanation. As he watched, a carriage with the Justerly crest on it drew to a halt before the building. He saw the duke peer out the window at the picketing women; then the protesters started toward the carriage shouting, "Save your soul! No more gambling!" Justerly pulled abruptly back and let the carriage curtains drop closed; then Stephen heard his shout to his driver to get them out of there. The coach lurched away and the women cheered at their success in saving one more soul.

"Damn!" Leaving Plunkett at the door, Stephen stormed out into the mob.

"YOU TRULY *ARE* out to ruin me, aren't you?"

Prudence turned slowly at those words, not at all surprised by Stephen's appearance. She had actually expected him earlier, and thought it very forbearing of him to wait so long to kick up a fuss. "Good evening, my lord. How are you this evening?"

"How am I?" He glared. "I am suffering a financial setback in the person of one Lady Prudence Prescott. No one dares come near this place. I have a total of ten guests in the club right now—all of them patrons who were inside before you and your league of sour-faced dowagers arrived. And they are all terrified to leave lest one of their wives or mothers is out here picketing."

"Is my father one of the men inside?" Prudence asked with a frown.

"Nay."

She smiled in relief at his snapped response. "Then I suppose I can say that your plan is working. Thank you."

"*My* plan?"

Prudence nodded with a smile. "The other night at Ellie's ball you said that if I had such strong feelings about gambling, I should picket and get the gambling establishments closed down."

"I meant that you should picket the House of Commons and get the laws changed and—" He regained control of himself with some effort, then said very calmly, "All you have accomplished, my lady, is another step toward ruining *my* business. Which will not aid *your* cause. Your father is gambling tonight, I guarantee it. Just not in Ballard's."

Prudence startled at that suggestion. "Faugh! Of course he isn't. He had to give up his membership to the clubs. He favors your establishment."

"You do not have to belong to the private clubs to get in; you merely need a friend to take you with him as a guest. Your father spends the first part of most nights at White's. He—"

"You are lying. I followed him here that first night, and both times I have been inside Ballard's since, he was—"

"Both times you were inside Ballard's it was late evening," he pointed out firmly.

Prudence frowned. What Stephen was saying was true enough. She had gone late deliberately. When she had first gone disguised as a man it had taken her a good portion of the night to tuck and pin the back of her father's breeches. Even with Ellie's help it had been quite late when she had finally set out. Then, the night she had gone disguised as a serving wench, she had gone late to avoid the kitchen staff, thinking it might be less risky. If what he said was true, and her father did not only gamble here, then she was wasting her time. Wasn't she?

"Ah, well, that is of no consequence. The important thing here is that my father, like the rest of your patrons, will not show up here tonight. My picketing is still a success."

Stephen glared at her in frustration, then snatched her hand and began dragging her along the sidewalk toward his carriage.

"What are you doing? Unhand me, my lord." She started to bring her sign down on his head, but he caught it with his free hand and tugged it from her, tossing it aside with disgust.

"Must you always carry something to brain men?"

"I do not carry things about with the intention of braining men," Prudence answered with affront.

"Oh? What about that umbrella you broke over Plunkett's head?"

"It was raining earlier in the evening. I brought the umbrella in case it started up again."

"Uh-huh." He sounded doubtful. "And the cane you clobbered Mershone with when you were disguised as a man?"

"Mershone?" Prudence echoed with confusion, then asked, "Was he that hawk-faced fellow?"

"Aye."

"What an awful man. He was mistreating one of your servants and deserved the koshing he got. But I only had that cane as part of my disguise; I thought it was most effective."

"Most effective," she heard him mutter. Prudence made a face at the back of his head.

"You batted me over the head with your fan at the Kindersleys' ball."

"I told you I was sorry about that. There was a rather large spider on your head and—"

"You were just about to beat on me with that sign you're carrying!"

Having no defense for that accusation, Prudence merely sighed and settled on the cushioned seat, then stiffened when she realized that while distracting her with his accusations, he had managed to get her into his carriage. She lunged for the door.

"Oh, no, you don't!" Stephen grasped her about the waist and tugged her onto his lap, holding her there firmly with one arm as he banged on the carriage wall with the other. The carriage was off at once and Prudence grabbed frantically at his arm to maintain her balance.

"You can release me now," she said once the carriage had settled into a steady trot.

"But I rather like holding you."

Prudence felt her insides melt at that husky announcement and allowed herself the luxury of briefly enjoying his embrace. When she felt his breath on her neck, little tingles of anticipation raced through her; then she let out a breathy sigh and turned in to the caress as his lips claimed the sensitive skin there. However, when his hands closed over her breasts through her gown and the warmth inside her started turning to red-hot heat, she forced herself to struggle out of his arms to the safety of the opposite seat.

Stephen let her go. He was smiling at her when she finally glanced across at him.

"I thought you liked my kisses?"

Prudence flushed. "Aye. Well, it is not proper to—"

"And you are so proper," he gently teased.

Prudence glanced away, trying not to squirm with embarrassment, and shrugged. "I may not always be proper, my lord, but I do have some sense. And once I was away from your . . . influence, I realized that I really did not wish to become involved with someone who is helping my father, and countless others, destroy their families by gambling. Especially a man who should know better. Your own father should have made you sympathetic to this plight!"

Stephen was silent for a moment, the smile gone from his face. She expected him to be angry and strike out at her verbally about her own shortcomings, but was surprised by his quiet reply. "I can understand that sentiment, my lady. I did not feel much differently about the gaming hells my father attended or their owners. I have realized since that the owners are not the ones to blame. Which I am about to prove to you."

Prudence turned her head and peered silently out the window.

"If he were not gambling at Ballard's, it would be somewhere else," Stephen said quietly. "I run an honest establishment and limit how much men are allowed to lose. Should they start to dig too deep, I cut them off and send them home."

Prudence turned back to face him. "Is that supposed to make it all right that you help ruin them—the fact that if it was not you taking their money, it would be someone else?"

Irritation flashed across his face. "That is not what I meant."

"What did you mean then?"

He opened his mouth to answer, then paused to glance out the window as the carriage slowed. "We are here. Come. You will see what I am trying to say."

Opening the carriage door, he stepped down and turned to help her out. Prudence ignored the hand he proffered and glanced at the building they had stopped before. As she stepped down from the carriage, she saw that he had brought her to White's.

"After our discussion at the Kindersleys' ball, I looked into your father's gambling." Stephen urged her up to the window to the side of the door. There was a table there with men seated around it. Prudence knew it was considered the best seat in the house, where one could be seen on display. Her father was not one of the men at the table, she saw with relief.

"As I told you, I do not allow my patrons to play too deep. For him to have lost the large amounts of money you are suggesting, I knew he must be gambling elsewhere. I looked into the matter. He usually comes here first. Then he goes to one or two of the other private clubs, depending on his mood. Then he goes to Ballard's, where he plays cards until well after midnight. At that point, he heads to some of the lesser establishments. He does not appear to gamble large amounts at any of his stops, but when added together, perhaps . . ." He shrugged, then suddenly pointed past the table in the front window toward one further in. "There he is."

Prudence stared at the man he was pointing to. It *was* her father. And he was playing cards. She felt her heart shrivel in her chest. Tonight had been a waste of time. Perhaps all of it had been. And perhaps she'd known all along and blindly done what seemed would help—no matter how ludicrous.

She remained silent and docile as he turned her away from the window and led her back to his carriage, getting inside automatically when the driver opened the door. She remained silent as Stephen gave his driver her address and instructions to take them there. Some part of her thought she should return to the picketing. She had organized it, after all, but now there seemed little use, and she did not have the heart for it. They had all been so excited and buoyed by the fact that they were driving Ballard's customers away that she didn't want to be the one to tell them it was for naught. No doubt *all* their husbands and fathers were merely gambling elsewhere.

"You should give it up, Prudence. Your father simply does not wish to listen. Nothing you say will sway him. It is some sort of illness. Believe me, I know."

"Aye, I know you do," she said quietly. "Which is precisely why it is so hard for me to comprehend how you can now do to others what was done to your family."

"I am not doing anything. I run an honest establishment. I do not cheat—"

"You say that it is some sort of illness. A compulsion. Are you not then taking advantage of this illness?" When he stared at her blankly, she turned her head away with a sigh. "I am not foolish enough to think that I can make him change his ways. Our talk at Ellie's ball convinced me that I could not do that. Tonight's efforts were an attempt to at least slow his losses down. Perhaps I would have been able to keep my family intact just a little bit longer. I thought—*hoped*—to keep us out of the poorhouse until at least the new year. I see now that even that is not possible."

Stephen pulled back sharply at her words, concern on his face. "Surely it is not so bad?"

Pru's answer was a painful silence, and Stephen frowned, taking in her broken expression.

"Prudence, please," he began, reaching out to caress her cheek, but the carriage stopped. They had reached her home. Pulling free of his touch as the driver opened the door, Prudence stepped out of the carriage and walked through the gate to her home.

Chapter Five

Stephen leaned back in his chair, the accounts open before him all but forgotten. His mind was not on what he should be doing, but instead taken up with thoughts of Prudence. He could not seem to get his last vision of her out of his mind. Her shoulders slumped, she had looked so defeated as she had walked away. That vision haunted him. *She* haunted him. Stephen hadn't known her long, but she had certainly made an impact on his life in a hurry. She had also livened it up. With her around, almost every day had been an adventure. It had gotten to the point where he had wondered what would come next. The answer now was nothing. She hadn't tried anything for a week, not since he had taken her to White's.

Pushing impatiently to his feet, he wandered through the kitchens of his establishment and into the gaming room. Servants were rushing about, cleaning up from last night's business and preparing for tonight's. It had picked up again now that Ballard's was no longer plagued with Pru's own particular brand of havoc.

He would trade it all to enjoy that havoc and her presence again.

Shaking his head at that thought, he walked to the front door and opened it. Plunkett turned questioningly as Stephen glanced around the street's inhabitants. No one would be coming for hours, but Plunkett started work each day as soon as Stephen unlocked the doors. He was there to prevent anyone from sneaking in to steal things while the servants were busy.

"Any trouble?" he asked almost hopefully.

"Nay, milord. Quiet as the dead."

"Hmm." Stephen couldn't deny his disappointment. He missed her. He missed her presence, her smell, her smile, her apologetic looks as she created chaos and left destruction in her wake.

"Maybe ye should call on her, milord."

Startled by the unsolicited advice, Stephen glanced to his doorman and found the beefy man looking flustered by his own temerity in making the suggestion. But, as uncomfortable as he appeared, it didn't stop him from offering more.

"I only say that because I've noticed how you've been hankering after her, sort of low since she ain't come back. *Everyone*'s noticed." Seeing Stephen's alarm, he added, "Not that anyone would be blaming ye. She's one of them wormy sorts."

"Wormy sorts?" Stephen echoed with amazement.

"Aye. One of them ones who worms under the skin by your heart and sticks there. Kind of charming and naughty and good all at the same time so's you don't know whether to spank her or kiss her."

Stephen considered the analogy solemnly, then nodded. It was somewhat scandalous for this door-man to speak so of a woman of Prudence's rank, but the man had the right of it. "Aye. She is definitely one of the wormy ones." Stepping out onto the stoop, he let the door close behind him. "Perhaps I *will* go call on the Prescotts."

"ARE YOU NOT going to skate?"

Prudence smiled at Ellie's rosy-cheeked face and shook her head. "You know I cannot."

"Aye, but you have your skates on. I thought mayhap you were going to give it a go. You will improve with practice, Pru."

"That is what you said when we were ten. You do recall, do you not, the time I fell and nearly bit my tongue off?"

"Ah, yes." The other girl grimaced. "Well, why do you have your skates on then?"

"In case Charlotte falls down and hurts herself or needs me. I wanted to be prepared."

"Oh. How sensible."

"There is no need to sound so surprised that I am being sensible, Ellie. I am not a complete nod-cock, you know."

"Nay, of course you aren't. I did not mean to make it sound as if you—Uh-oh."

"Uh-oh what?" Prudence asked with a frown.

"Well, fancy meeting you ladies here."

Pru stiffened at that cheerful voice, then turned to glance over her shoulder at Stephen as he joined them at the edge of the ice rink. She hadn't seen him since he had taken her to White's. And had missed him horribly, she admitted to herself, then berated herself for being an idiot. She shouldn't miss him. He was helping to ruin her family, whether deliberately or not. She should loathe the man. But he was so damned handsome, and he had such a nice smile and sweet eyes and—*Damn!*

Without really considering what she was doing, Prudence propelled herself out onto the ice.

STEPHEN GAPED AFTER Prudence in amazement. He had arrived at the Prescott home only to learn that Pru had taken her younger sister skating. Not one to give up easily, he had left the Prescotts', headed straight to the shops to purchase himself a pair of skates, then had come to find her. And find her he had, though he had to wonder at the state of his mind, for it was obvious the woman he was pursuing was quite mad.

"What the devil is she doing?" he asked, watching her perform some sort of dance on the ice. At least he thought it was a dance, though it was one he had never seen before. It consisted of repetitive jerking, then skidding motions of her feet and a wild swinging and flapping of her arms. She careened across the ice.

"Hmmm," Eleanore Kindersley murmured consideringly beside him. "I believe she is attempting to skate, my lord."

"She is?" He let his gaze drift over the other people gliding around the rink. "No one else appears to be skating like that."

"Well, I did say *attempting* to skate."

Stephen raised his eyebrows at Pru's friend, but she didn't notice. She was wincing at something out on the ice. Following her gaze, Stephen winced as well. Prudence had taken a tumble and was now trying to pick herself up. She managed to get halfway back up before her feet slid out from beneath her and she ended back on her behind.

"She doesn't appear to be very good at it."

"Nay," Ellie agreed quietly. "But then she doesn't care to skate. In fact, she did not originally intend to skate today. She only wore her skates in case Charlotte needed her."

"I see," Stephen said softly, watching Prudence gain her feet only to do something like a pirouette and again land on her bottom. Shaking his head, he turned abruptly and moved to the nearest log. Settling on it, he began to undo his boots.

"What are you doing?"

Stephen glanced up at Eleanore Kindersley, then went back to what he was doing. "Putting on my skates."

"Ah. You have never tied skate laces before, have you?"

"Nay." He glanced up with surprise. "How did you know?"

"You are doing it wrong," she explained. Kneeling before him, she took the strings. "Here, let me assist you." Swatting his hands out of the way, she made quick work of the task.

"I hesitate to ask this, my lord," she said, stepping back as he got to his feet. "But have you ever been skating before?"

He paused, looking uncertain, then nodded. "Yes. I am sure I did as a child. At least, I recall drinking hot cider in the cold."

"Oh, dear. Well, perhaps you should remain here. I am sure Prudence—" She turned and fixed on something on the ice. Following her gaze again, Stephen saw that a rather dashing-looking fellow had stopped to help Pru.

"There. You see. There is no need for you to—"

Cursing under his breath, Stephen did not stick around to hear more. He sailed out onto the rink in a manner rather similar to the way Prudence had done moments before, and no doubt looking just as mad as he wheeled his arms and pedaled his feet. Not that he cared. He was more concerned with staying upright on the ridiculously slippery surface and rescuing Prudence from the randy bastard presently using the excuse of helping her as a chance to maul her.

The man was holding her far too close to his chest, in Stephen's opinion. And Prudence, grateful for his assistance, was probably wholly unaware of his no doubt salacious intent.

"Lecher," Stephen muttered under his breath as Prudence started to slip again and the man hugged her closer until they were chest-to-chest. When he got there, he would—

His thoughts ended abruptly as a young boy swished past, bumping him. Stephen promptly lost his precarious balance and landed flat on his back. Grimacing at the pain in his tailbone, he sat up, then glanced irritably around at a raucous laugh. The young beast who had knocked him off his feet was now skating in circles about him, laughing uproariously. The little demon only reached the top of Stephen's head where he sat on the ice, but he skated like the wind.

Deciding that if the little guttersnipe could skate like that, he himself could, Stephen ignored the brat and started to his feet. He was halfway back up when his feet slid out from beneath him again. The second time he ended up doing half a split. Deciding that he needed something to keep his first skate steady while he regained his feet, Stephen hesitated, slid his glove off and set it on the ice before his right skate, then tried again.

Much to his satisfaction, that worked nicely. The glove held the skate in place, allowing him to regain his feet. But then he teetered there, peering down at the glove still lying on the ice. He knew without a doubt that if he tried to retrieve it, he would end up back on his butt. After all the trouble he had gone to getting here, he wasn't risking falling again for one stupid glove.

He would just leave it, he decided as he glanced over to snarl at the way the libertine was holding Prudence. It was indecent. If anyone was going to hold her that way, it was him and him alone!

Stepping over his glove, he launched himself forward. Careening across the ice at a rather satisfying, if terrifying speed, he reached Prudence and her would-be rescuer in a trice. Unfortunately, once he was sailing along, he had no idea how to slow or stop himself. He was going to crash into the pair. Just moments before impact, he managed to adjust the angle of his skates, thereby sending himself hurtling into only the fellow.

"Stephen!"

It did his heart good to hear that concerned cry from Prudence as he crashed down on top of her would-be rescuer. He gave her a reassuring smile over his shoulder, then glanced back at the fellow who had thoughtfully, if unintentionally, cushioned his fall.

"So sorry about that," he apologized, crawling off and bracing his skate against the man's leg to get back to his feet. "I meant to come to Pru's aid; however I am just getting used to skates again. Need a little practice, I guess. Are you all right?"

Taking the man's groan for a yes, Stephen nodded with satisfaction. Turning, he took Pru's hands.

"Wait. I do not think he is—"

"He is fine. You heard him. Come along. We had best get off the ice before one or both of us suffers an injury. Thanks again, young man," he called, then urged her away, both of them teetering and slipping across the ice.

"Where is your other glove?"

"Hmm? What?" He glanced down at the cold bare hand she was clutching and grimaced. "Oh, yes. Well, I appear to have lost—" He paused as Prudence suddenly tumbled to her knees.

Stephen stared down at her with a dismay that turned to chagrin as he saw the glove she was picking up, the one that had caught her skate and tripped her.

"You found it." Taking the ice-covered glove from her, he shoved it into his pocket, then took her elbow to help her to her feet. He managed to get her up without falling himself, then urged her to the edge of the rink, noting with some pride that he was actually almost skating.

"What are you doing here?" Prudence said in a hiss, pulling free of his hold the moment they stepped off the ice and onto the more stable snowy ground. "I believe I made it plain that I am uncomfortable seeing you when you are aiding in ruining—"

"I know," Stephen interrupted as he followed her to the log he had sat on earlier to don his skates. "You were right."

"About what, my lord?"

"About . . . I did not really realize that . . . When I started Ballard's, I was desperate to regain some of the money my father had lost. He left my mother and me in a bad way and we needed income to survive. I found I was good at gambling. Ironic, since my father was not. After making a small amount, seeing how much certain clubs could take in, starting Ballard's seemed the swiftest way to return my family's estate to what it was. But after that, I was tainted. It seemed only fitting that the club should remain open. I did not consider that I was taking advantage of others just like my father had been taken advantage of. But you are right. I am making money off of the frailties of others."

She considered that silently, then asked, "What shall you do now that you realize that?"

Stephen scowled and wished he could see her face. She was bent forward, undoing her skates, and he couldn't see her expression. He hadn't really planned what he wanted to say to her. He was stumbling around blind. "Well, I suppose I could ban your father from the club."

"Why bother? As you proved, he will just gamble elsewhere."

Stephen frowned, his gaze moving absently over the skaters before he glanced back and complained, "I do not know what else I can possibly do."

"Nay. Of course you do not." She sounded bitter, and Stephen felt at a loss until she straightened and added, "This is not about my father, Stephen.

At least not just my father. This is about you—how you make your way in the world."

There was a regret in her eyes that made his heart shrivel. "I—"

"Pru! Guess what?"

Stephen watched helplessly as she turned away toward a young girl who had rushed over to address her. She was a younger version of Prudence, with the same chestnut hair and gamine features. Stephen had the brief thought that Prudence's daughter would probably look very much the same.

"Good. You have already removed your skates," Prudence said, getting to her feet. "'Tis time to return home. Where is Eleanore?"

"Oh, but Pru!" the girl protested.

"Where is Eleanore?" she repeated firmly.

"She said to tell you she had gone home."

"Gone home?" Prudence echoed with disbelief.

"Aye. She said that no doubt Lord Stockton would take us home, and she was growing cold."

"Growing cold, my eye," Stephen heard her mutter irritably as he got to his feet.

"I would be pleased to see you home," he said. He saw the inner struggle take place on her face, but then her gaze landed on her sister and resignation set in. Even as she agreed, he got the distinct impression that she would have walked rather than accept his offer—and would have, were it not for her sister's presence. Ironically, that made young

Charlotte one of Stephen's favorite people, and he teased and chatted with her easily, listening with a smile to her chatter all the way to the Prescotts'.

When the carriage stopped in front of their home, the little whirlwind was out the door at once. But when Prudence made to follow, Stephen caught her arm and drew her back, pulling her into his arms for a kiss before she could protest. It was a desperate kiss, a last-ditch effort to bring her back to him, and at first, as she kissed him back, he felt hope that it might succeed. But then he felt her become still and withdraw, and her expression when he reluctantly released her killed his brief hope. He saw on her face that he was one of the bad guys. Just as he had seen the owners of the gaming hells his father had frequented, so she saw him—as a vulture.

She exited the coach without a word.

Stephen's mood was grim when he returned to his club. He found dissatisfaction plucking at him as he peered around the gaming room. It was late enough that the place was filling up, and everywhere he looked were the desperate gazes of men risking more than they should, the slumped shoulders of losers. At times like this, it all seemed terribly tawdry and unpalatable, and he seriously considered alternative professions. It was also at times like this that he saw his father everywhere. Right that moment, he was even seeing his father in the face of Lord Prescott, and the man's very presence seemed to mock him.

PRUDENCE ROLLED ONTO her back and sighed miserably. Sleep seemed to be beyond her. Her mind was too full to allow it. She kept thinking of Stephen, seeing his handsome face, remembering his kisses, his touch, his scent, his smile. He had such gentle eyes. She wished—

She threw the bedcovers aside impatiently and sat up to swing her feet off of the bed. There was no use in wishing for things she couldn't have. It was doubtful that Stephen's interest in her went beyond the carnal, and even should he wish more, she could not, in good conscience, have any sort of marriage with a man who made his living off of the weaknesses of people like her father.

Standing, she found her robe and pulled it on, then made her way cautiously through the dark to the door. It was Christmas Eve. She had gone to bed early. The whole household had, except for her father. He was no doubt out losing the last of their possessions. The creditors had stopped allowing Bentley, their butler, to brush them off. The day before, they had started to take things away in lieu of payment. Which was why Prudence had taken Charlotte skating—to keep her from having to witness those nasty encounters.

She had intended to take her little sister somewhere else today, perhaps to visit Ellie, but other than two large bill collectors who had visited rather early, no one had come around. The day had turned out well, and she and her mother had decided to take advantage of their home while they still had it, stringing popcorn to finish decorating the tree. Prudence supposed even creditors had hearts if they were waiting until after Christmas to empty the Prescott home.

She had made her way along the dark hall and down the stairs before spotting the light shining from beneath the kitchen door. Suspecting it was her mother, and knowing she would need cheering, Prudence forced a smile to her face and pushed into the room. Inside she froze. It wasn't her mother; instead, her father sat at the table, looking dazed.

"Father, whatever are you doing home?" she asked with surprise. "Why are you not out . . ."

"I have been banned from everywhere, that is why. Where has all the liquor in this house gone?"

"You *drank* it," she answered distractedly. "Did you say you were banned from *everywhere?*"

He nodded morosely. "Someone went around and paid all my debts, every last one. But in exchange, the owners were to bar me from entry." He shook his head miserably. "I am not even allowed in to drink! Who the hell would do a thing like that?"

"Papa, you are sober."

He glanced up with a startled expression. "Aye. Why does that surprise you?"

"I have not seen you sober in a long time," she

said gently. Surprised realization crossed his face; then his gaze moved to the door as his wife entered.

"What is this about?" she asked upon seeing her husband. Her face showed the same surprise at his presence that Prudence had felt.

"Papa has been banned from the clubs. Someone has paid his debts, but he is no longer allowed in them—even to drink." Prudence spoke quietly, then rushed to comfort her mother as she burst into sudden tears. "This is good news, Mam. Everything will be well now."

"I know!" the woman wailed. "It is just that I have been so frightened. When those creditors came and took . . . I feared we would be in the poorhouse by year's end, and—oh, Prudence, we are saved!" She threw her arms around her daughter and held her tightly, sobbing into her shoulder, and Prudence peered over the woman at her father, unable to keep the accusation out of her eyes. It was not softened by the stunned and slightly horrified look on his face.

He looked away from her angry eyes for a moment, then stood and moved forward to pat awkwardly at his wife's shoulder. "Ah, now, Meg. Don't carry on so," he said uncomfortably. "Things had not got that bad."

"Not got that bad?!" Lady Prescott shrieked, turning on him in the first show of temper Prudence had ever seen from her. "The creditors were here yesterday and this morning. They took my mother's diamond necklace and—"

"What?" Lord Prescott interrupted, looking thunderous. "Why did no one tell me?"

"Because you were never here to tell!" she roared. "You have been avoiding us for weeks now. Dragging yourself back in the middle of the night, passing out in the guest chambers, sneaking out the moment the way was clear . . ."

He flushed guiltily at the accusations, then wearily sank back into his seat.

"I have been an ass, haven't I? I've made you both so miserable." Grasping his wife's hand, he pressed it to his forehead and closed his eyes. "I do not know how it started. John died and I just didn't want to think about it. At first the drink worked for that, but then it wasn't enough. I started gambling. Before I knew it, I had gotten so far in debt that I could not stop. I kept hoping that the next hand would be enough to get me out, but instead I just kept getting in deeper and deeper and . . ." He shook his head, then opened his eyes and peered up at his wife. "I am sorry."

A sob breaking from her lips, Lady Prescott bent to hug her husband tightly around the neck. "I know it was hard losing Johnny like that. I still ache over it as well. But dear God, Edward, this last while I felt sure we had lost you, too."

"Nay." He patted her back soothingly. "Well, mayhap for a while. But I am back now." He blinked, as if looking at the world through new eyes. Sober eyes.

"Thank you, God," Lady Prescott whispered, then added with a smile, "Just in time for Christmas."

"Christmas?" Lord Prescott looked stunned, then vexed. "Damn me, I forgot all about Christmas. I have no gifts for you."

"It does not matter." Prudence's mother gave a watery laugh, joy spreading on her face. "I got all I wanted for Christmas."

Her husband's confusion was plain to see. "What was that?"

"I prayed that you would stop drinking and gambling, that we wouldn't spend Christmas in debtors' prison. And I have that now."

"Damn." He sighed miserably. "I *have* been an ass. I am sorry, love. I will try to be a better husband. I will try very hard."

"That's all a woman could ask," Lady Prescott said quietly, and helped him to his feet.

Prudence watched them head up the stairs, a soft smile on her face. She knew it wouldn't be easy; there were still hard times ahead. There were days her father would be miserable and unhappy for want of the liquor, but there was finally hope . . . and her mother looked so happy. Almost as happy as Prudence felt.

A thought coming to her, she headed for her own room, but not to go to bed. She needed to get dressed. She had someone to thank for this miracle. Someone unexpected.

Chapter Six

My lord?"

Stephen glanced up from the fire he had been morosely contemplating, and lifted an eyebrow at the sight of his butler.

"You have a guest, my lord," the man announced.

Stephen started to say that he had no wish for company, to send whoever it was away, when he spotted Pru's gamine face peeking around his butler's ample girth. He lurched out of his seat.

"Prudence! What are you doing here?" he cried in astonishment, waving the butler away as he hurried forward to greet her.

"I had to talk to you."

"But you could be ruined if anyone—"

"No one saw me," she assured him quickly. "And I will stay only a moment."

His expression easing somewhat, Stephen nodded and led the way toward the two chairs in front of the fire, gesturing for her to take one. He waited politely while she seated herself, then moved to lean against the fireplace.

"*You* did it, didn't you?" she asked the moment he was settled.

Stephen shrugged, not bothering to ask what she spoke of. He knew she meant her father and his gambling debts.

"Why?"

Uncomfortable under her shining gaze, he turned away, bracing his hand on the mantel and peering down into the flames. "You were right when you accused me of refilling my coffers at the expense of others. For some it is just gaming. Good fun. But for others—like your father—they are suffering an illness. And, as you pointed out, I was taking advantage of that. Once I admitted that to myself, I found I could no longer pretend I wasn't harming anyone."

"So you paid off my father's debts?"

He shrugged as if it were of no real consequence; then a smile tugged at his lips as he admitted, "I managed to save his reputation, I think. I gave a rather clever explanation as to why I was paying all your father's debts." Before she could question him on that, he added, "I also told them that he was not to be allowed inside the gaming hells anymore."

"And they agreed to this?"

His expression turned wry at her obvious surprise. "I do have some influence around town. Most everyone owes me money." He scuffed at the corner of the rug before the fire with his boot, then added, "And then I sold Ballard's."

Prudence leaned forward in her seat. "You what?"

"Well, it shan't be Ballard's much longer. The new owner is renaming it." Sticking his hands in the pockets of his coat, he shrugged again. "I am looking into other ventures. I already have several I may invest in." He turned back to the fire. "Would I be right in supposing that your father is now grumpy as hell, but at home and sober?"

"Aye." When she fell silent, he glanced over his shoulder to see her biting her lip uncertainly, her gaze sliding around the warm and cozy room they were in. Then she heaved a little sigh, straightened her shoulders in a habit he was coming to recognize, and faced him to ask, "Did you do this because you felt guilty?"

Stephen considered her question solemnly as he turned his back to the fireplace. "That may have influenced me; however, I have considered getting out of the business for a while. As for paying your father's debts, that I did for you. I could hardly let the woman I love end up in debtors' prison for Christmas."

"Love?" She looked as if she were holding her breath.

"Aye."

"Oh, Stephen!" Launching out of her chair, she threw herself at him. He staggered back against the fireplace as she pressed tiny little kisses all over his face.

"Thank you, thank you, thank you!" she cried

between kisses to his nose, his cheeks, his eyes, his chin, and finally his lips. There he brought the spate of little butterfly kisses to an end. Catching the back of her head, he held her still when she would have continued on with her exuberant rampage, and he moved his mouth on hers. Prudence didn't seem to mind. She gave no resistance. In fact, Stephen felt her smile against his mouth before she opened to him, inviting a deeper kiss. He immediately took advantage of the invitation, devouring her with a passion that had him hardening to shameful proportions. His body was reacting like an untried lad's, and he was heeding its plaintive urgings. Within moments he had Prudence on her back on the fur rug in front of the fire, his hands busy everywhere. One was pushing the skirt of her gown up, the other tugging the top of it down. His lips were leaping from hers to the curve of one breast, then back, eager to taste everything as she writhed, arched, moaned, and sighed beneath him.

"This is not good," he muttered, kissing his way over the curve of her breast. Prudence sighed dreamily and arched against him as he took one erect nipple into his mouth.

"It feels very good to me," she purred.

Stephen smiled against her flesh. She felt it, apparently, and slid her hand into his dark hair. "You are smiling," she said.

"I have been doing that a lot since I met you," he admitted, his smile widening.

"It is the same for me," Prudence confessed on a half giggle, half sigh. He laved her nipple. "I must thank you."

Stephen raised his head to peer at her questioningly. "For making you smile?"

"Aye. For that, and for—"

"This?" he asked, catching the tip of her breast between his teeth and licking it. Releasing it, he added, "Or this?" The hand that had been resting on her thigh rose up to cup the center of her.

"Oh." Prudence pressed into his touch and shook her head a touch frantically on the fur. "If this is being ruined, I think I like it."

Stephen stilled at those words, concern for her gripping him, but she opened her eyes and smiled at him gently.

"Pray, do not stop. I do not wish you to stop." She hesitated, then added, "But I do want to thank you for giving my mother everything she wanted for Christmas."

"Ah." Aroused and pleased by the good he'd done, Stephen rubbed a thumb over the damp nipple he had been suckling, enjoying the way she arched and purred in response. "And what do *you* want for Christmas?"

"Me?" She seemed surprised.

"Aye. You," he said. Then he stilled as he realized that it was Christmas Eve. He could not buy her a gift until the shops reopened. Vexed that he hadn't thought of a gift before this, he warned, "I shan't be able to procure it until after the shops reopen, but—"

"What I want cannot be purchased."

Stephen drew back at that soft assurance. "What?"

"I would like more of *this*," she said huskily. Laughing, she drew his head toward her own.

Stephen allowed her to pull him forward until his mouth was a bare inch away, then paused and murmured, "I am not sure."

"What?"

He couldn't tell if she was more affronted or shocked by his refusal to take what she offered, and he nearly smiled at her reaction, but managed to keep a solemn demeanor. "Well," he amended. "Perhaps I could be persuaded . . . if you were to agree to give me what I want for Christmas in return."

Prudence suddenly looked wary. "What do *you* want for Christmas?"

"All I want in the world for Christmas is for you to make an honest man of me. Marry me, Prudence."

PRU CAUGHT HER breath at Stephen's proposal, nearly squeezing him silly. She wanted to shriek, "Yes," but she hesitated and pushed at his chest until he eased the embrace. Solemnly she said, "You do not have to marry me. We can stop this right now. No one would ever know. I have escaped notice for far worse. You do not have to feel honor-bound to marry me."

"On the other hand," he said slowly, "I could enjoy you now, tonight, on this Christmas Eve, and every other night so long as we both shall live. I could share your life, have children with you who will look as sweet and be just as cussedly stubborn as you. And I can have you and your harebrained schemes to make the rest of my life an adventure." He smiled crookedly. "It is not a hard choice."

"Truly?"

"Truly," he assured her. "Besides, that clever reason I gave for why I was paying your father's debts . . ."

Confusion covered her expression at the seeming change of subject. "Yes?"

"I said it was because we were marrying and he had to save up for a huge wedding."

"Stephen!" she cried, slapping at his chest.

He grinned unrepentantly and pulled her closer in his arms. "I do love you, Pru, and I want to share my life with you. What of you?"

"Me?" She smiled crookedly at the uncertainty on his face as he asked the question, then made a serious face and tapped her chin thoughtfully. "Hmmm, let me see. Marry my own personal hero? The man who saved my family?"

"No," Stephen said at once, "I do not wish you to marry me for what I did. I do not wish you to marry me out of simple gratitude."

"Ah." Prudence nodded her head with understanding. "Then how about because you make me burn? Raise my passions? Test my mind? Make me smile? Or because my heart sings when you are near? Because when you are away I think of you and wonder what you are doing, and when you are near I wonder what you are thinking and wish you would touch me? Would that be reason enough? Or perhaps because I love you?"

She gasped when he hugged her tightly, then rolled on the floor with her until she lay atop him. Pulling her head down, he kissed her until they were both aching with want; then he leaned his forehead against hers and held her close. Doing so, he whispered, "I do love you. You make me very happy, Pru."

"Ahhhh," Prudence sighed in a quavery voice. "I have changed my mind."

"About what?" he asked, brushing the hair back behind her ears, a loving smile on his face for her and only her.

"All I want for Christmas is for you to say that again," she murmured, a smile trembling on her lips.

Stephen's lips widened. "I believe that can be arranged. In fact, lucky girl that you are, I think I can give you both things."

And he did.

Three French Hens

Chapter One

December 24

"Ye'd best set that aside and wipe yer hands, girl. Cook'll be wantin' ye in a minute."

"Hmm?" Brinna glanced up from the pot she had been scrubbing and frowned slightly at the old woman now setting to work beside her. "Why?"

"I was talkin' to Mabel ere I came back to the kitchen and she says one o' them guests His Lordship brought with him don't have no maid. Fell ill or something and they left her at court."

"So?"

"So, Lady Menton sent Christina in here to fetch a woman to replace her," she said dryly, and nodded toward the opposite end of the kitchen.

Following the gesture, Brinna saw that Aggie was right. Lady Christina was indeed in the kitchen speaking with Cook. A rare sight, that. You were more likely to find the daughter of the house with her nose buried in one of those musty old books she was forever dragging about than sniffing near anything domestic. It had been a bone of contention between her and her mother since the girl's return from the convent school.

"I still don't see what that's to do with me," Brinna muttered, turning to frown at the older woman again, and Aggie tut-tutted impatiently.

"I didn't raise ye to be a fool, girl. Just look about. Do you see any likely lady's maids 'sides yerself?"

Letting the pot she had been scrubbing slide down to rest on the table before her, Brinna glanced around the kitchen. Two boys ground herbs with a mortar and pestle in a corner, while another boy worked at the monotonous task of turning a pig on its spit over the fire. But other than Lady Christina and Cook, she and Aggie were the only women present at the moment. The others were all rushing about trying to finish preparations for the sudden influx of guests that Lord Menton had brought home with him. Aggie herself was just returning from one such task.

"From what I heard as I entered, they've settled on ye as the most likely lady's maid," Aggie murmured.

"Mayhap they'll send you now that yer back," Brinna murmured. "That would make a nice change fer ye."

"Oh, aye," Aggie said dryly. "Me runnin' up an' down those stairs, chasin' after some spoilt little girl. A nice change, that. Here it comes," Aggie added with satisfaction as Lady Christina left and Cook turned toward them.

"Brinna!"

"See. Now, off with ye and make me proud."

Releasing her breath in a sigh, Brinna wiped her hands dry on her skirts and hurried to Cook's side as she returned to the table that she had been working at before Lady Christina's arrival. "Ma'am?"

"Lady Christina was just here," the older woman announced as she bent to open a bag squirming beneath the table.

"Aye, ma'am. I saw her."

"Hmm." She straightened from the bag, holding a frantically squawking and flapping chicken by its legs. "Well, it seems one of the lady's maids fell ill and remained behind at court. A replacement is needed while the girl is here. You're that replacement."

"Oh. But, well, yer awful short-staffed at the moment and—"

"Aye. I said as much to Lady Christina," Cook interrupted dryly as she picked up a small hatchet with her free hand. "And she suggested I go down to the village in search of extra help . . . just as soon as I dispatch you to assist the lady in question."

"But—oh, nay, ma'am, I never could. Why, I can't. I . . ."

"You could, you can, and you will," Cook declared, slamming the bird she held on the table with enough force to stun it, stilling it for the moment necessary for her to sever its head from its body with one smooth stroke of her ax. Pushing the twitching body aside, she wiped her hands on her apron, then removed it and set it aside before catching Brinna's elbow in her strong hand and directing her toward the door.

"Ye've been a scullery maid under me now for ten of yer twenty years, Brinna, and I've watched ye turn away one chance after another to advance up the ranks. And yet God has seen fit to send ye another, and if you think to turn this away for yer dear Aggie's sake—"

She paused and rolled her eyes skyward at Brinna's gasp of surprise. "Did ye think I was so dense that I'd believe ye actually enjoy washing pans all day every day? Or did ye think I was too blind to notice that ye start afore the others have risen and stay at it until well after they've quit for the night—all in an effort to cover the fact that Aggie has slowed down in her old age?" Sighing, the cook shook her head and continued forward, propelling Brinna along with her. "I know you are reluctant to leave Aggie. She raised ye from a babe, mothered ye through chills, colds, and childhood injuries. And I know too that ye've been the best daughter a woman could hope for, mothering and caring for her in return these last many years. Covering for her as age crept over her, making the job too hard for her old body. But ye needn't have bothered. I am not so cruel that I would throw an old woman out on her duff after years of faithful service because she cannot work as she used to. She does her best, as do you, and that leaves me well satisfied.

"So . . ." Pausing, she eyed Brinna grimly. "If you don't accept this opportunity to prove yourself and maybe move up the ranks through it, I'll swat ye up the side o' the head with me favorite ladle. And don't think I won't. Now." Cook turned her abruptly, showing Brinna that while she had been distracted by the woman's words, Cook had marched her out to the great hall and to the foot of the stairs leading to the bedchambers. "Get upstairs and be the best lady's maid ye can be. It's Lady Joan Laythem, third room on the right. Get to it."

She gave her a little push, and Brinna stumbled up several steps before turning to glance down at the woman uncertainly. "Ye'll really keep Aggie on, despite her being a bit slower than she used to be?"

"I told you so, didn't I?"

Brinna nodded, then cocked her head. "Why're ye only telling me now and not sooner?"

Surprise crossed the other woman's face. "What? And lose the best scullion I've ever had? Why, it will take two women to replace you. Speaking of which, I'd best get down to the village and find half a dozen or so girls to help out while the guests are here. You get on up there now and do your best."

Nodding, Brinna turned away and hurried upstairs, not slowing until she reached the door Cook had directed her to. Pausing then, she glanced down at her stained and threadbare skirt, brushed it a couple of times in the vain hope that some of the stains might be crumbs she could easily brush away, then gave up the task with a sigh and knocked at the door. Hearing a muffled murmur to enter, she pasted a bright smile on her lips, opened the door, and stepped inside the room.

"Oh, fustian!" The snarled words preceded the crash of a water basin hitting the floor as Lady Joan bumped it while peeling off her glove. Stomping her foot, the girl gave a moan of frustration. "Now look what I have done. My hands are so frozen they will not do what I want and—"

"I'll tend it, m'lady." Pushing the door closed, Brinna rushed around the bed toward the mess. "Why don't you cozy yerself by the fire for a bit and warm up."

Heaving a sigh, Lady Laythem moved away to stand by the fire as Brinna knelt to tend to the mess. She had set the basin back on the chest and gathered the worst of the soaked rushes up to take them below to discard, when the bedroom door burst open and a pretty brunette bustled into the room.

"What a relief to be spending the night within the walls of a castle again. I swear! One more night camping by the roadside and—" Spying Brinna's head poking up curiously over the side of the bed, the woman came to a halt, eyes round with amazement. "Joan! What on earth are you doing on the floor?"

"Whatever are you talking about, Sabrina? I am over here."

Whirling toward the fireplace, the newcomer gasped. "Joan! I thought—" She turned abruptly back toward Brinna as if suddenly doubting that she had seen what she thought she had. She shook her head in amazement as Brinna straightened slowly, the damp rushes in her hands. "Good Lord," Sabrina breathed. "Who are you?"

"I-I was sent to replace Lady Laythem's maid," Brinna murmured uncertainly.

This news was accepted with silence; then the brunette glanced toward Lady Laythem, who was now staring at Brinna with a rather stunned expression as well. "It is not just me," the cousin said with relief. "You see it too."

"Aye," Lady Joan murmured, moving slowly forward. "I did not really look at her when she entered, but there is a resemblance."

"A resemblance?" the brunette cried in amazement, her gaze sliding back to Brinna again. "She is almost a mirror image of you, Joan. Except for that hair, of course. Yours has never been so limp and dirty."

Brinna raised a hand self-consciously to her head, glancing around in dismay as she realized that the ratty old strip of cloth that usually covered her head was gone. Seeing it lying on the floor, she bent quickly to pick it up, dropping the rushes so that she could quickly replace it. The cloth kept the hair out of her face while she scrubbed pots in the steaming kitchen, and half-hid the length of time between baths during the winter when the cold made daily dips in the river impossible. She, like the rest of the servants, had to make do with pots of water and a quick scrub for most of the winter. The opportunity to actually wash her hair was rare during this season.

"She does look like me, does she not?" Lady Laythem murmured slowly now, and hearing her, Brinna shook her head. She herself didn't see a resemblance. Lady Joan's hair was as fine as flax and fell in waves around her fair face. Her eyes were green, while Brinna had always been told that her own were gray. She supposed their noses and lips were similar, but she wasn't really sure. She had only ever seen her reflection in the surface of water, and didn't believe she was anywhere near as lovely as Lady Laythem.

"Aye." The cousin circled Brinna, inspecting every inch of her. "She could almost be your twin. In fact, had she been wearing one of your dresses and not those pitiful rags, you could have fooled me into thinking she was you."

Lady Laythem seemed to suck in a shaky gasp at that, her body stilling briefly before a sudden smile split her face. "That is a brilliant idea, Sabrina."

"It is?" The brunette glanced at her with the beginnings of excitement, then frowned slightly. "What is?"

"That we dress her up as me and let her take my place during this horrid holiday."

"What?" Brinna and Sabrina gasped as one; then Sabrina rushed to her cousin's side anxiously. "Oh, Joan, what are you thinking of?"

"Just what I said." Smiling brightly, she moved to stand in front of Brinna. "It will be grand. You can wear my gowns, eat at the high table with the other nobles. Why, 'twill be a wonderful experience for you! Aye. I think it might actually even work. Of course, your speech needs a little work, and your hands—"

When the lady reached for her callused and chapped hands, Brinna put them quickly behind her back and out of reach as she began to shake her head frantically. "Oh, nay. 'Tis sorry I am, m'lady, but I couldn't be takin' yer place. Why, it's a punishable offense fer a free woman to pass herself off as a noble. Why, they'd—well, I'm not sure what they'd do, but 'tis sure I am 'twould be horrible."

"Do you think so?" Lady Laythem glanced toward her cousin questioningly, but found no help there. Her cousin was gaping at them both as if they had sprouted a third head between them. Sighing, Joan turned back to beam at Brinna reassuringly. "Well, it does not matter. 'Twill not be a worry. If you are discovered, I shall simply say 'twas all my idea. That 'twas a jest."

"Aye, well . . ." Eyes wide and wary, Brinna began backing away. "I don't think—"

"I will pay you."

Pausing, she blinked at that. "Pay me?"

"Handsomely," Joan assured her, then mentioned a sum that made Brinna press a hand to her chest and drop onto the end of the bed to sit as her head spun. With that sum, Aggie could retire. She could while away the rest of her days in relative comfort and peace. Aggie deserved such a boon.

"Joan!" Dismay covering her face, Sabrina hurried forward now. "Whatever do you think you are doing? You can't have this—this *maid* impersonate you!"

"Of course I can. Don't you see? If she is me, I won't have to suffer the clumsy wooing of that backwoods oaf to whom my father is determined to marry me off. I may even find a way out of this mess."

"There is no way out of this mess—I mean, marriage. It was contracted when you were but a babe. It is—"

"There is always a way out of things," Joan insisted grimly. "And I will find it if I just have time to think. Having her pretend to be me will give me that time. I would already have figured a way out of it if Father had deigned to mention this betrothal ere he did. Why, when he sent for me from court, I thought, I thought—well, I certainly did not think it was simply to ship me here so that some country bumpkin could look me over for a marriage I did not even know about."

"I understand you are upset," Sabrina murmured gently. "But you have yet to even meet Royce of Thurleah. He may be a very nice man. He may be—"

"He is a lesser baron of Lord Menton's. He was the son of a wealthy land baron some fifteen years ago when my father made the betrothal, but his father ran the estate into the ground and left his son with a burdensome debt and a passel of trouble. He made a name for himself in battle while in service to the king, then retired to his estates where he is said to work as hard as his few vassals. He does not attend court, and does not travel much. In fact, he spends most of his time out there on his estate trying to wring some profit from his land."

Sabrina bit her lip guiltily. It was she herself who had gained all this information for Joan during the trip here from court. It had been easy enough to attain, a question here, a question there. Everyone seemed to know and respect the man. She pointed that out now, adding, "And he is succeeding at the task he has set for himself. He is slowly rebuilding the estate to its original glory."

"Oh, aye, with my dower, Thurleah shall no doubt be returned to its original wealth and grandeur . . . in about five, maybe ten years. But by the time that happens, I shall have died at childbirth or be too old to enjoy the benefits. Nay. I'll not marry him, cousin. This is the first time in my nineteen and a half years that I have even set foot outside of

Laythem. I have dreamed my whole life that some-day things would be different. That I would marry, leave Laythem, and visit court whenever I wish. I will not trade one prison for another and marry a man who stays on his estate all the time, a man who will expect me to work myself to death beside him."

"But—" Sabrina glanced between her cousin and Brinna with a frown. "Well, can you not simply go along with meeting and getting to know him until you come up with a plan to avoid the wedding? Why must you make the girl take your place?"

"Because 'twill give me more time to think. Besides, why should I suffer the wooing of a country bumpkin who probably does not even know what courtly love is? Let him woo the maid. His coarse words and ignorant manners will no doubt seem charming to her after the rough attentions she probably suffers daily as a serf."

"I am a free woman," Brinna said with quiet dignity. But neither woman seemed to hear, much less care, about what she had to say, as Sabrina frowned, her eyes narrowing on Joan.

"I have never said anyone called Thurleah a country bumpkin or said that his manners were poor," Sabrina declared.

"Did you not?" Joan was suddenly avoiding her cousin's gaze. "Well, it does not matter. Someone did, and this maid can save me from all that by taking my place."

"Nay. She cannot," Sabrina said firmly. "It would not work. While you are similar in looks, you are not identical. She is even an inch or two taller than you."

"You are right, of course. If Father were here I would never dare try it, but it's almost providential that he fell ill and had to remain behind at court. But no one here has seen me before except for Lord Menton on the journey here, and then I was bundled up in my mantle and hood, with furs wrapped around me to keep warm. The only thing he saw was my nose poking out into the cold, and she has the same nose. The same is true of Lady Menton when we arrived. She greeted us on arrival, but 'twas only for a mere moment or two and I was still all bundled up."

"Mayhap, but what of the difference in height?"

Joan shrugged. "I was on my horse most of the journey and no doubt my mantle adds some height to me. They will not notice. It will work."

"But she is a *peasant*, Joan. She does not know how to behave as a lady."

"We will teach her what she needs to know," Joan announced blithely.

"You expect to instill nineteen years' worth of training into her in a matter of hours?" Sabrina gasped in disbelief.

"Well . . ." The first signs of doubt played on Joan's face. "Perhaps not in hours. We can claim that I am weary from the journey and wish to rest in my room rather than join the others below for dinner tonight. And I shall tutor her all evening." At Sabrina's doubtful look, she gestured impatiently. "It is not as if I must teach her to run a household or play the harp. She need only walk and talk like a lady, remember to say as little as possible, and not disgrace me. Besides she need only fool Lord Thurleah, and he could not possibly spend much time around proper ladies. He does not even go to court," she muttered with disgust. She turned to the maid.

"Girl?" Joan began, then frowned. "What is your name?"

"Brinna, m'lady."

"Well, Brinna, will you agree to be me?" When Brinna hesitated briefly, Joan moved quickly to a chest at the foot of the bed and tossed it open. Riffling through the contents, she found a small purse, opened it, and poured out several coins. "This is half of what I promised you. Agree and I will give them to you now. I shall give you the other half when 'tis over."

Brinna stared at those coins and swallowed as visions of Aggie resting in a chair by the fire in a cozy cottage filled her mind. The old woman had worked hard to feed and clothe Brinna and deserved to enjoy her last days so. With the coins from this chore, she could see that she did. And it wasn't as if it was dangerous. Lady Joan would explain that it was her idea if they got caught, she assured herself, then quickly nodded her head before she could lose her courage.

"Marvelous!" Grabbing her hand, Joan dropped the coins into her open palm, then folded her fingers closed over them and squeezed firmly. "Now, the first thing we must do is—"

The three of them froze, gazes shooting guiltily to the door, as a knock sounded. At Joan's muttered "Enter," the door opened and Lady Christina peered in.

"Mother sent me to see that all is well with your maid."

"Aye. She will do fine," Joan said quickly, a panicked look about her face. Brinna realized at once that the girl feared that seeing them together, Lady Christina might notice the similarity in their looks and somehow put paid to her plans. There was no way to reassure her that the other girl wasn't likely to notice such things. It was well known at Menton that Lady Christina paid little attention to the world around her unless it had something to do with her beloved books. Which was the reason Brinna was so startled when the girl suddenly tilted her head to the side, her deep blue eyes actually focusing for a moment as she gave a light laugh and murmured, "Look at the three of you. All huddled together with your heads cocked up. You look like three French hens at the arrival of the butcher. Except, of course, only two of you are from Normandy and therefore French. Still . . ."

Brinna felt Joan stiffen beside her as an odd expression crossed over Christina's face. But then it faded and her gaze slid around the room. "They have not brought your bath up yet? I shall see about that for you." Turning, she slid out of the room as quickly as she had entered, leaving the women sighing after her.

"WHY YE'VE MADE me as beautiful as yerself," Brinna breathed in wonder as she was finally allowed to peer in the looking glass at herself.

It was dawn of the morning after Brinna had stepped through the door of Lady Joan's room as her temporary maid. The hours since then had been incredibly busy ones. While Sabrina had carried Joan's message that she was too tired to dine with the others to the dinner table, Brinna had reported to the kitchens, informing Cook that the lady required her to sleep on the floor in front of her door in her room as her own maid usually did. She had then grabbed a quick bite to eat from the kitchen and spared a moment to assure herself that all was well with Aggie before preparing a trencher and delivering it to the lady, only to find her in the bath Lady Christina had had sent up. After tending her in the bath, then helping her out, Brinna had found herself ordered into the now-chill water.

Ignoring her meal, Joan had seen to it that Brinna scrubbed herself from head to toe, then again, and yet again, until Brinna was sure that half of her skin had been taken off with the dirt. Joan had even insisted on scrubbing Brinna's long tresses and rinsing them three times before allowing her to get out of the water. Once out, however, she had not been allowed to redon her "filthy peasant's clothes," but had been given one of Joan's old shifts instead. They had dried their hair before the fire, brushing each other's tresses by turn.

The situation had become extremely odd for Brinna at that point as the boundary between lady and servant became blurred by Joan's asking her about her childhood and life in service, then volunteering information about her own life. To Brinna, the other girl's life had sounded poor indeed. For while she had had everything wealth and privilege could buy, it did seem that Joan had been terribly lonely. Her mother had died while she was still a child and her father seemed always away on court business. This had left the girl in the care and company of the servants. Brinna may not have had the lovely clothes and jewels the other girl had, but she'd had Aggie, had always known she was loved, had always had the woman to run to with scraped knees or for a hug. From Joan's descriptions of her childhood, she'd never had that. It seemed sad to Brinna. She actually felt sorry for the girl . . . until their hair was dry and the actual "lessons" began. Brinna quickly lost all sympathy for the little tyrant as the girl barked out orders, slapped her, smacked her, and prodded and poked her in an effort to get her to walk, talk, and hold her head "properly." It was obvious that she was determined that this should work. It was also equally obvious to Brinna that it would not. Lady Sabrina had not helped with her snide comments and dark predictions once she had returned to the room. By the time dawn had rolled around, Brinna was positive that this was the most foolish thing she had ever agreed to. . . .

Until she saw herself in that looking glass. She had thought, on first looking into the glass that Lady Joan held between them, that 'twas just an empty gilt frame and that 'twas Lady Joan herself she peered at. But then she realized that the eyes looking back at her were a soft blue gray, not the sharp green of the other girl's. Other than that, she did look almost exactly like Lady Joan. It was enough to boost her confidence.

"You see?" Joan laughed, lowering the mirror and moving away to set it on her chest before turning back to survey Brinna in the dark blue gown she had made her don. "Aye. You will do," she decided with satisfaction. "Now, one more time. When you meet Lord Thurleah you . . . ?" She raised a brow questioningly and Brinna, still a little dazed by what she had seen in that glass, bobbed quickly and murmured, "Greetings, m'lord. I—"

"Nay, nay, nay." Joan snapped impatiently. "Why can you not remember? When you first greet him you must curtsy low, lower your eyes to the floor, then sweep them back up and say—"

"Greetings, my lord. I am honored to finally meet you," Brinna interrupted impatiently. "Aye. I remember now. I only forgot it for a moment because—"

"It doesn't matter why you forgot. You *must* remember, else you will shame me with your ignorance."

Brinna sighed, feeling all of the confidence that the glimpse of herself in the looking glass had briefly given her seep away like water out of a leaky pail. "Mayhap we'd best be fergettin' all about this tomfoolery."

"Mayhap we had best forget all about this foolishness," Joan corrected her automatically, then frowned. "You must remember to try to speak with—"

"Enough," Brinna interrupted impatiently. "Ye know ye can't be makin' a lady of me. 'Tis hopeless."

"Nay," Joan assured her quickly. "You were doing wonderfully well. You are a quick study. 'Tis just that you are tired now."

"We are all tired now," Sabrina muttered wearily from where she sat slumped on the bed. "Why do you not give it up while you can?"

"She is right," Brinna admitted with a sigh. "'Tisn't workin'. We should give it all up for the foolishness it is and—" A knock at the door made her pause. She moved automatically to open it, then stood blinking in amazement at the man before her.

He was a glorious vision. His hair was a nimbus of gold in the torchlight that lit the halls in the early morning gloom. His tall, strong body was encased in a fine amber-colored outfit. His skin glowed with the health and vitality of a man used to the outdoors, and his eyes shone down on her as true a blue as the northern English sky on a cloudless summer day. He was the most beautiful human Brinna had ever laid eyes on.

"Lady Joan? I am Lord Royce of Thurleah."

"Gor," Brinna breathed, her eyes wide. This was the backwoods oaf? The country bumpkin whose clumsy attentions they wanted her to suffer? She could die smiling while suffering such attentions. When his eyebrows flew up in surprise, and a pinch of her behind came from Joan, who was hiding out of sight behind the door, she realized what had slipped from her lips, and alarm entered her face briefly before she remembered to curtsy, performing the move flawlessly and glancing briefly at the floor before sweeping her eyes up to his face and smiling.

"My lord," she breathed, her smile widening as he took her hand to help her up, but that smile slipped when she saw his expression.

He was frowning, not looking the least pleased, and Brinna bit her lips uncertainly, racking her brain for the reason behind it. Had she muffed the curtsy? Said the words wrong? What? she wondered with dismay, until he shifted impatiently.

"I arrived but a moment ago," he said.

Brinna's eyes dilated somewhat as she tried to think of what she should say to that.

"*I hope your journey was pleasant.*" She glanced around at those hissed words, her wide eyes blank as they took in Joan's impatient face peeking at her from behind the door. "*Say it. I hope your journey—*"

"Who are you talking to?"

Brinna turned back to him abruptly, stepping forward to block his entrance as he would have tried to peek around the door. The move stopped his advance, but also put them extremely close to each other, and Brinna felt a quiver go through her as she caught the musky outdoors scent of him. "Just a servant," she lied huskily, ignoring the indignant gasp from behind the door.

"Oh." Royce stared at the girl, his mind gone blank as he took in her features. She was not what he had expected. His cousin, Phillip of Radfurn, had spent several months in France in late fall, had traveled through Normandy on his way home, and had stopped awhile at Laythem on his travels. He had then hied his way to Thurleah to regale Royce with his impressions of his betrothed. He had spoken a lot about her unpleasant nature, her snobbery, the airs she put on, the fact that she ran her father's home as similarly to court as she could manage. . . .

He had never once mentioned the impish, turned-up nose she had, the sweet bow-shaped lips, the large dewy eyes, or that her hair was like spun sunshine. Damn. He could have prepared a body and mentioned such things. Realizing that he had stood there for several moments merely gaping at the girl, Royce cleared his throat. "I came to escort you to Mass."

"Oh." She cast one uncertain glance back into the room, then seemed to make a decision and stepped into the hall. Pulling the door closed behind her, she rested her hand on the muscled arm he extended and smiled a bit uncertainly as he led her down the hallway.

"Well?"

Sabrina turned away from the door she had cracked open to spy on the departing couple and glanced questioningly at Joan. "Well, what?"

"You are going with her, are you not? She will need help to carry this off."

Sabrina's eyes widened in surprise. "But I am your companion. I am not to leave you alone."

"Aye. And she is me just now. It will look odd if you leave her alone with him."

Sabrina opened her mouth to argue the point, then closed it with a sigh as she realized Joan was right. Sighing again, she hurried out the door after Royce and Brinna.

Chapter Two

"The things I do for Joan."

Brinna sighed inwardly as Sabrina continued her tirade. The woman seemed to have a lot to say on the subject. Brinna just wished she wasn't the one to have to listen to it. Unfortunately, she was rather a captive audience, unable to escape the other girl. Sabrina attached herself to Brinna every time she left Lady Joan's room, and did not unattach herself until they returned.

It was the day after Christmas, the day after Lord Thurleah had arrived at Menton and come to Lady Joan's room to escort her to Holy Mass. And that was the last moment of peace Brinna had had. Mass had been longer than usual, it being Christmas Day, and Brinna had spent the entire time allowing the priest's words to flow over her as she had stared rather bemusedly at Lord Thurleah from beneath her lashes. He truly was a beautiful man, and Brinna could have continued to stare at him all day long, but of course, Mass had eventually come to an end and Lord Thurleah had turned to smile at her and ask if she would not like to take a walk to stretch their legs after the long ceremony.

Brinna had smiled back and opened her mouth to speak, only to snap it closed again as Sabrina had suddenly appeared beside her, declining the offer. Using the risk of getting a chill as an excuse, she had then grabbed Brinna's arm and dragged her from the chapel and back to the great hall, hissing at her to remember to keep her head down to hide her gray eyes, and to try to slouch a bit to hide the difference in height.

Brinna had spent the rest of that first day as Lady Joan, staring at her feet and keeping her shoulders hunched as Sabrina had led her in a game of what appeared to be musical chairs. She would insist they sit one place, spend several moments hissing about "the things I do for Joan," then suddenly leap up and drag her off to another spot should anyone dare to come near them or approach to speak to her. Eventually, of course, there had been nowhere left to hide in plain view, and Sabrina had stopped moving about, switching her tactics to simply blocking any communication with Brinna/Joan by answering every single question addressed to Brinna as if she were a deaf mute. Most of those questions she answered had been addressed by Lord Thurleah, who had followed them around the great hall determinedly, then had seated himself beside Sabrina at dinner. He had tried to sit beside Brinna—who he thought was his betrothed

Joan—but Sabrina had promptly stood and made Brinna switch seats on some lame pretext or other that Brinna hadn't even really caught. She had been too distracted by the frustration and anger that had flashed briefly on Lord Thurleah's face at Sabrina's antics to notice. It had been a great relief to her when the meal had been over and Sabrina had suggested, meaningfully and quite loudly, that she looked tired and might wish to retire early for the night.

Leaving Sabrina behind to beam obliviously at an obviously irate Lord Thurleah, Brinna had returned to Joan's room to find it empty of the lady who was supposed to occupy it. After a moment of uncertainty, Brinna had shrugged inwardly and set to work putting the room to rights, finding that she actually enjoyed the task. Working in the kitchen, and usually sleeping there as well on a bed of straw with the other kitchen help, made solitude a rare and valued commodity to Brinna. She had reveled in the silence and peace as she had puttered about the room, putting things away, then removing Lady Joan's fine gown and lying down to sleep on the pallet by the door in her shift. She had dozed off, only to awaken hours later when the door had cracked open to allow Joan to slip inside.

Brinna's eyes had widened in amazement as the dying embers from the fireplace had revealed her own worn clothes on the girl and that the strip of cloth she usually wore on her head was now hid-

ing Joan's golden curls. But she had not said anything to let Joan know that she had seen her return
dressed so when Joan had removed the tired old
rags. It wasn't her place to question the lady as to
her goings-on. Besides, the stealthy way she had
crept about and crawled into bed warned Brinna
that her questions wouldn't be welcome. Pretending she hadn't seen her, Brinna had merely closed
her eyes and drifted back to sleep.

Joan had still been sleeping when Lord Thurleah
had arrived at the room that morning, but Brinna
had been up and dressed and ready to continue the
charade. Once again he had escorted her to Mass,
and once again, as they had prepared to leave the
chapel, Sabrina had whisked her away into her
game of musical chairs until the nooning meal,
when Lady Menton had announced a need for
more mistletoe. Christina had quickly arranged a
party of the younger set to go out in search of the
"kissing boughs." Most of the guests, Lord Royce
included, were on horseback, but a wagon had
been brought along to put the mistletoe in and Sabrina had managed to make some excuse to Lady
Christina as to why she and "Joan" would rather
ride in the wagon. So here Brinna sat, trapped in
the back of a wagon with Sabrina, stuck listening
to her rant about her cousin.

Who would have thought that being a lady could
be so *boring*? she thought idly, her gaze slipping
over the rest of the group traveling ahead of the

wagon. Well, at least she was just bored and not miserable like that poor Lady Gibert, she thought wryly as her gaze settled on the other woman.

Eleanor was the girl's name. She had tried to introduce herself to Brinna/Joan the day before, and Sabrina had blocked her as she had everyone else. It was one of the few times that Brinna had been really angry at Joan's cousin and not just irritated. Eleanor was obviously terribly unhappy and in need of a friend, and Brinna felt Sabrina could have been a bit kinder about it.

Her gaze slid to the man who rode beside Lady Eleanor, and Brinna grimaced. James Glencairn. He was the girl's betrothed and also the one to blame for Eleanor's misery. The man had come to Menton as a boy, and had had a chip on his shoulders as wide as Menton's moat since arriving. Not surprising perhaps since, despite being treated well, he had been and still was a virtual hostage, kept and trained at Menton to ensure his father's good behavior in Scotland. Sadly, it appeared he was making the unfortunate Lady Eleanor just as miserable.

"You are not even listening to me," Sabrina hissed suddenly, elbowing Brinna in an effort to get her attention.

Taken by surprise by that blow to her stomach, Brinna swung back in her seat on the edge of the wagon, lost her balance, and tumbled backward out of the cart to Sabrina's distressed squeak. She landed on her back in the hard-packed snow of the lane and was left gasping for the breath that had been knocked out of her as Sabrina's assurances caroled in her ears. "Nay, nay, all is fine. Lady Joan and I have merely decided to walk. You keep on going."

"But—" the anxious driver's voice sounded before Sabrina cut him off.

"Go on now. Off with you."

Sighing as she was finally able to suck some small amount of air into her lungs, Brinna lifted her head slightly to see that the riders on horseback had not noticed her mishap and only the wagon driver was peering anxiously over his shoulder at her as he reluctantly urged his horses back into a walk. Sabrina was trudging back toward her through the snow, glaring daggers.

"What on earth are you trying to do? Kill me with embarrassment? Ruin Joan?"

"Me?" Brinna squealed in amazement.

"Aye, you. Ladies do not muck about in the snow, you know."

"I—"

"I do not want to hear your excuses," Sabrina interrupted sharply, perching her hands on her hips to mutter with disgust, "Peasants! Honestly! Get up off your—"

"Is everything all right, ladies?"

Sabrina's mouth snapped closed on whatever she had been about to say, her eyes widening in horror as Lord Thurleah's voice sounded behind her. They had both been too distracted to realize that he and his man had taken note of their predicament and ridden back to assist. Forcing a wide, obviously strained smile to her lips, Sabrina whirled to face both men as they dismounted. "Oh, my, yes. Everything is fine. Why ever would you think otherwise?"

Brinna rolled her eyes at the panicky sound in the other girl's voice and the way her hands slid down to clutch at her skirts, tugging them to the side as if she thought she might hide Brinna's undignified position in the snow. By craning her neck, Brinna could just see Lord Thurleah's face as he arched one eyebrow, his lips appearing to struggle to hold back an amused smile. "Mayhap because Lady Joan has fallen in the snow?"

"Fallen?" Lady Sabrina's genuine horror seemed to suggest ladies simply did not *do* anything as embarrassing as fall off the back of the wagon into the snow. . . . And if they did, gentlemen shouldn't deign to notice or mention it. Sabrina's fingers twitched briefly where they held her skirts, then suddenly tugged them out wider as she gasped, "Oh, nay. You must be mistaken, my lord. Why, Lady Joan would never have fallen. She is the epitome of grace and beauty. She is as nimble as a fawn, as graceful as a swan. She is—"

"Presently lying in the snow," Lord Thurleah pointed out dryly.

Sabrina whirled around at that, feigning surprise as she peered at Brinna. "Oh, dear! However did that happen? It must have been the driver's fault. Oh, do get up, dear."

Leaning forward, she clasped Brinna's arm and began a useless tugging even as Lord Thurleah bent to catch Brinna under the arms and lift her to her feet, then quickly helped Sabrina brush down her skirts before straightening to smile at Brinna gently. "Better?"

"Oh, yes, that is much better," Sabrina assured him, cutting off any reply Brinna might have given. "Thank you for your aid, my lord. Lady Joan is usually—"

"The epitome of grace," Royce murmured wryly.

"Aye. Exactly." She beamed at him as if he were a student who had just figured out a difficult sum. "Why, she has been trained in dance."

"Has she?" he asked politely, turning to smile down at Brinna.

"Aye. And that is not all," Sabrina assured him, stepping between him and Brinna to block his view of the girl. Apparently eager to convince him that this little mishap was an aberration, she began to rattle off Lady Joan's abilities. "She speaks French, Latin, and German. Knows her herbs and medicinals like the back of her hand. Is meticulous in the running of the household. Is trained in the harp and lute—"

"The harp?" Lord Thurleah interrupted, leaning sideways to peer around the brunette at Brinna.

"Oh, aye. She plays it like a dream," Sabrina assured him, shifting to block his vision again.

"Really?" Straightening, he smiled at Brinna. "Then mayhap you could be persuaded to play for us tonight after our meal? 'Twould make a nice break from that minstrel who attempted to sing for us last night."

"Aye, it would, would it not?" Sabrina laughed gaily.

Brinna's mouth dropped open in horror as the brunette continued. "Why, he was absolutely horrid. Joan would be much more pleasant to listen to." She glanced to the side then, as if to look proudly at Brinna, then frowned as she caught the girl's expression. "What are you—" she began anxiously, turning toward her fully. Then her eyes rounded as she suddenly grasped the reason for Brinna's abject horror. Her own face suddenly mirroring it, she whirled back toward Lord Thurleah, shaking her head frantically. "Oh, nay. Nay! She couldn't possibly play. Why she . . . er . . . she . . ."

When Sabrina peered at her wild-eyed, Brinna sighed and moved forward, murmuring, "I am afraid I injured my hand quite recently. I would be no good at the harp just now. Mayhap later on during the holidays."

"Aye," Sabrina gasped with relief, and turned to beam at Royce. "She hurt her hand." Realizing that she looked far too pleased as she said that,

Sabrina managed a frown. "Terrible, really. Awful accident. Sad. Horribly painful. She almost lost full use of her hand."

Brinna rolled her eyes as the girl raved on, not terribly surprised when her comments made Lord Thurleah lean forward to glance down at the hands she was presently hiding within Lady Joan's cloak. "It sounds awful. Whatever happened?" he asked.

"Happened?" Sabrina blinked at the question, her face going blank briefly, then filling with desperation. "She . . . er . . . she . . . er . . . pricked her finger doing embroidery!" she finished triumphantly, and Brinna nearly groaned aloud as what sounded suspiciously like a snort of laughter burst from Lord Thurleah, before he could cover his mouth with his hand. Turning away, he made a great show of coughing violently, then cleared his throat several times before turning a solemn face back to them.

"Aye. Well, that *is* tragic." His voice broke on the last word, and he had to turn away again for a few more chortling coughs. By the time he turned back, Brinna was biting her upper lip to keep from laughing herself at the ridiculous story. Unaware that her eyes were sparkling with merriment as she met his gaze, that her cheeks were pink with health, and that she seemed almost to glow with vitality, she blinked in confusion when he suddenly gasped and stilled.

Frowning now, Sabrina glanced at the man, her

mouth working briefly before she assured him, "Aye, well, it may not sound like much, but 'twas an awful prick."

Royce blinked at that, seeming startled out of his reverie. For a moment, Brinna thought he might have to turn away for another coughing fit, but he managed to restrain himself and murmur, "Aye, well, then we must not let her play the harp. Mayhap something less strenuous on her *pricked* finger. Chess perhaps?"

"I am sorry, my lord," Sabrina answered. "I fear chess is out of the question as well. Joan has . . . a . . . er . . . tendency to suffer the . . . er . . . aching head." At his startled glance, she nodded solemnly. "They come on any time she thinks too hard."

Brinna closed her eyes and groaned at that one. She couldn't help it. Really! It was hard to imagine that the girl was supposed to be on Lady Joan's side.

"So, thinking is out of the question?" she heard Lord Thurleah murmur with unmistakable amusement.

"I am afraid so."

"Aye. Well, it must be a family trait."

Brinna's eyes popped open at that. She was hardly able to believe that he had said that. To her it sounded as if he had just insulted Sabrina. Surely he hadn't meant it that way, she thought, but when she glanced at his face, he gave her a wink that assured her that she was brighter than Lady Sabrina would have him believe. He had just insulted the girl. Fortunately, Sabrina obviously hadn't caught on to the insult. Making a sad grimace with her lips, she nodded solemnly and murmured, "Aye, I believe the aching head does run in the family."

"Ah," Lord Thurleah murmured, then gestured up the path to where the others were now disappearing around a curve in the lane. "Mayhap we should catch up to the others?"

"Oh, dear." Sabrina frowned. "They *have* left us quite far behind, have they not?"

"Aye, but my man and I can take the two of you on our horses and catch up rather quickly, I am sure," he said gently, taking Sabrina's arm and leading her the few steps to where his man waited by the horses. Brinna followed more slowly, her gaze dropping of its own accord over his wide strong back, his firm buttocks, and his muscled legs as he assisted Lady Sabrina onto his mount.

At least she had assumed it was his mount. Sabrina apparently had too, Brinna realized as he suddenly stepped out of the way to allow his man to mount behind the girl and the brunette gasped anxiously. "Oh, but—"

"Lady Joan and I will be right behind you," Lord Thurleah said gaily over her protests, nodding to his man, then slapping the horse on the derriere so that it took off with a burst of speed, carrying away the suddenly struggling and protesting Lady Sabrina. She was squawking and flapping her arms not unlike the chicken Cook had held by the legs while talking to her the other day, and Brinna bit her lip to keep from laughing aloud at the wicked comparison. Lord Thurleah turned to face her.

"Now," he began, then paused, his thoughts arrested as he took in her amused expression.

"My lord?" she questioned gently after an uncomfortable moment had passed.

"I have heard people speak of eyes that twinkle merrily, but never really knew what it meant until today," he said quietly. "Your eyes sparkle with life and laughter when you are amused. Did you know that?"

Brinna swallowed and shook her head. This must be the rough wooing Joan had spoken of, she realized, but for the life of her she could find no fault with it. His voice and even his words seemed as smooth as the softest down to her.

"They do," he assured her solemnly, reaching out to brush a feather-light tress away from her cheek. "And your hair . . . It's as soft as a duckling's down, and seems to reflect the sun's light with a thousand different shades of gold. It's, quite simply, beautiful."

"Gor—" Brinna murmured faintly enough that he could not have caught the word, then paused uncertainly and swallowed as his eyes turned their focus on her mouth.

"And your lips. All I can think of when I peer at them is what it would feel like to kiss you."

"Oh," she breathed shakily, a blush suffusing her face even as her chest seemed to constrict somewhat and made it harder to breathe.

"Aye, you might very well blush did you know my thoughts. How I imagine covering your mouth with my own, nibbling at the edges, sucking your lower lip into my mouth, then slipping my tongue—"

"Oh, Mother," Brinna gasped, beginning to fan her suddenly heated face as if it were a hot summer day instead of a frigid winter one. His voice and what he was saying were having an amazing effect on her body, making it tingle in spots, and sending bursts of warm gushy feelings to others. Maybe she was coming down with something, she thought with a bit of distress as his face began to lower toward hers.

"Joan! Oh, Joan!"

Royce and Brinna both straightened abruptly and turned to see Lady Sabrina walking determinedly toward them, Lord Thurleah's mounted man following behind, an apologetic expression on his face as he met his lord's glance.

"Your cousin appears to be most persistent," Royce muttered dryly, and Brinna sighed.

"Aye. She's rather like a dog with a bone, isn't she?"

"The group has stopped just beyond that bend," Sabrina announced triumphantly as she neared. "It seems the spot is just crawling with mistletoe. Even as I speak, servants are climbing and shimmying up trees to bring down some of the vines."

Reaching them, Sabrina hooked her arm firmly through Brinna's and turned to lead her determinedly in the direction from which she had come, trilling, "It is fortunate, is it not? Else you may have gotten separated from the group and not caught up at all. Then you would have missed all the fun. Imagine that."

"Aye, just imagine." Royce sighed as he watched the brunette march his betrothed off around the bend.

"He is—"

"Aye, I know," Joan interrupted Brinna dryly. "He is a very nice man. You have said so at least ten times since returning to this room."

"Well, he is," Brinna insisted determinedly. They had arrived back at Menton nearly an hour ago. Sabrina had rushed her upstairs, then insisted Brinna wait in the hall while she went in and spoke to Joan alone. Brinna had stood there, alternately worrying over what was being said inside the room and fretting over how she would explain why she was loitering about in the hall should anyone happen upon her. Fortunately, no one had come along before Sabrina had reappeared. Stepping into the hall, she had gestured for Brinna to enter the room, then walked off, leaving her staring after.

A moment later, Brinna had straightened her

shoulders and slid into the room to find Joan seated in the chair by the fire awaiting her. Brinna had not hesitated then, but had walked determinedly toward her. After rejoining the group, she had spent the better part of that afternoon considering everything she had learned to date. And it had seemed to her that, while Lady Joan was reluctant to marry Royce, it was due to some obvious misconceptions. Someone had misled her. Lord Thurleah was neither a backward oaf nor a country bumpkin given to rough wooing. He was just as polite and polished as any of the other lords. And it seemed to Brinna that she was in a position to correct this situation. All she had to do was tell Lady Joan the truth about Lord Thurleah's nature and the girl would resign herself to being his bride. Lady Joan, however, did not appear to wish to hear what she was trying to tell her. Still, she'd decided she had to try. "He isn't what you said. He doesn't woo roughly. He—"

"Brinna, please." Joan laughed, digging through her chest for Lord knows what as she went on gently. "My dear girl, you are hardly in a position to judge that. It is not as if you have spent a great deal of time around nobility."

"Aye, but, he-he spoke real pretty. He—"

"You mean he was very complimentary?" Joan asked, pausing to frown at her as Brinna nodded quickly. "Well, then, say that. Ladies do not say things like 'he spoke real pretty.' And do try to slow your speech somewhat. That is when you make the most mistakes."

Brinna sighed in frustration, then took a moment to calm herself before continuing in the modulated tones Joan had spent that first night trying to hammer into her head. "You are correct, of course," she enunciated grimly. "I apologize. But he truly is not the way you think he is. He was very *complimentary*. He said your eyes twinkled, your hair was as soft as down, and your lips—"

"It doesn't matter. I am not marrying him," Joan declared firmly, then closed the lid of the chest with a sigh and turned to face her. "Now, Sabrina told me about the little incident of your falling out of the wagon."

Brinna felt herself flush and sighed unhappily. "Aye. She nudged me and—"

"It doesn't matter. All I wanted to say was to be more careful in the future. And try to remember that you are a lady while pretending to be me and should comport yourself accordingly."

"Aye, my lady," she murmured.

"So, you'd best change quickly and make your way down to the meal."

Brinna's eyes widened at that. "Should I not go below and fetch you something to eat first?"

Joan arched an eyebrow at that. "That would look odd, do you not think? A lady fetching a meal for her servant?"

"Nay, I meant that I could change into my own dress and—"

"That will not be necessary. I have already eaten."

Brinna stilled at that news, confusion on her face as she considered how that could have come about. One look at Lady Joan's closed expression told her that she was not to dare ask. Sighing, she shook her head. "Still, I should at least go down to the kitchens for a minute. They will wonder if they don't see me every once in a while."

"They saw you today." When Brinna blinked at that news, the other girl smiled wryly and admitted, "I donned your dress and the cloth you wore over your hair in case anyone came looking for you while you were out on the mistletoe hunt as me. Someone did. I think it was your Aggie. At least she seemed a lot like the old woman you described to me."

"What happened?" Brinna gasped.

Joan shrugged. "Nothing. She said Cook had said 'twas all right for her to bring you something to eat and check on you. I told her that 'Lady Joan' had left a whole list of chores to do while she was gone and thanked her for the food. They won't expect to see you again today. That is why I told you to inform them that I wanted you to sleep in my room. So they wouldn't expect to see much of you."

"And she didn't suspect that you were not me?" Brinna asked with disbelief.

"Who else would she have thought I was?" Joan laughed dryly. "No one would suspect that a lady of nobility would willingly don the clothes of the servant class."

"Nay, I suppose not," Brinna agreed slowly, but felt an odd pinch somewhere in the vicinity of her chest. Aggie had raised her. Watched her grow into womanhood. Surely the woman could tell the difference between her own daughter and an impostor?

"Come now." Joan clapped her hands together. "Change and get downstairs, else you will be late for the meal."

"Aye, my lady."

Chapter Three

"Riding? On that great beast?"

Brinna stared at the mount before her with nothing short of terror. This was the fourth day of her escapade, but it was the first day that she did not have Sabrina dragging her about, lecturing her as she avoided the rest of the guests while a frustrated Lord Thurleah trailed them, doing his best to be charming and friendly to the back of Brinna's head. Brinna had actually begun to feel sorry for the poor man as he'd tried to shower attendance on her while Sabrina blocked his every advance. His Lordship was not finding this courting easy. Or at least he hadn't been until this morning, for this morning Sabrina was bundled up in bed, attempting to fight off the same chills and nausea that had kept Lady Joan's maid and father from accompanying the others to Menton for Christmas.

Sabrina had started coming down ill the day before, and it had shown. She had lacked her usual bulldog-like promptness in blocking any speech between Brinna and the others, to the point that Brinna had actually had the opportunity to murmur, "Aye, my lord," twice. Brinna had also made their excuses when, after sitting down to sup with the others, Sabrina had stared at the food before them, her face turning several shades of an interesting green before she had suddenly clawed at Brinna's arm, gasping that they had to leave the table . . . at once!

Recognizing the urgency in her tone, Brinna had risen quickly and escorted Joan's cousin upstairs, where the girl had made brief friends with the chamber pot before collapsing onto the bed clutching the stomach she had just emptied, proclaiming that she was surely dying. And if she wasn't, she wished she were.

She hadn't looked much better this morning. If anything she had seemed weaker, which was hardly surprising since she had spent the better part of the night with her head hanging over the chamber pot until there had simply been nothing left for her stomach to toss into it. Perhaps it was due to that weakness that she had not fought too hard to convince Joan to keep Brinna from impersonating her that day and to send a message that they were both ill. Whatever the case, she had not argued too vigorously, and Joan had decided that Brinna should go ahead, saying that Brinna had had several days in the company of the other nobles and would most likely be fine. Joan had merely reminded Brinna to try to say as little as possible, keep her head bowed, and not allow herself to be alone with Lord Thurleah.

Trying to tamp down the excitement whirling inside her, Brinna had nodded solemnly, then gone to the door to greet Lord Thurleah as he had arrived to escort her to Mass. If she had felt a secret pleasure at the idea of spending the day alone with Lord Thurleah—well, as alone as one could be in the company of the rest of the Menton guests—he had looked decidedly pleased by the news that Sabrina was too ill to accompany them that day.

Smiling charmingly, he had clasped her hand on his arm and escorted her to Mass as usual, but afterward, rather than steer her toward the great hall as he had every other morning, he instead had led her here to the stables, explaining that he had planned a surprise for her and Sabrina that morning. He had thought that a ride might be a nice change and had sent word to the stables to prepare their horses. Which was how she found herself standing before the three great beasts now eyeing her suspiciously, her heart stuck somewhere in the vicinity of her throat as she contemplated dying trampled beneath their hooves. For surely that was what would happen should she attempt to ride one of the saddled animals before her. Lord Thurleah might think that a ride would be a nice change, but Brinna could not help but disagree with him. Scullery maids did not have reason to be around the beasts much, and certainly didn't get the chance to ride them.

"Did I make a mistake, m'lady? This is your mount, isn't it?" the stable boy asked anxiously. Brinna cleared her throat and forced a smile.

"Aye. 'Tis my horse. I . . . I just thought . . . Well, 'twas a long journey here. Mayhap 'twould be better if she was allowed to rest," she finished lamely, and wasn't surprised when the stable lad and Royce exchanged slightly amused smiles before Royce murmured, "I was told you arrived at noon the day before I did. If so, then your mount has had four days to rest, my lady. No doubt she would enjoy a bit of exercise about now."

"Oh, aye," she murmured reluctantly, and wondered what to do. Lady Joan had not prepared her for a situation like this. Though she probably would have had she had a horse handy in her room at the time, Brinna thought wryly. She blinked suddenly as a thought came to her. Mayhap the girl had prepared her. Managing a grimace of disappointment, she turned to face Royce and the stable boy.

"What a lovely surprise, and it would have made a nice change too," she said, careful to enunciate clearly as Joan had taught her. "But as Sabrina is too ill to accompany us, and it isn't proper for a lady to be alone with a man who isn't her husband, well . . ." She paused to add a dramatic little sigh before finishing with, "I fear the ride shall have to be put off until Sabrina can accompany us."

"Aye, you are right, of course." Frowning thoughtfully, Royce turned to pace several steps away, and Brinna was just beginning to relax when he suddenly snapped his fingers and whirled back. "My man can accompany us."

"What?" she cried in alarm.

"My man Cedric can accompany us. He will make a fine chaperone. Unsaddle Lady Sabrina's mount, lad, and prepare Cedric's instead," he instructed as Brinna's eyes widened in horror.

"Oh, but—" she began, panic stealing any sensible argument she might have come up with. She was left gaping after him as he strode out of the stables determinedly.

"Bloody hell," she breathed as he disappeared, then turned back to eye the mount that would be hers as the stable boy led Sabrina's horse off. Joan's mare didn't look any happier at this turn of events than she felt. The beast was eyeing her rather suspiciously, and Brinna couldn't help thinking the horse knew that she wasn't Joan and was wondering what had become of the girl. Brinna was so sure of what the look in the beast's eyes meant that she shifted uncomfortably and murmured, "I haven't harmed 'er. Yer lady's alive and well." Noting that the horse didn't look particularly convinced, Brinna frowned. "It's true. 'Sides, this is all her doin'. She—"

"Who are you talking to?"

Brinna gave a start at that question, and glanced

over her shoulder to find that Royce had returned and now towered over her shoulder. He was big. Very big. Why, she imagined if they stood in the sun side by side, he would cast a fine patch of shade for her to stand in. "My mare," she murmured absently, trying to judge how much wider he was. Probably twice as wide as she, she decided a bit breathlessly, not noticing the way he shook his head before sharing an amused glance with the older man who now accompanied him.

"This is my man Cedric. You may remember him from the mistletoe hunt?"

"Oh, aye. Greetings, my lord," Brinna murmured, and recalling her lessons on greeting people, started to sweep into a graceful curtsy that Lord Thurleah halted by catching her elbow.

"He is a knight, not a lord," Thurleah explained gently, and Brinna felt herself flush.

"Oh, well." She hesitated, unsure how to greet the man now, then merely nodded and offered a smile, which was gently returned.

"Here you are, m'lord. I returned the lady's horse to its stall and prepared Sir Cedric's." The stable lad led the new horse forward to join the other two.

"Ah. Very good. Fast work, boy." Giving him an approving nod, Royce turned Brinna toward the door and led her out of the stables, offering her a smile as he went. Swallowing, Brinna managed a weak smile in return, but her attention was on the three horses Sir Cedric was now leading out behind them.

"I . . ." Brinna began faintly as he brought the horses to a halt beside them, but whatever she would have said died in her throat and she nearly bit her tongue off as Royce suddenly turned, caught her at the waist, and lifted her up onto the animal that was Lady Joan's. Once he had set her down on the sidesaddle, he paused to eye her solemnly, his eyebrows rising slightly.

"Are you all right, Lady Joan? You have gone white as a clean linen."

"Fine," Brinna squeaked.

"You are not afraid of horses, are you?"

"Nay, nay," she gasped.

"Nay, of course not," he murmured to himself. "You rode here on this beast."

"Ahhhaye." The lie came out as a moan.

Royce nodded almost to himself, then cleared his throat and murmured, "Then, if you are not afraid, my lady, why is it you are clutching me so tightly?"

Brinna blinked at the question, then shot her eyes to her hands. They had tangled themselves in the material of his golden tunic and now clawed into it with all the determination of someone who was positive that should he release her, she would surely fall to her death. Lady Joan would not do that, of course, she told herself firmly. Forcing a smile that felt as stiff as wood, she forced her hands to release their death grip and smoothed the material down. "'Tis fair soft material, my lord. Quite good quality."

"Ah." Looking unsure as to what to make of her behavior, he released his hold on her waist and started to move away, only to step quickly back and catch her once more as she immediately started to slip off the sidesaddle. "I am sorry. I thought you had already braced your feet," he muttered, easing her back onto the saddle again.

Swallowing, Brinna dug about the animal's side with her feet under her skirts in search of whatever it was he thought would be there to brace her feet. She found it after a moment, an inch or so higher than her feet fell. Of course, Lady Joan was a couple of inches shorter than her, and of course that would have been the perfect height for *her*. For Brinna it meant bending her legs more than she should have had to and resting at a most awkward position. This time when he released her, she managed to keep her seat, and even summoned a wobbly smile as she accepted the reins he handed her.

As he turned to mount his own horse, Brinna wrapped the reins desperately around her hands to be sure she did not lose them. Only then did she risk a glance toward the ground. As she had feared, it appeared to be a mile or more away. Aye, the ground was a long, long way down, and she could actually almost see it rushing toward her as if she were already falling off the beast. Shutting her eyes, she sat perfectly still, afraid to even breathe as she frantically wondered what the order was to make the animal move when the time came to do so. She needn't have worried. The moment Royce urged his own mount forward, and his man Cedric followed, the mare fell into line behind them.

They started at a sedate pace, but even that was enough to make Brinna wobble precariously in her seat and tighten her grasp on the reins desperately as they moved through the bailey. She was positive she would not make it out of the gates, but much to her amazement she did, and even began to relax a bit. But then they crossed the bridge and reached the land surrounding the castle and Royce suddenly urged his mount into a canter.

Brinna's horse followed suit at once, and she began to bounce around on the animal's back like a sack of turnips in the back of a cart on a rutted path. Every bone in her body was soon aching from the jarring they were taking. Still, she held on, her teeth gritting together, as she told herself that it would soon be over. It seemed to her that they had been riding for hours when Royce and his man suddenly turned to glance back at her. Forcing her lips into a tight smile, she freed a hand to wave at them in what she hoped was a careless manner. They had barely turned forward again when her foot slipped off the bar brace and she slid off the horse. All would have been well had she not wrapped the reins around her hands as she had. She would have tumbled from the horse into a nice pile of snow and that would have been that. Unfortunately, the reins were wrapped around her hand and she didn't at first have the presence of mind to unwrap them. She hung down the side of the mount, shrieking in terror as her feet and lower legs were dragged through the snow. Her shrieks, of course, just managed to terrify her mount and urge it into a faster run, which made her scream all the louder.

ROYCE GLANCED OVER his shoulder toward Lady Laythem, saw her wave, and glanced back the way he was heading. He had decided on this ride in an effort to get her alone. He had heard a great deal about her being spoiled and snobbish from his cousin, but so far the woman had not quite fit that description. While it was true she was silent most of the time, which could be mistaken for snobbery, he was beginning to think it merely shyness. Truly, the girl seemed to shrink within herself when in the company of others. Of course, that cousin of hers didn't help any. Sabrina answered every question he addressed to the girl in an effort to draw her out, and usually positioned herself between the two of them. It was most annoying. He was hoping that once alone Lady Laythem would shed some of that shyness and show her true nature.

"She's not much of a rider," Cedric commented, drawing Royce from his thoughts and making him nod in silent agreement. "When do you want me to drop back and give you some privacy?" Cedric asked, having been apprised of his lord's wishes when he had fetched him.

Before Royce could respond, a sudden shrieking made them both turn back again. They were just in time to see the lady's mount come flying up and pass them, dragging the lady herself behind, kicking and screaming like a madwoman.

"My God." They both gaped after the fleeing horse briefly, until Lady Laythem finally managed to regain her scattered wits and untangle her hand from the reins. She slid free of the mount, disappearing into the deep snow alongside the trail as the mare raced wildly off into the woods.

"I shall fetch the mare," Cedric choked out around what sounded suspiciously like laughter before urging his horse into a gallop and chasing off into the woods after the beast.

Shaking his head, Royce bit his lip in his own amusement and urged his mount forward along the trail until he reached the spot where Lady Joan had disappeared. It was easy enough to find; she had left a trail as she had been dragged along through the snow. Where the trail ended was where she must have slid off the horse. But as he stopped his mount, Royce couldn't see any evidence of her presence. His amusement replaced by concern, Royce slid off of his horse and waded into the snow calling her name, shocked to find himself waist-deep in snow as fluffy as a newborn lamb's wool. Stumbling forward, he nearly tripped over her body, then bent quickly, shoveling some of the top snow away with his bare hands before reaching into the icy fluff to find her and drag her upward, turning her at the same time until he had her head resting against his bent knee.

"Joan?" he murmured worriedly, taking in her closed eyes and the icy pallor of her cheeks. She opened one eye to peer at him, then closed it again on a groan. "Are you all right? Is anything broken?"

"Only me pride," she muttered, then opened both eyes to admit wryly, "I was rather hoping ye'd just leave me here to die in shame alone."

Royce blinked at that, then felt his mouth stretch into a slow smile before he asked again, "Were you hurt? Is anything broken?"

"Nay." She sighed wryly. "But the snow went up me skirts so far me arse is a block of ice." When his eyes widened incredulously at that and a choked sound slid from his throat, Brinna stiffened anxiously. She supposed ladies wouldn't refer to their behinds as arses. Or mayhap they wouldn't mention them at all. Arses or what they were called had not come up during Lady Joan's lessons. Still, from Lord Thurleah's reaction, she was pretty sure that she hadn't chosen the right word to use. The poor man looked as if he were choking on a stone.

Sitting up in his arms, she reached around to pat his back solicitously. The next moment, she clutched at his shirt with both hands under his mantle as he suddenly lunged to his feet, dragging her with him until they both stood in the small clearing he had made in the snow while digging her out. Once she was standing, he immediately began brushing down her skirts, but Brinna couldn't help noticing the way he avoided looking at her and the fact that his face was terribly red. She was trying to decide if this was from anger or embarrassment when he straightened and cleared his throat.

"Better?"

Brinna hesitated, gave her skirts a shake, then wiggled her bottom about a bit beneath them to allow the snow underneath to fall back out before allowing her skirts to drop back around her legs. Then she gave a wry shrug. "'Tis as good as 'tis likely to get 'til I can change, my lord."

"Aye." He sighed as he saw his plans to get her alone being dashed. "We had best head right back to see to that."

Taking her arm, he led her to his horse, mounted, then bent to the side and down, grasped her beneath her arms, and lifted her onto the horse before him. Settling her there with one arm around her waist to anchor her, he reached with the other for the reins.

Clutching his arm nervously, Brinna tried to relax and get her mind off the fact that she was actually on a horse again. It was as he started to turn his mount back the way that they had come when she realized that one of the sounds that she was hearing didn't quite belong. "What is that?"

Royce paused and glanced at her, then glanced around as he too became aware of the muffled sounds she had noticed just moments earlier. It sounded like someone cursing up a blue streak. After a brief hesitation, Royce turned his horse away from the castle again and urged his mount forward until they turned the bend and came upon a loaded-down wagon stopped at the side of the path. At first it looked abandoned, but then a man straightened up from the rear, shaking his head and muttering under his breath with disgust.

"A problem?" Royce asked, drawing the man's startled gaze to them and bringing him around the wagon.

"I'm sorry, m'lord. Is my wagon in yer way?"

"Nay. There's more than enough room to get by you should I wish to," Royce assured him. "Are you stuck?"

"Aye." He glanced back to his wagon with a sigh. "I was trying to stay to the side of the path to be sure there was room fer others to pass, but it seems I strayed too far. The wagon slid off to the side and now she won't budge."

Royce shifted behind her, and she glanced up just as a decision entered his eyes. "Wait here, my lady. I won't be a moment," he murmured, then slid from the mount.

Brinna hesitated, clutched the pommel of his mount as the animal shifted restlessly beneath her, then slid from the saddle and followed to where the two men examined the situation. "Can I help?"

Both men glanced up with surprise at her question, but it was Royce who answered with a surprised smile. "Nay, Lady Joan, just stand you over there out of the way. We shall have this fellow out and on his way in a moment."

Biting her lip, Brinna nodded and moved aside, aware that ladies wouldn't trouble themselves with such problems. She stayed there as the men decided on a course of action, and even managed to restrain herself when Royce put his shoulder to the cart while the wagon driver moved to the horse's head to urge the animal forward. The wagon moved forward a bare inch or so, but then Royce's foot slid on the icy path and the wagon promptly slid back into its rut. When they paused long enough for Royce to reposition himself, Brinna couldn't restrain herself further. She wasn't used to standing on the sidelines twiddling her thumbs when there was work to be done. Giving up her lady-like pose, she hurried forward, positioning herself beside Royce to add her weight and strength to the task at hand. Royce straightened at once, alarm on his face.

"Oh, nay, Joan. Wait you over there. This is no job for a lady."

"He's right, m'lady. 'Tis kind of ye to wish to

assist, but yer more like to be a hindrance than a help. You might get hurt."

Brinna rolled her eyes at that. A decade working in the kitchens carting heavy pots and vats around had made her quite strong. Of course they could hardly know that, and she could hardly tell them as much, so she merely lifted her chin stubbornly and murmured, "I am stronger than I look, sirs. And while I may not be of much help, it would seem to me you could use any little help you can get at the moment." On that note, she put her shoulder to the cart once more and arched a brow at first one man, then the other. "Are we ready? On the count of three, then."

After exchanging a glance, the two men shrugged and gave up trying to dissuade her from helping. Instead, they waited as she counted off, then applied their energies to shifting the wagon when she reached three. Brinna dug her heels into the icy ground and put all of her slight weight behind the cart, straining muscles that had been lax these last several days, grunting along with the men under the effort as the cart finally shifted, at first just an inch, then another, and another, until it suddenly began to roll smoothly forward and right back onto the path. She nearly tumbled to the ground then as the cart pulled away, but Royce reached out, catching her arm to steady her as he straightened.

"Whew." Brinna laughed, grinning at him

widely before turning to the wagon driver as he hurried back to them.

"Thank ye, m'lord, and you too, m'lady," he gushed gratefully. "Thank ye so much. I didn't know how I was going to get out of that one."

"You are welcome," Royce assured him. "Just stick to the center of the path the rest of the way to the castle."

"Aye, m'lord. Aye." Tugging off his hat, the fellow made a quick bow to them both, then hurried back around the wagon to mount the driver's bench again and set off.

"Well—" Brinna straightened as the cart disappeared around the bend in the path, the clip-clop of the horse's hooves fading to silence. "That was fun."

"Fun?" Royce peered at her doubtfully.

"Well, perhaps not fun," she admitted uncertainly. "But there's a certain feeling of satisfaction when you get a job done well."

He nodded solemn agreement, then frowned as his gaze slid over her. " Your dress is ruined."

Brinna glanced down with disinterest, noting that aside from being soaked, it was now mud-splattered. "'Tis but mud. 'Twill wash out," she said lightly, then glanced back up, her eyebrows rising at his expression.

"You are a surprise, Lady Laythem," he murmured, then explained. "When you fell off the horse and were soaked, you did not cry that your gown was ruined, coif destroyed, or curse all four-legged beasts. You picked yourself up, dried your-self off, and said 'twas the best to be done until you could change."

"Actually, you picked me up," Brinna pointed out teasingly and he smiled, but continued.

"Then, when we came across the farmer with his wagon stuck in the snow, you did not whine that I would stop to help him before seeing you safely back to the castle, changed, and ensconced before the fire. Nay. You put your own shoulder to the man's wagon in an effort to help free it."

"Ah," Brinna murmured on a sigh as she con-sidered just how out of character her actions must seem for a lady of nobility. "I suppose most ladies wouldn't have behaved so . . . um . . . hoydenishly." She voiced the last word uncertainly, for while Aggie had often called her a hoyden as a child, Brinna wasn't sure if "hoydenishly" was a word.

"Hoydenishly?" Royce murmured with a laugh that had Brinna convinced that it wasn't a word until he added, "'Twas not hoydenish behavior. 'Twas unselfish and thoughtful, and completely opposed to the behavior I expected from a woman who was described as a snobbish little brat to me."

"Who called me that?" Brinna demanded before she could recall that it wasn't herself that had been described that way, but Joan.

"My cousin. Phillip of Radfurn." When she peered at him blankly, he added, "He visited Lay-them some weeks ago."

"Oh. Of course."

"Aye, well, I fear he took your shyness and reticence as signs of snobbery and a . . . er, slightly spoilt nature. He had me quite convinced you were a terror."

"Really?" she asked curiously. "Then why did you come to Menton?" Her eyes widened. "Did you come here to cancel the betrothal?" That would be a fine thing, wouldn't it? If he had come to cancel it and she had put paid to his intentions with her actions.

"Oh, nay, I could never cancel it. My people are counting on your dower." The last word was followed by silence as his eyes widened in alarm. "I mean—"

"'Tis all right," Brinna assured him gently when he began to look rather guilty. "I already knew that you needed the dower."

He sighed unhappily, looking not the least reassured. "Aye, well, without it I fear my people will not fare well through this spring."

"And you will do your best to provide them with what they need? Whether you want to or not?"

"Well . . ." Taking her arm, he turned to lead her back toward his horse. "It is the responsibility we have as members of the nobility, is it not? Tending to our people, fulfilling their needs to the best of our ability."

"Some of the nobility do not see it that way," she pointed out gently, and he grimaced.

"Aye. Well, some of them have no more honor than a gnat."

"But you are different."

When he gave a start at the certainty in her tone, she shrugged. "Most *lords* would not have troubled themselves to offer aid to a poor farmer either."

He smiled wryly. "I suppose not."

"But then from what I have heard, you are not like other lords. I was told that you are trying to correct neglect and damage done by those who came before you."

He remained silent, but grimaced, and she went on. "I was also told that you work very hard, even side by side with your vassals, in an effort to better things?"

His gaze turned wary, but he nodded. "I do what must be done and am not ashamed to work hard." He hesitated. "I realize that some ladies would be upset to have their husbands work side by side with the servants, but—"

"I think it is admirable," Brinna interrupted quickly, wishing to remove the worry from his face. It wasn't until she saw his tension ease that she recalled that Lady Joan had not seemed to be at all impressed by it. Before she could worry overly much about that, Royce turned to face her, taking her hands in his own.

"I need the dower. My people need it desperately. And to be honest, I would have married you for it whether you were hag, brat, whore, or simpleton—just to see my people fed and safe." He grimaced as her eyes widened incredulously at his words, then went on. "But you are none of those. You have proven to be giving and to be willing to do whatever is necessary when the need arises to help those less fortunate around you. And I want you to know that, the dower aside, I am beginning to see that I and my people will be fortunate to have you as their lady, Joan. I think we shall deal well together."

Joan. Brinna felt the name prick at her like the sharp end of a sword. She too was beginning to think that they would have dealt well together. Unfortunately, she wasn't the one he was going to marry. It was Joan. Her thoughts died abruptly as his face suddenly lowered, blocking the winter sun as his lips covered her own.

Heat. That was the first thing Brinna noticed. While her lips were chill and even seemed a bit stiff with cold, his were warm and soft as they slid across hers. They were also incredibly skilled, she realized with a sigh as he urged her own lips open and his tongue slid in to invade and conquer.

The kiss could have lasted mere moments or hours for all Brinna knew. Time seemed to have no meaning as she was overwhelmed with purely tactile sensations. She was lost in the musky scent of him, the taste and feel of him. She wanted the kiss to go on forever, and released an unabashed sigh of disappointment when it ended. When she finally opened her eyes, it was to find him eyeing her with a bit of bemusement as he caressed her cheek with his chill fingers.

"You are not at all what I expected, Joan Lay-them. You are as lovely as a newly bloomed rose. Sweet. Unselfish . . . I never thought to meet a woman like you, let alone be lucky enough to marry her." With that he drew her into his arms again, kissing her with a passion that fairly stole her breath, made her dizzy, and left her clutching weakly at his tunic when he lifted his head and smiled at her. "We had best return. Else they will wonder what became of us."

"Aye," Brinna murmured, following docilely when he led her by the hand back to his mount. She would have followed him to the ends of the earth at that moment.

"Good Lord!"

Brinna turned from closing the bedroom door to spy Joan pushing herself from the seat by the fireplace and rushing toward her. She was wearing Brinna's own dress. The fact that Joan was there took Brinna a bit by surprise. The other girl had usually been absent until late at night, when she'd crept in like a thief and slid silently into bed to awake the next morning and act as if nothing were amiss. But then, Sabrina wasn't usually around this room either, and that was the cause. Brinna supposed it was possible Joan had stuck around to keep an eye on the ailing girl. On the other hand, it was equally possible that she had stuck around to avoid having the fact discovered that she usually slipped out as soon as they were gone. The lady was up to something.

"Look at you!" Joan cried now, clasping her hands and taking in her sodden clothes with a frown. "You are soaked through. What did he do to you?"

"He didn't do anything," Brinna assured her quickly. "I fell off your horse and—"

"Fell off my horse!" Joan screeched, interrupting her. "You don't ride. Do you?" she asked uncertainly.

"Nay. That is why I fell off," Brinna said dryly, and pulled away to move to the chest at the end of the bed.

Joan took a moment to digest that, then her eyes narrowed. "You didn't go out with him alone, did you?"

"Nay. Of course not. His man accompanied us," Brinna assured her as she sifted through the gowns in the chest. Picking one, she straightened and turned to face Joan unhappily. "Mayhap you should play you from now on."

Joan blinked at that. "Whatever for?"

"Well . . ." Brinna turned away and began to remove the gown she wore. "You are to be married. You really should get to know him."

Joan grimaced at that. "Not bloody likely. I'll not marry him. I shall join a convent before consenting to marry an oaf like that."

"He's not an oaf," Brinna got out from between

gritted teeth as she flung the dress on the bed. She turned to face Joan grimly. "He's a very nice man. You could do worse than marry him."

Joan's eyes widened at her ferocious expression and attitude, then rounded in amazement. "Why, you are sweet on him."

"I am not," Brinna snapped stiffly.

"Aye, you are," she insisted with amusement, then tilted her head to the side and eyed Brinna consideringly. "Your color seems a bit high and you had a dreamy expression on your face when you came into the room. Are you falling in love with him?"

Brinna turned away, her mind running rife with memories of his body pressed close to hers, his lips soft on her own. Aye, she had most likely looked dreamy-eyed when she had entered. She had certainly felt dreamy-eyed until Joan had started screeching. And she would even admit to herself that she might very well be falling in love with him. It was hard not to. He was as handsome as sin, with a voice like Scottish whiskey, and kisses just as intoxicating. But even worse, he was a good man. She had been told as much of course, or if not exactly told, she had heard Lady Joan and her cousin discussing what they considered to be his flaws. Which to her were recommendations of his character. The fact that he worked so hard to help his people, that he was determined to better things for them . . . He put their needs before his own, even in matters of marriage. How could one not admire that?

Aside from that, he had been nothing but gentleness itself in all his dealings with her. He was no backward oaf or country idiot. Or at least, if he was, Brinna couldn't tell. Nay, he had treated her sweetly and well, staying near her side during Mass and throughout every day since Christmas morning. Despite Sabrina's interference, she had felt protected. And he had not taken advantage of her reaction to those kisses in the woods, though the Good Lord knows he could have. Brinna suspected that had he wished it, she would have let the man throw her skirts up and have her right there at the side of the path, and all it would have taken was a couple more kisses. She suspected he had known as much too, but he hadn't taken advantage of that fact. Nay, he was a good man. A man she could easily love with her whole heart. But if she gave her heart to him, it would be lost forever, for he was engaged to Joan, and he had to marry her, else he would lose the dower that his people needed so desperately.

He couldn't do that. She knew it. He wouldn't do it. She had not known him long, but she knew already that he was a man who took his responsibilities seriously. His people needed that dower, so he would marry to attain it and Brinna had no hope of having him. She couldn't go on with this charade. Couldn't risk her heart so. Not even for Aggie and the possibility of seeing her comfortable. She would not do this anymore. She had to convince Joan to resign herself to this marriage, but to do that, she had to convince her that he wasn't the backward oaf someone had led her to believe he was.

"Who is it that told you that Lord Thurleah was a country bumpkin and oaf?" Brinna asked determinedly, and Joan got a wary look about her suddenly.

"Who?" she echoed faintly, then shrugged. "It must have been Sabrina. She questioned people on the journey here to find out more about him for me."

Brinna's gaze narrowed suspiciously. "But didn't she say the day I became your maid that she hadn't said that he was an oaf—just that he worked hard to improve his lot in life?"

Joan shrugged, avoiding her eyes. "Then someone else must have mentioned it."

"Could it have been Phillip of Radfurn?" Brinna asked carefully, feeling triumph steal up within her as the other girl gave a guilty start, her eyes wide with shock. "It *was* him, wasn't it? He is deliberately making trouble between the two of you. He visited you at Laythem, told you that Royce was a backward oaf, with no social graces, then went on to his cousin's to tell him that you were a—"

When she cut herself off abruptly, Joan's gaze narrowed. "To tell him that I was what?"

"Oh, well . . ." Now it was Brinna's turn to avoid eye contact. "I don't really recall exactly."

"You are lying," Joan accused grimly. "What did he say?"

Brinna hesitated, then decided to follow one of Aggie's maxims. The one that went, *If yer in a spot and don't know what to do or say, honesty is yer best option.* "He told Lord Thurleah that you were a selfish, spoilt brat."

"What?" The blood rushed out of Joan's face, leaving her looking slightly gray for a moment, then poured back in to color her red with rage. "Why, that—" Her eyes, cold and flinty, jerked to Brinna. "Change and return below," she ordered coldly, moving to the door. "And no more riding or anything else alone with Lord Thurleah. His man is not a suitable chaperone." Then she slid out of the room, pulling the door closed with a snap.

Chapter Four

I think you are improving."

"Oh, aye." Brinna laughed dryly as she clutched at the hands Royce held at her waist to steady her as they skimmed along on the lake's frozen surface on the narrow-edged bones he had insisted she try. Royce called them skates, and claimed that what they were doing was skating. It was something he had picked up while on his travels in the Nordic countries. Brinna called it foolish, for a body was sure to fall and break something trying to balance on the sharp edge of the bones that he had strapped to her soft leather boots and his own.

He had been trying for days to convince her to try skating. Ever since the afternoon they had gone for the ride. The day Sabrina had felt under the weather. But it wasn't until today that she had given in and agreed, and that was only because she had wanted to please him. She caught herself doing that more and more often these days; doing things to try to please him. It was worrisome when she thought about it, so she tried not to.

"Nay, he is right, you are improving," Sabrina

called. Having overheard his comment and Brinna's answer as they had skated past where she stood on the edge of the frozen lake, Sabrina had called out the words cheerfully. "At least you have stopped screaming."

Brinna laughed good-naturedly at the taunt. Sabrina had relaxed somewhat during the past several days. She had recovered quickly from her illness and returned to her chore as chaperone the morning after the ride. But she had taken a different approach on her return. She still accompanied Brinna everywhere, but no longer bothered to try to keep her from talking to everyone, Royce included. She had also stopped forcing herself between the two of them when they walked about or sat for a bit. Brinna supposed she had decided it wasn't worth the trouble when they had already spent a day together without her interference.

"You are starting to shiver," Royce murmured by her ear. "We have been out here quite awhile. Mayhap we should head back to the castle to warm up."

"Aye," Brinna agreed as he steered them both back toward Sabrina. "Mayhap we should. 'Tis almost time to sup anyway."

Sabrina seemed to greet the decision to return with relief. She herself had refused to be persuaded to try the "sharp bones," as she called them, so she had stood on the side, watching Brinna's antics instead. While it had been amusing, her lack of activity meant that she was a bit chill and so was eager to return to the warmth of the castle. She waited a bit impatiently as they removed the bones from their feet, then accompanied them back to the castle, teasing "Lady Joan" gently about her ineptitude on the ice.

As it turned out, it was later than any of them had realized, and the others were already seated at table when Brinna, Royce, and Sabrina entered. They were laughing over Brinna's less-than-stellar performance on skates that afternoon, but fell silent as they realized that they were late. Not that most people noticed their entrance—the great hall was abuzz with excited chatter and laughter—but Lady Menton spotted them arriving.

Casting apologetic glances toward their hostess, the three of them hurried to the nearest spot with an opening and managed to squeeze themselves in. It meant they ended up seated among the knights and villeins at the low tables, but such things couldn't be helped—besides, the high table seemed quite full even without them.

"It looks like a celebratory feast," Brinna murmured as the kitchen doors opened and six women filed out, each bearing a tray holding a succulent roast goose on it.

"Aye," Sabrina agreed with surprise. "I don't recall Lady Menton saying anything this morning about—"

Brinna glanced at the brunette sharply when

her unfinished sentence was interrupted by a gasp. Spotting the alarm on Sabrina's face and the way she had blanched, Brinna frowned and touched her hand gently. "What is it? Are you not feeling well again?"

Sabrina turned to her, mouth working but nothing coming out.

"Joan? My lady?"

Brinna glanced distractedly at Royce when he touched her arm. "Aye?"

"Is that not your father?"

"My father?" she asked blankly, but followed his gesture to the head table. Her gaze slid over the people seated there, and she suddenly understood why the table was full even without them. William of Menton and an older man now helped fill it. Her gaze fixed on the older man. He was handsome with blond hair graying at the temples, strong features, and a nice smile. Brinna would have recognized him anywhere. He was Lord Edmund Laythem, a good friend of Lord Menton's and a frequent visitor at Menton. He was also Joan's father.

Brinna's gaze was drawn to Lady Menton as the woman leaned toward her husband to murmur something. Whatever it was made the two men glance across the room toward Brinna. For a moment she felt frozen, pinned to her seat like a bug stuck in sticky syrup as her heart began to hammer in panic and her breathing became fast and shallow. What if he stood and came to greet her? He would know. They would all know. But he didn't rise. Edmund Laythem merely smiled slightly and nodded a greeting.

It took an elbow in her side from Sabrina to make Brinna nod back and force what she hoped was a smile to her own lips.

"Mayhap we should go greet him," Royce murmured beside her and started to rise, but Brinna clawed at his arm at once.

"Oh, nay! Nay. I—there is no sense disrupting Lady Menton's feast. Time enough to greet him afterward."

Royce hesitated, then settled in his seat reluctantly. "As you say, my lady," he murmured, then smiled wryly. "Well, now we know the reason behind the feast. Lady Menton must have put it on to welcome your father and her son."

"Aye," Brinna murmured faintly, then tore her eyes away from the high table and swiveled abruptly toward Sabrina.

"What are we going to do?" Sabrina asked in a panic before she could say a word, and Brinna's heart sank as she realized the brunette would be of little help.

"Are you not going to eat?"

Forcing a smile, Brinna turned to face forward at Royce's question. "Of course. Aye. We shall eat," she murmured, casting Sabrina a meaningful sideways glance.

Nodding, Sabrina set to her meal, but there was

a frown between her eyes as she did, and she was still as tense as the strings on a harp as she cast nervous glances toward the head table. Brinna was aware of her actions, but avoided looking at the head table herself at all costs. She kept her head bowed, eyes fastened on her meal as she ate, and slowly began to shrink in her seat.

It was the most excruciating meal Brinna had ever sat through. Worse even than her first night as Joan's fill-in. She wasn't even sure what she ate. It all tasted like dust in her mouth as her mind raced about in circles like a dog chasing its tail, desperately searching for a way out of this mess. An excuse to hurry upstairs right after the meal and avoid Lord Laythem was needed, but her mind seemed consumed with the fact that this was the end of the road for her. She had thought she had a couple more days at least to bask in the warmth of Lord Thurleah's attention, but this was it. The end. These were her last moments with him. If only—

She cut the wish off abruptly. It was no good. She could not have Royce. He was a lord and she just a scullery maid. He needed a large dower such as Joan could provide. She had nothing but the ragged clothes presently on Lady Joan's back. Still, he had come to her on Christmas Day like a gift from God that had brightened her life and made her experience things she had never thought to feel. It broke her heart that he was a gift meant for someone else and that she could not keep him.

"Are you done?" Royce asked after finishing off the last of his ale. The meal was coming to a close. Several people at the lower tables around them had already risen to return to their chores, or to find a place to relax and listen to the minstrel, who was even now preparing to torture them some more with his version of music. Even Brinna had finished off what Royce had served her with, though she couldn't recall actually eating a thing. "Shall we go greet your father now?"

"Oh, I-I should . . . er . . ."

"Aye, we should," Royce agreed, misunderstanding her stammering and taking her arm as he rose to his feet.

Brinna remained silent, following reluctantly as he led her toward the head table where most of the guests sat chatting over their ales, her mind still squirming about in search of escape. Luck lent a hand as the others began to rise in groups now to leave the tables, slowing them down and making Royce and Brinna proceed in single file as they weaved through the crowd. Royce let go of her hand then, and Brinna walked behind him for a couple of steps, then simply turned on her heel and made a beeline for the steps that led upstairs.

She had to get to Joan's room. She had to find Joan, and the only place she could think to look was the room. Not that she would normally be there at this hour. Joan didn't even sleep in her own room anymore. She had fallen into the pattern of leaving as soon as Brinna departed with Royce for Mass, then not returning until just ere dawn on the next morning. She had been doing so since the day Brinna had told her what Royce's cousin, Phillip of Radfurn, had said. The girl had stormed out in a fury, been absent through the night, then returned just moments before Royce had arrived to escort the woman he thought was Lady Joan to Mass. The fact that Lady Joan had been out all night had been worrisome enough to Brinna, but the fact that she had returned in a fabulous mood, and had actually glowed with satisfaction and happiness as she had insisted that they continue with the charade, had made Brinna fear that whatever was going on did not bode well for Royce.

Now, Brinna just hoped that the girl, wherever she normally spent her time, had heard about her father's arrival and had returned to the room, prepared to take over her role as a member of nobility.

ROYCE STEPPED ONTO the dais directly behind Lord Laythem and tapped the man on the shoulder, offering a polite smile when he turned on his seat to glance at him.

"Royce. Greetings, son." The older man stood at once, as did Lord Menton and his son, William. "I hope you are having a good Christmas here with Robert and his family? I am sorry I haven't been here from the beginning, but I fear the ague and chills felled me where many men have failed."

Royce smiled at his wry words and nodded reassuringly. "I was told that you were ill. I hope you are recovered now?"

"Aye, aye. I'm still regaining my strength and I've a stone or two to put back on, but I feel much better."

"I'm glad to hear it. Your daughter and I—" He turned slightly to gesture Joan forward as he spoke, then paused, blinking in surprise as he saw that she was no longer with him. "Where did she—" he began in bewilderment, and Lord Laythem clapped a hand on his shoulder and smiled wryly.

"I think she slipped away when you moved through that one group halfway up the room," Edmund Laythem told him dryly, revealing that he had watched their approach.

Royce's eyes widened at this news. "Why would she—"

"She was none too pleased with me when last we met," the older man confessed, then shrugged. "I fear I handled things badly. I never really bothered to mention the betrothal agreement until she arrived at court on her way here. It was all a great surprise to her and she was understandably upset by my neglect."

"I see," Royce murmured thoughtfully.

"Aye, well, I am sorry if she has caused you any trouble because of it?" It was a question as well as an apology, and Royce reassured him quickly.

"Oh, nay. She has been delightful. Of course,

Lady Sabrina was another matter at first. She would not even let me talk to Joan for the first few days."

Lord Laythem's eyebrows rose at that, but he shrugged. "Sabrina can be a bit overeager when a task is set to her. No doubt that is all that was." He smiled wryly, his gaze moving to the brunette, who still sat in her seat at the table, watching them anxiously. "Actually, I must have a word with her. Her father was at court over the holidays and arranged a marriage for her. He sent some men with me to retrieve her back to prepare for it. If you will excuse me?"

"Of course." Royce stepped aside to allow the man past him, then took a moment to greet William of Menton and compliment Lord and Lady Menton on the feast he had just enjoyed before turning to survey the room in search of Joan. Catching a glimpse of her disappearing up the stairs, he excused himself and hurried after her.

BRINNA OPENED THE door to enter Joan's room, and found herself pushed back out by a hand on her chest.

"I just have to check on something," Joan trilled gaily before allowing her body to follow her arm out of the room.

"What—" Brinna began in confusion as the girl pulled the door closed, but Joan waved her to silence, then glanced quickly up and down the hall before dragging her to the shadows near the top of the stairs to keep an eye on the people below.

"My father arrived today," Joan said.

"Aye, I know. 'Tis why I came up here. To avoid him."

Joan nodded at that, but frowned as she rubbed her forehead. "This complicates things."

"Complicates things?" Brinna goggled at her, but Joan didn't notice.

"Aye. My maid came with him. That is who I was talking to in our room."

"Your room," Brinna said firmly. "And to my mind this doesn't complicate things. It ends them. You shall have to go back to being you. 'Tis for the best anyway."

Joan did not appear to see the sense behind the suggestion as she shook her head grimly. "Nay. I cannot. I need to—" Her expression closed as she caught herself, then said more calmly, "There is no need to end it now. I shall insist my maid rest for the remainder of my stay to recover from her recent illness and the journey here. That way you will not be expected to return to the kitchens, she will not get in the way, and we can continue with our agreement."

"What of your father?"

"Oh, damn, here comes Lord Thurleah."

Brinna glanced down the stairs at Joan's anxious tones, her heart skipping a beat as she saw him start up the stairs toward them. Her gaze returned to the other girl in a panic. They were both dressed as Lady Joan at the moment. It would not do to be seen together. "What—"

Joan cut her off by giving her a shove toward the stairs. "Get him out of here. He must not see us together."

"But your father!" Brinna cried in dismay, resisting her push.

"Just avoid him," Joan snapped impatiently. "Now, get going."

The shove she gave her this time nearly sent Brinna tumbling down the stairs. Catching herself at the last moment, she cast a glare back toward the shadows that hid Joan, then hurried down the stairs to meet Royce.

"Where did you go?" were his first words. "One moment you were behind me and the next you were gone."

"Oh . . . I . . . I went to my room to greet my maid," she lied lamely, not surprised when Royce arched one eyebrow doubtfully.

"Before greeting your father?"

"Well, she was very ill when I left her at court."

"As was your father," he pointed out dryly, and Brinna grimaced.

"Aye, but—"

"Your father told me that you were angered with him for keeping the news of our betrothal to himself and not giving you warning," he interrupted before she could say something else stupid.

"Aye, well . . ."

"And while he should have perhaps given you more warning, he seems to regret the rift between you."

"Yes, well—"

"Besides, you do not mind so much, do you? About marrying me, I mean?"

"Nay, of course not," she assured him quickly.

"There you are then. 'Tis only polite to greet him. Now, where has he got to?" Pausing halfway up the stairs, he peered about until he spotted Lord Laythem below talking to Sabrina. "Oh. He is still with your cousin. He is passing on a message from her father, your uncle." Hesitating, he glanced back at Brinna, smiling wryly. "Mayhap we should leave them in peace until they finish. Would you care for a beverage while we wait?"

"Aye," she murmured, then continued down the stairs with him until they reached the bottom and she spied a knight and one of the kitchen girls slipping outside. An idea springing to mind, Brinna stopped abruptly, tugging on his hand. "Nay."

He turned to her in surprise. "Nay?"

"Nay." She paled slightly as her gaze slid past him to see that Lord Laythem had finished speaking to Sabrina and was now rising, his gaze on where she and Royce stood. "I-I need . . . air."

Frowning with concern, Royce clasped her lightly by the arms. "Are you all right? You've gone quite pale."

Brinna dragged her gaze away from the approaching Lord Laythem and focused on Royce. "Nay," she said firmly. "I am not all right. 'Tis the heat. Do I not get out into the fresh air this minute, I'm sure to faint."

It was all she had to say. She barely had time for one more glance over his shoulder at Lord Laythem as he weaved his way toward them; then Royce had whirled her toward the great hall's doors and propelled her to and through them.

"Better?" he asked solicitously as the doors closed behind them.

Her arms moving automatically to hug herself against the cold winter night, Brinna glanced uncertainly about the courtyard. Lord Laythem had been close enough to see where they had gone to, and she very much feared his following them. Standing on the steps, handy for him to find on exiting the hall, hardly seemed the wisest thing to do.

"Perhaps the stables," she murmured thoughtfully. Surely Lord Laythem would never look for them there? Certainly it was the last place Brinna would have chosen to go were she not desperate to hide.

"The stables?"

"What a wonderful idea." Brinna beamed at him as if it had been his idea. "No doubt the stables shall make me feel better." Taking his arm, she attempted to move him down the steps. It was like trying to shift a centuries-old tree. The man was immovable.

Certainly too damn big for her slight weight. "My lord? Will you not come with me to the stables? 'Tis warmer there," she coaxed, tugging at his arm.

Heaving a sigh, he started forward down the stairs. "I thought you said that the castle was too hot and you needed to be outside else you might faint. Now you wish to go to the stables because 'tis warmer?"

"Aye, well, the castle is too warm, and the night too cold. The stables shall be just right, I am sure," she muttered, dragging at his arm in an effort to speed him up. "Do you not think we might walk faster?"

"You were faint a moment ago," he protested.

"Aye, but the exercise will do me good."

Muttering under his breath, he picked up his pace a bit, hurrying across the courtyard behind her as she began a jog toward the stables.

"I am not sure this is a good idea," Royce complained as they reached the stables.

Ignoring him, Brinna tugged the stable doors open and slid inside. Turning to glance back the way they had come as he slid in behind her, she spied a dark shape that could have been Lord Laythem standing on the stairs staring after them, and felt her heart skip a beat. Whirling away as he closed the door, she eyed the stables almost desperately, searching for somewhere to hide lest Joan's father follow them. Then she started down the row of stalls determinedly.

"What are you doing?" Royce asked curiously, following her the length of the building until they reached the last stall.

"I thought to check on my mare," she lied grimly.

"She was back near the door," he pointed out dryly, and Brinna rolled her eyes at that bit of news, then for want of any other thought of what to do, whirled, caught him by the tunic, and reached up onto her tiptoes to plaster her lips on his. It was the only thing she could think to do. His kisses made her thought processes fuzzy and scattered and made her willing to follow him anywhere unquestioningly. She could only hope they had the same effect on him and would stop his questions. Unfortunately, it did seem to her that he was better at this. While their earlier kisses had been fiery and passionate, now, without his participation, it did seem to be a wasted exercise. Brinna was about to pull away when he suddenly relaxed and kissed her back.

Sighing in relief, Brinna leaned into him and let her arms creep up about his neck. She had the curious urge to arch and stretch against him like a cat, but he pulled away before she could, a question in his eyes.

"How do you feel now?"

"Wonderful," Brinna purred, leaning her head on his chest with a small sigh, only to stiffen at his next words.

"Then mayhap we should head back."

"Oh, nay," she gasped anxiously.

"We shouldn't be here alone. It isn't proper, Joan."

Joan. She stared at him silently. He was Joan's. But for just this moment in time, she wanted to pretend he was hers. Joan wouldn't care. She didn't want him. But Brinna did. She wanted to hold him close for one night. Then hold those memories close for all the days of her future as she worked in her little cottage.

"Joan?"

"Mayhap I don't feel proper," she whispered huskily, and Royce's eyes widened incredulously. For a moment they stood frozen in silence. Then he suddenly groaned and pulled her back into his arms, his mouth lowering to cover hers in a kiss that made her legs weak. This time there was no restraint. Nothing held back. He gave her all his passion, overwhelming her with it as his hands closed over her breasts through her gown.

Pressing her back against the stall, he broke the kiss and turned his attention briefly to undo the lacings of her dress. Brinna gasped as the neckline slid apart and he tugged the collar of her shift down, revealing her naked breasts. Cold winter air chilled them briefly before Royce covered them with his hands. Growling deep in his throat, he cupped them, his thumbs running over her erect nipples as he pressed another hard, fast kiss to her lips. Then he made a trail down her throat, across her collarbone, and down to the erect tip of one breast, which he sucked into his mouth hungrily.

Brinna shuddered. Her hands clenched in his hair, then dragged his face back up for a kiss, and she thrust her own tongue into his mouth as he had done to her. Releasing his head, she dropped her hands down to slide her fingers beneath his tunic, fanning them over his hard flat stomach, then running them up over his ribs to his chest.

She felt the cool breeze creep its way up her left leg with some peripheral part of her mind, but really didn't realize what it meant until his hand brushed against her hip. Before she could register surprise, his hand had slid around between her legs and up the inside of her thigh, a warm caress. Brinna gasped into his mouth, jerking in his arms as his hand covered her womanhood, cupping it briefly before he slid a finger between her folds to investigate her warmth and heat as he urged her legs further apart with a knee between her own.

She heard the keening whimpers for quite a while before she realized that they were coming from her own throat. Suddenly embarrassed, she tugged her mouth away and turned her head until she found his shoulder. Pressing her mouth against it, she retrieved her hands from beneath his shirt, then wasn't sure what to do with them. When Royce caught one of her hands and drew it down to the front of his braies, pressing it against the solid hardness that had grown there, she froze, raising fear-filled eyes to him. He met her gaze, read her fear, and paused, his hand stilling between her legs. She saw uncertainty burst to life in his eyes, and would have kicked herself had she been able to.

"You are afraid. Mayhap we should stop and—" he began, his voice dying, eyes widening in shock as she suddenly moved the hand that clasped him through his braies, and slid it down the front of his braies to touch his bare flesh.

"Move to the straw," she suggested huskily, giving him a gentle squeeze.

Uncertainty fleeing under passion, Royce caught her by the backs of her thighs and lifted her up. Brinna wrapped her legs around his hips, and caught them at the ankles to help hold them up as he turned to walk to the back corner of the stables where several bales of hay rested. He set her on one that would keep her at the same height, then reached up to tug her gown and shift off her shoulders as she released her legs and flattened them against the front of the bale she sat on. Once the cloth lay in a pool around her waist, Brinna leaned back, tilting her head back as she arched her breasts upward for his attention.

He did not disappoint her. His hands and mouth paid homage, touching, caressing, licking, nibbling, and sucking at her goose-bumped flesh until she moaned aloud with her desire for him. It wasn't until then that he caught at the hem of her skirt again. Sliding his hands beneath it, he clasped her ankles, then ran his hands up the flesh of her calves to her thighs, pushing the material before him, urging her legs apart as he did. His mouth moved to cover her gasps as she shuddered beneath his touch, and she drank of him deeply, then bit his lower lip as his hands met at her center. He caressed her, then slid one finger smoothly into her, and Brinna arched into the invasion, her hands shifting to his shoulders and clutching him desperately as she wriggled into the caress.

Tearing her mouth away then, she shook her head desperately and gasped as he slid his finger out, then back in. Reaching down into his braies again, she grasped him almost roughly, trying to tell him what she wanted as she bit into his shoulder to prevent crying out. She felt the cloth loosen around her hand, then felt it no longer as he sprang free in her hand. Brinna ran her hand the length of his shaft, then pressed her feet against the bale, sliding her behind to the edge of it in search of him.

Chuckling roughly at her eagerness, Royce gave in to her request and edged closer, brushing her hand away to grasp his manhood himself and steer it on the course it needed to follow. She felt him rub against her, caressing her as his hand had done a moment ago, and wiggled impatiently, but still he did not enter her, but teased and caressed and rubbed until Brinna thought she would go mad. It was at that point that the tension that had been building inside of her suddenly broke. Taken by surprise, Brinna cried out, her legs snapping closed on either side of his hips as she arched backward.

Covering her mouth with his own, Royce chose that moment to thrust into her. A sudden sharp pain flared briefly where they joined, and Brinna stiffened against it, then gasped and relaxed somewhat as it passed. When he began to draw himself out then, Brinna's eyes popped open, dismay covering her face as she clutched at his buttocks to keep him inside her.

"Nay," she gasped in protest, then blinked in surprise as he drove into her again. "Oh," she breathed, arching automatically and returning his smile a bit distractedly as she felt the tension begin to build again. "Oh."

"Aye," Royce murmured, slipping his hands beneath her buttocks and lifting her into his thrusts.

"JOAN?"

Brinna blinked her eyes open with a sigh, sorry to see her stolen moment pass so swiftly. They had just finished the ride she had started. Royce had spilled his seed with a triumphant cry that had made the horses shift and whinny nervously in their stalls in response. Brinna had followed him quickly, biting into the cloth of his tunic as her body spasmed and twitched around him. Then he had slumped against her slightly, holding her even as she held him. Now it was over, it seemed, and he had brought reality back with that one name. *Joan.*

"Joan?" Straightening, he smiled down at her with a combination of uncertainty and gentleness. "Are you all right? I did not hurt—"

"Joan?"

They both stiffened at that shout from out of the darkness.

Brinna peered anxiously over Royce's shoulder even as he cast a glance that way himself. They both saw that the stable door was open and someone was walking up the shadowed aisle toward them. Cursing, Royce pulled out of her and quickly tugged her skirt down into place. Replacing himself inside his braies, he turned away, hiding her with his back as he faced the approaching man.

"Who goes there?" he asked tensely, reaching for his sword.

"Lord Laythem."

Brinna heard the breath whoosh out of Royce at that announcement, and bit her lip as she clasped Joan's gown to her breasts and ducked fully behind him. There was a moment of tense silence as the man approached, then the crunch of straw under his feet ended and there was a weary sigh.

"Well, it would seem I waited too long to see if you would return to the hall," he murmured, then added wryly, "Or perhaps not long enough."

"I am sorry, my lord," Royce began grimly. "I—"

"Do not be sorry, lad. I was young once myself. Besides, this makes me feel better. At least now I won't have to feel that I forced Joan into something."

Brinna saw Royce's hands unclench as he relaxed. Then Lord Laythem cleared his throat and murmured, "Though it may be a good idea to move the wedding date forward a bit."

"Aye. Of course," Royce agreed promptly. "Tomorrow?"

"Eager, are you?" Lord Laythem laughed. "I shall talk to Robert, but I do not think tomorrow is likely. We crown the Lord of Misrule tomorrow," he reminded him. "I'll see what I can arrange and let you know."

"As you wish, my lord." Brinna could hear the grin in Royce's voice and knew he was pleased. Her own heart seemed suddenly leaden. But then, she wasn't the one he would be marrying.

"Aye. Well, you had best collect yourselves and return to the hall. I would not want anyone else to catch the two of you so."

"Aye, my lord."

"Good." There was a rustle as he turned to leave, then he paused. "Joan, I want to talk to you ere Mass on the morrow . . . Joan?"

"Aye," Brinna whispered, afraid to speak lest he notice that her voice differed from his daughter's. Apparently not noticing anything amiss, he wished them good night and left.

Royce whirled to face her as soon as Lord Laythem was gone. He was jubilant as he helped her redon Joan's gown, talking excitedly about how this was a wonderful thing. How the arrival of the dower early would aid his people. They would leave the day after the wedding. They would travel to Thurleah, purchase this, repair that, and spend every spare moment in bed. Brinna listened to all this, forcing herself to smile and nod, and doing her best to hide the fact that her heart was breaking.

Chapter Five

*H*ere, put this on."

Brinna turned from straightening the bed linens as Lady Joan slammed into the room. "My lady?"

"Put this on," Joan repeated grimly, stripping her gown even as she spoke. "And give me your dress."

"But—"

"Now, Brinna. There is no time."

Brinna started to undress, responding automatically to the authority in Joan's voice, then halted. "Nay. We cannot do this. *I* cannot. Your father is here now. He will—"

"Today they appoint the Lord of Misrule. All will be chaos all day. 'Sides, he will not bother with me—*you*. He will be drinking and carousing with Lord Menton. You can easily avoid him."

Brinna shook her head grimly. "I cannot."

"You must," Joan hissed, grabbing her hand desperately and giving it a squeeze. "Just this one last time."

"But—"

"You got me into this," Joan said accusingly, her

patience snapping, and Brinna's eyes widened in amazement.

"Me?"

"Aye, you. If you hadn't let Royce drag you off to the stables for a quick tumble like some cheap—" She snapped her mouth closed on the rest of what she was going to say and sighed.

"How did you find out?" Brinna asked, her voice heavy with guilt.

"What do you think Father wished to speak to me about?" she asked grimacing, then bit her lip miserably. "The wedding is tomorrow. I have to warn—" She snapped her mouth closed again and frowned, then turned away, took two steps, then turned back. "Please? Just this one last time. You will not be discovered. I promise. Truly, you know as well as I that 'twill be chaotic today."

"Not at Mass it won't be."

Sensing that she was weakening, Joan pounced. "You shall leave late for Mass. That way, Father will be seated at the front with Lord and Lady Menton, and you and Lord Thurleah will be at the back of the chapel. Just don't let Thurleah dawdle once Mass is over and it should be all right."

Brinna blew her breath out on a sigh, then nodded and continued to undress, wondering as she did why she had even hesitated. She wanted to do this. She was eager to spend any little moment of time with Royce that she could while she could.

"Oh, good," Joan said.

Brinna whirled from closing the bedroom door to stare at Joan in amazement as she rushed toward her. Truly, she had not expected the other girl to be there yet. She had thought Joan would spend every last moment of freedom she had as far from this room as possible. Actually, she had rather hoped that Joan would. After the day she had had, Brinna could have used a few moments of peace and quiet.

As per Joan's instructions, Brinna had kept Royce waiting that morning, leaving him cooling his heels in the hall as she and Joan had paced nervously inside the room until Joan had determined that enough time had passed so that Brinna and Royce would be late for Mass and end up seated far from Lord Laythem and the possibility of his noticing something amiss. And the girl had been right. Mass was already started when they reached the chapel. Royce ushered her to the nearest seat, as far from her "father" as Brinna could have wished, and they had sat silently through the Mass.

Royce would have waited then to return to the great hall with the other Menton guests, but Brinna had exited the moment it was over, forcing him to follow or leave her without an escort. She had apologized prettily once they were out of the chapel, claiming a need for air with a suggestive smile that had made his eyes glow with the memory of the last time she had proclaimed a desire for air. Moments later Brinna had found herself locked in his arms in a handy alcove, being kissed silly. And so the day had gone, with Brinna spending half her time dodging Joan's father and the other half locked in Royce's arms in some handy secluded spot. The only chance she had had to relax was during the feast itself. She, along with everyone else, had cheered the crowning of the kitchen lad who usually manned the spit as the Lord of Misrule, then had helped Lord and Lady Menton and most of their younger guests in serving the servants while Joan's father and another guest had taken on the role of minstrels and attempted to provide music for the celebrants.

Once it was over, however, Brinna had again found herself dodging Lord Laythem and spending more and more time in dim corners and dark alcoves, her head growing increasingly fuzzy with a combination of drink and lust. Royce had not gone unaffected by the revelry and their passion himself. The last time she had dragged him off to avoid Lord Laythem, he had nearly taken her in the shadows at the head of the stairs before recalling himself and putting an end to their embrace. Then he had suggested a little breathlessly that mayhap they should end that evening early so that their wedding day would come that much quicker. Which was why Brinna was now back in Joan's room before the usual time.

"I am glad you are here," Joan went on, clasping her hands with a smile. "I was afraid I would not have the opportunity to thank you and say goodbye ere I left."

"Left?" Brinna echoed faintly.

"Aye. I am leaving. Phillip and I are running away to be married."

"Phillip?" Brinna stared at her blankly, sure the drink had affected her more than she had realized.

"Phillip of Radfurn. Lord Thurleah's cousin?" Joan prompted with amusement. "When he visited Laythem we—" She shrugged. "We fell in love. He followed me to court, then on here, and has been staying in the village so that we could see each other."

"But he told Royce that you were a spoiled brat," Brinna reminded her in confusion.

"Aye. He was hoping to convince him to break the contract. He wanted me for himself, you see."

"I see," Brinna murmured, but shook her head. She didn't really see at all. "Did you say you were running away?"

"Aye. To be married. Phillip is fetching the horses now."

"But you can't. You are supposed to marry Royce tomorrow morning."

"Well, obviously I will not be there."

"But you cannot do this. He's—"

"I know, I know." Joan rolled her eyes as she moved to the window to peer down into the darkness of the courtyard below. "He is a nice man. Well, if you like him so much, why do you not marry him? He will be looking for a wife now that I am out of the picture anyway. As for me, Phillip is more my sort. We understand each other. And we will not spend our days moldering out on some old estate. He adores court as much as I do."

"What of your father?"

Joan grimaced. "He will be furious. He may even withhold my dower. But Phillip does not care. He loves me and will take me with or without—" She paused suddenly, then smiled. "There he is. He has the horses. Well, I'm off."

Whirling away from the window, she pulled the hood of her mantle over her head and hurried to the door. Pausing there, she glanced back. "I left the rest of the coins I promised you in the chest. Thank you for everything, Brinna."

She was gone before Brinna could think of a thing to say to stop her. Sighing as the door snapped closed, Brinna sank down on the edge of the bed in dismay.

What a mess. It was all a mess. Joan was rushing off with Lord Radfurn. Royce's plans would be ruined. His hopes for his people crushed. And she was at fault, she realized with horror. She had ruined everything for him. If she had not masqueraded as Joan, Joan would have been forced to remain here and spend time with him and—

Oh, dear Lord, how could she have done this to him?

"Joan!" Sabrina rushed into the room, slamming the door behind her with a sigh. "It is madness out there. Everyone is drunk and I thought I saw Brinna slipping out of the keep—" She paused as she drew close enough to see the color of Brinna's eyes and the miserable expression on her face. "Brinna?"

She nodded solemnly.

"Then that was Joan I saw slipping out of the keep?"

"Aye," Brinna sighed. "She is running off with Phillip of Radfurn."

"What?" Sabrina shrieked. "Oh, I knew that man was trouble."

Brinna's eyes widened in surprise. "Phillip of Radfurn?"

"Aye. He was all over her at Laythem. Trailing after her like a puppy dog. Going on and on about how grand Henry's court is. As if Joan's head wasn't already stuffed with the thought herself." She shook her head in disgust and dropped to sit on the bed beside Brinna. "He must have followed us here."

"Aye, he did."

"Then she has probably been slipping out to see him every day. No wonder she wanted me to accompany you. That way she could flit about unchaperoned. Lord knows what they have been getting up to. They—oh, my God!" Sabrina turned on her in horror as if just understanding the significance of Joan's running away. "What are we going to do? Lord Laythem will be furious when he finds out."

"No doubt," Brinna agreed, thinking that the man would also be mightily confused after coming across someone he thought was Joan messing about with Royce in the stables just last night. He would be furious to think that after that, she had then run off with Radfurn. Royce would be just as confused and angry.

"Oh, dear Lord." Sabrina stood abruptly and moved toward the door. "I am getting out of here."

"Out of here?" Brinna stood up anxiously. "What do you mean out of here?"

"My father sent men with Uncle Edmund to escort me home to be married. I had insisted that we wait until after the wedding to go, but now . . ." Pausing at the door, she turned back to shake her head. "I will insist we leave first thing on the morrow. I do not want to be here when Uncle Edmund discovers this. He will skin me alive for my involvement. And I would rather be far and away from here before he finds out."

"But should we not tell them? They will worry and—"

"Worry? Girl, what are you thinking of? Forget their worry and think of yourself."

Brinna blinked in surprise. "I have nothing to worry about. I am just a servant."

"Who has been parading as a noble for the past nearly two weeks," Sabrina pointed out, then bit her lip. "Oh, dear Lord, I knew I should have told you this sooner."

"What?" Brinna asked warily.

Sabrina shook her head. "I was talking to Christina that first night at table. The night Joan stayed up here to train you to be a lady," she explained. "She happened to mention that a neighbor's smithy got caught impersonating Lord Menton this last summer. It seems the lord had commissioned a new suit of mail. The smithy finished it earlier than expected, but rather than take it at once to his lord, he donned it and paraded about, masquerading as him. He was caught, and they buried him alive with the mail, saying that since he coveted it so much he could spend eternity with it."

Brinna paled and winced at the story, then shook her head. "Aye, but that was different. Lady Joan insisted I masquerade as her. She said she would say 'twas all a jest and all would be well. She—"

"She is not here to tell anyone that, is she? And as it turns out, 'tis not much of a jest. At least I don't think Lord Laythem or Lord Thurleah will see it as one." Sabrina nodded as Brinna's eyes widened in dawning horror. "Mark my words. Dirty your face and hair with soot, redon your kerchief and clothes, then get you on that pallet by the door and feign sleep until the morrow. When they come looking for Joan, claim she did not return last night and you know not where she is, then just get out of the way. As for me, I am going to speak to my father's man and see if 'tis too late to leave tonight."

Brinna leapt into action the moment the door was closed, rushing to the chest to begin digging through it for her ratty old gown and the strip of cloth to cover her hair. She had just sunk to her knees by the chest in horror as she recalled that Joan had been wearing her clothes when she left, when the door to the room opened again.

"Ah, yer here already," the old crone who entered murmured with disappointment as she spotted Brinna by the chest. "I was hoping to beat ye here and see yer bed turned down ere ye arrived."

Brinna made a choking sound and the old woman smiled benignly. "Now, now. I know ye insisted I rest a bit longer to be sure I'm recovered, but really, I am well now and ready to take on my duties again. 'Sides, I wouldn't leave ye in the hands of some inexperienced little kitchen maid on the eve of yer wedding."

Brinna held her breath in horror as the woman, who could only be Joan's maid, approached. At any moment the woman would cry out in horror once she saw Brinna up close and realized that her eye color was all wrong and her features just a touch off—but it never happened. Instead, Brinna's eyes were the ones to widen in realization as she saw the clouds that obscured the woman's eyes leaving her nearly blind. Brinna was safe for now, so long as she kept her mouth shut. But she had to figure a way out of this mess by morning, else she might find herself spending the day watching them dig a grave to bury her alive in.

BRINNA STOOD SILENTLY between Royce and Lord Laythem, her head bowed to hide the color of her eyes and her shaking knees. She couldn't be sure whether they shook from her fear of discovery, or the fact that she had been standing with her knees slightly bent all throughout the priest's short morning Mass in an effort to appear an inch or so shorter so as not to give herself away to Joan's father.

It was fate that had brought her here. Fickle fate, blocking her at every turn, making escape impossible. First her clothes had left the room on Joan's back; then Joan's maid had arrived to usher her to bed before settling herself on the pallet before the door, ensuring that no one entered . . . and that Brinna couldn't leave. She had spent the night wide awake, tossing and turning, as she tried to find a way out of this cauldron of trouble. The only thing she had been able to come up with was to simply slip away at her first opportunity, find Aggie, get her to find her something more appropriate for a servant to wear, then do as Sabrina had suggested.

Fate had stepped in to remove that opportunity as well. She simply had not been given the chance. Joan's maid had barely risen in the morning and begun to fuss around Brinna before the door had burst open to allow Lady Menton and a bevy of servants to enter. Aggie had been among them, and Brinna had waited stiffly for her to say something, but the woman who had raised her from birth seemed not to recognize her as Brinna was bathed, dressed, and primped. It wasn't until just before Royce arrived that Brinna had realized that the woman had known who she was all along. The bath had been removed and Lady Menton and the rest of the servants had left with it when Aggie had suddenly stepped up to her and placed a silver chain about her neck.

"Yer necklace, m'lady. Ye can't be getting married without this," she had murmured. "'Twas yer mother's."

Brinna had lifted the amulet that hung from the chain in her hand and peered down at it, her eyes widening as she recognized it as the one that Aggie had worn for as long as she had known her.

"All will be well," the old woman had whispered gently, and Brinna had gasped.

"You know!"

Giving her a sharp look of warning, Aggie had gestured to Joan's maid, who was busy digging through the chest, then chided Brinna gently. "I've known from the beginning. Did ye think I wouldn't when I met that other girl in here?"

"But what do I do?"

"You love him, don't you?"

Brinna's answer had been in her eyes, and Aggie had smiled. "Then marry him."

"But—"

"Here we are." Joan's maid had approached then with a veil for her to wear, and Aggie had merely offered Brinna a reassuring smile and slipped from the room. Then Joan's maid had veiled her, Royce had arrived, and she had found herself making the walk she had made every day since taking on this foolish masquerade. Only this morning she had known she was walking to her death.

Mass this morning had been delayed and shortened due to the wedding, but now the priest had finished it and moved on to the ceremony while Brinna struggled with what to do. She knew what she *should* do. Throw off the veil that half-hid her features and proclaim who she really was before this went any further. Unfortunately, fear was riding her just now. While Brinna loved Royce, she certainly did not think that she could not live without him. She was quite attached to living actually. In fact, the more she considered how some poor smithy had been killed for daring to misrepresent himself as his lord, the more she loved life.

"Do you, Joan Jean Laythem, take Royce to be your . . ."

A rushing in her ears drowned out the priest's voice briefly, and Brinna felt the sweat break out on her forehead as she swallowed some of the bile rising up in her throat.

"Love, honor, and obey . . ."

Love, she thought faintly. Aye, she loved him.

And she thought he might actually love her too. But how long would that last once he realized how she had tricked him? Good Lord, he would loathe her. How could he not when she was taking the choice away from him. Tricking him into marriage with a scullery maid.

"My lady?"

Blinking, she peered at the priest, suddenly aware of the silence that surrounded her. They were waiting for her answer. Her gaze slid to Royce, taking in the expression on his face. It was two parts loving admiration, and one part concern as he awaited her response. Swallowing, she tried to get the words out. *I do*, she thought. *I do. I do.* "I don't."

"What?"

Brinna hardly heard Lord Laythem's indignant roar as she watched the shock and alarm fill Royce's face. Shaking her head, she gave up her slouching and stood up straight and tall, wondering even as she did what madness had overcome her. "I cannot do it."

"Joan?" The confusion and pain on Royce's face tore at her.

"You need the dower for your people. If that were not so . . . But it is, and I cannot do this to you. You would never forgive me. And you shouldn't forgive a woman who could do that to you."

Royce shook his head in confusion. "What are you saying?"

"I am not Joan."

There was silence for a moment, then Royce gave an incredulous laugh. "You jest!"

"Nay. I am not Joan Laythem!" Brinna insisted, and her heart thundering in her chest, she ripped the veil from her head. As those there to witness the occasion leaned forward in confusion, wondering what they were supposed to be seeing, she whirled to face Lord Laythem. "I am naught but a scullery maid. I—your daughter—I was sent to tend to Lady Laythem when she arrived because her lady's maid was ill. When she realized how similar we were in looks, she insisted I take her place for Lord Royce to woo," she ended lamely, despair and resignation on her face.

"Joan." Lord Laythem turned her to face him, then paused in surprise as he noted the extra inches she suddenly sported. Frowning, he shook his head and looked her grimly in the eyes. "Joan, I—green," he declared with dismay.

Royce frowned, his stomach clenching in concern at the expression on the man's face. "My lord?" he asked warily.

"Her eyes are green," Lord Laythem said faintly.

"Nay, my lord." Royce frowned at him, his own eyes moving to the lovely gray orbs now filling with tears of fear and loss. "Her eyes are as gray as your own."

"Aye, but my daughter's are green."

Royce blinked at that, then shook his head with horror. "Are you saying this is not your daughter?"

"Aye," he murmured, his gaze now moving slowly over her features, taking in the tiniest differences, the smallest variations with amazement, before he recalled the problem before them and asked. "Girl—what is your name?"

"Brinna," she breathed miserably.

"Well, Brinna, are you saying that since my daughter has arrived here, you have been Joan?"

"Aye," she confessed, shamefaced.

"Even in the stables?"

Her face suffusing with color, Brinna nodded, wincing as Royce cursed harshly.

"And where is my daughter now?" Lord Laythem asked, ignoring the younger man.

"She ran off to marry Phillip of Radfurn last night," Brinna murmured, turning to peer at Royce as she said the words and wincing at the way he blanched. Knowing that all his hopes for his people were now ashes at his feet, she turned away in shame, flinching when he grasped her arm and jerked her back around.

"You knew her plan all along? You helped her?" he said accusingly with bewildered hurt, and Brinna bit her lip as she shook her head.

"I helped her, aye, but I didn't know of her plan. Well, I mean, I knew she did not want to marry you and that she was looking for a way to avoid it, but I did not know how she planned to do so. And . . . and had I—I didn't know you when I agreed to help her, I just—she offered me more coins than

I had ever hoped to see and I thought I could use them to make Aggie comfortable and—" Recognizing the contempt on his face and the fact that nothing she was saying was helping any, Brinna unconsciously clutched her mother's amulet and whispered, "I'm sorry."

"Look, girl," Lord Laythem began impatiently, only to pause as his gaze landed on the amulet she was clutching so desperately. Stilling, he reached a trembling hand to snatch at the charm. "Where did you get this?" he asked shakily, and Brinna swallowed nervously, afraid of next being accused of being a thief.

"It is my mother's," she murmured, recalling what Aggie had said as she placed it around her neck. Brinna had always known that Aggie was not the woman who had birthed her, but since Aggie had always avoided speaking of it, Brinna had never questioned her on the subject.

"Your mother's?" Paling, Lord Laythem stared at her blankly for a moment. Then, "What is her name?"

"I don't know."

"Of course you know, you must know." He gave her an impatient little shake. "What is her name?"

"She doesn't know."

They all turned at those words to see Aggie framed in the chapel door. Mouth tight with anger, she moved her wretched old body slowly through the parting crowd toward them. "She's telling the truth. She doesn't know. I never told her. What good would it have done?"

"Aggie?" Brinna stepped to the old woman's side, uncertainty on her face.

"I am sorry, child. There was no sense in yer knowing until now. I feared ye would grow bitter and angry. But now ye must know." Turning, she glared at Lord Laythem grimly. "Her mother was a fine lady. A real and true lady in every sense of the word. She arrived in the village twenty-one years ago, young and as beautiful as Brinna herself. The only difference between the two was that her eyes were green."

Her gaze moved from Brinna's gray eyes to Lord Laythem's own eyes of the same gray-blue shade before she continued. "I was the first person she met when she arrived. She told me she was looking to buy a cottage and perhaps set up shop. My husband had just passed on and we had no children. We used to run an alehouse from our cottage, but it was too much for a woman alone to handle, so I sold her our cottage. When she asked me to stay on and work with her, I agreed.

"As time passed, we became friends and she told me a tale, of a pretty young girl, the older of two daughters born to a fine lord and lady in the south. The girl was sent to foster with another fine lord and lady in the north, where she stayed until her eighteenth year, when the son of this lord and lady got married. The son returned from earning his knight's spurs three months before the wedding."

She glanced at Lord Menton meaningfully, nodding when his eyes widened at the realization that she spoke of him. Then her gaze slid to Lord Laythem again. "He brought with him a friend—and it was this friend who changed our girl's life. She fell in love with him. And he claimed to love her, and to want to marry her. Young as she was, she believed him," Aggie spat bitterly, making Lord Laythem wince despite his confusion.

"They became lovers, and then just before his friend's marriage, her lover was called home. His father had died and he had to take up his role as lord of the manor. He left, but not before once again vowing his undying love and giving our girl *that*." She pointed to the amulet that hung around Brinna's neck and grimaced. "He swore to return for her. Two weeks later a messenger arrived to collect our girl and take her home. She returned reluctantly only to learn that her parents had arranged a marriage for her. She refused, of course, for she loved another. But her parents would hear none of it. Marriage was about position, not love. Then she found out she was pregnant. She thought surely her parents would cancel the marriage and send for her lover then, but they merely pushed up the date of the marriage, hoping that the intended groom would think the babe his own. Our girl collected all the jewels she had and took part of the coins meant for her dower and fled for here, where she knew her 'love' would eventually return for her as he had promised.

"She came to the village because she knew that if she approached Lady Menton . . . your mother, my lord"—she explained, with a glance at Robert—"she would have sent her home. She thought that if she hid in the village, she would hear news of when her lover returned, yet not be noticed by the people in the castle. So, she waited and worked, and grew daily with child.

"Time passed, and I began to doubt her lover, but she never did. 'Oh, Aggie,' she'd laugh lightly. 'Do not be silly. He loves me. He will come.'" She was glaring so fiercely at Lord Laythem as she said that, that Brinna was getting the uncomfortable feeling that she knew how this was going to end.

"He didn't, of course, but she kept her faith right up until the day she died. The day Brinna was born. She had walked to the village market as she did every day for news, and she returned pale and sobbing, desperately clutching her stomach. She was in labor. A month early and angry at the upset that had brought about her birth, the babe came hard and fast. She was barely a handful when she was out. So wee I didn't think she'd survive the night."

Aggie smiled affectionately at the tall strong girl beside her as she spoke. "But you did. It was your mother who didn't. She was bleeding inside and nothing I did could stop it. She held you in her arms and named you Brinna, telling you and me both that it meant of nobility. Then as her life bled out of her, she told me what had upset her and brought about her early labor. She had heard in the village that her lover had returned. He was here visiting the young Lord Menton. He had arrived early that morning . . . with his new bride, our girl's own younger sister." Aggie's hard eyes fixed on Edmund Laythem. "Brinna's mother was Sarah Margaret Atherton, whose sister was Louise May Atherton Laythem."

Brinna gasped and turned accusing eyes on the older man standing beside Royce. She was blind at first to the tears coursing down his face.

"They told me she was dead," he whispered brokenly, then met Brinna's gaze beseechingly. "Robert knew of my love for your mother and sent word to me that she had been called home. I moved as quickly as I could, but winter struck before I got affairs in order and could leave. As soon as the spring thaw set in I hied my way south to Atherton, but when I arrived, it was only to be told that she was dead. Her parents offered me her younger sister, Louise, in her place. I was the lord now and expected to produce heirs as quickly as possible to ensure the line, and she looked so like Sarah I thought I could pretend . . ." His voice trailed away in misery. "It didn't work, of course. In the end I simply made her miserable. She wasn't my Sarah.

Sarah was full of laughter and joy, she had a love for life. Louise was more sullen in nature and shy, and all her presence managed to do was remind me of what I had lost. In the end I couldn't bear to be around her, to even see her. I avoided Laythem to avoid the pain of that reminder."

Taking Brinna's hands, he met her pained gaze firmly. "I loved your mother with all of my heart. She was the one bright light in my life. I would give anything to be able to change the way things worked out in the past, but I can only work with the now. I am pleased to claim you as my daughter." Pausing, he glanced at Royce, then squeezed her hands and asked, "You love him?"

"Aye," Brinna whispered, lowering her eyes unhappily.

Nodding, he then turned to Royce. "Am I right in assuming that you love my daughter?"

Royce hesitated, then said grimly, "I don't know who your daughter is. I thought she"—he gestured toward Brinna unhappily—"I thought this was your daughter, Joan. Now, it seems she is a scullery maid who is your illegitimate daughter and that she was pretending to be Joan so that the real Joan could run off with my own cousin. I won't be married, I won't get the dower my people need, I—" He paused in his angry tirade as Brinna gave a despairing sob and turned to hurry out of the church.

Lord Laythem watched his daughter flee, then turning determinedly on Royce, he straightened his shoulders. "Leave your anger at her deception aside and search your heart. Do you love Brinna?"

Royce didn't have to think long at all before saying, "Aye, I love the girl, whether she is Joan or Brinna, lady or scullery maid. I love her. But it matters not one whit. My people depend upon me. I have a duty to them. I have to marry a woman with a large dower." He heaved a sigh, then straightened grimly. "Now if you will excuse me, I shall leave and see if I cannot accomplish that duty and at least—"

"You have the dower." At Royce's startled look, Laythem nodded. "We had a contract. Joan has broken it. Her dower is forfeit. Now you need not marry for a dower. You may marry as you wish. If you love Brinna, I would still be proud to have you for a son-in-law."

Royce blinked once as that knowledge sank in, then whirled to the priest and grabbed him by the lower arms. "Wait here, Father. We'll be right back," he assured him, then whirled to chase after Brinna.

Lord Laythem watched him go with a sigh, then smiled at his friend Lord Menton as he and his wife stepped forward to join him.

"I didn't know," Robert murmured, and Lady Menton stepped forward to squeeze Edmund's hand. "Had I realized that Sarah was in the village, I would have sent a messenger to you at once. And had I known she had a daughter here—"

"I know," Edmund interrupted quietly, then

arched an eyebrow at his friend's daughter, Christina, as she stared after the absent Royce, shaking her head with slight bemusement. "What is it?" he asked her.

"Oh, nothing really," she murmured, giving a small laugh. "I was just thinking that if Brinna is your daughter, she too is half-Norman and they really were three French hens after all." When he and her parents stared at her blankly, she opened her mouth to explain about the day she had found Sabrina, Brinna, and Joan in a huddle, and the comment she had made about "three French hens," then shook her head and murmured, "Never mind. 'Twas nothing."

Royce rushed out of the chapel just in time to see Brinna disappear into the stables. Following, he found her kneeling in the straw where they had made love, sobbing miserably. Swallowing, he moved silently up behind her and knelt at her side. "J-Brinna?"

Her sobs dying an abrupt death, she straightened and turned, her eyes growing wide as she peered at him. Then she scrambled to her feet, turning away to face the wall as she wiped the tears from her face. "Is there something you wished, my lord? A pot you need scrubbed or a—" Her voice died in her throat as he turned her to face him.

"I need you," he told her gently. "If you will have me."

Her face crumpled like an empty gown, and she shook her head miserably as tears welled in her eyes. "'Tis cruel of you to jest so, my lord."

"I am not jesting."

"Aye, you are. You must marry someone with a dower. Your people need that to survive the winter and I—" Pausing suddenly, she bent to dig under her skirt until she found the small sack she had fastened at her waist. The sack jingled with the coins Joan had given her as she held them out to him. "I have this. It is not much, and I know it won't make up for what you lost with Joan, but mayhap it will help until you find a bride with a dower large enough—"

"I have the dower." He pushed the hand holding the sack away and drew her closer. "Now I need the bride."

"I-I don't understand," Brinna stuttered as his arms closed around her.

"Joan broke the contract. The dower is mine even though we won't marry. My responsibility to my people is fulfilled. Now I can marry whom I wish," he whispered into her ear before dropping a kiss on the lobe of that shell-like appendage.

"You can?" she asked huskily.

"Aye, and I wish to marry you."

"Oh, Royce," she half-sobbed, pressing her face into his neck. "You don't know . . . I hoped, I dreamed, I prayed that if God would just let me have this one gift, I would never ask for anything ever again."

"This gift?" Royce asked uncertainly, leaning back to peer down at her.

"You," Brinna explained. "You came to me on Christmas Day, my lord. And you were the most wonderful Christmas gift I could ever have hoped for." She laughed suddenly, happiness glowing in her face. "And I even get to keep you."

"That you do, my love. That you do."

The Fairy Godmother

Chapter One

The lid of the sarcophagus settled into place with a deep, low grinding of stone. There was silence for a moment, then everyone began to drift out, back to their daily chores and lives, leaving Odel alone. She was aware of their leave-taking and thought how funny it was that others still had chores to do. Unlike herself, life continued for them much as it had before the death of their lord and master, her father.

The priest patted her shoulder and Odel smiled at him stiffly, then watched him follow the others out of the building. He was leaving her alone to deal with her grief. Most considerate, she thought, almost ashamed that she was not feeling any. All she seemed filled with was an empty confusion, a sort of loss as to what to do next.

It seemed the whole of her life had been centered around the selfish wants and needs of the man who now lay entombed here. Without him to order her about, she really hadn't a clue what to do. At a loss, she stayed where she was, staring dry-eyed at the stone likeness laid out before her, waiting.

She was still standing there several moments later when the door opened again. An icy winter wind blew in, ruffling the black veil that shrouded Odel's still-dry eyes. Positive it was the priest returned, she did not look about. But when a woman's voice rang out behind her, she nearly jumped out of her skin.

"Well, here I am. Late again as usual. But then, better late than not here at all, I always say," the high, clear voice chimed, sounding almost bell-like in the small stone building.

Lifting the black veil that covered her face, Odel tossed it back over her head and whirled toward the door. A round, little gray-haired lady dressed in the most horrid pink confection Odel had ever seen was trundling toward her. She was positive she had never met her before, but the woman's words seemed to suggest otherwise. The way she now charged up and enveloped Odel in a pink silk and perfumed hug also seemed to indicate they were not strangers. Eyes wide, Odel stood stiff in her embrace and racked her brain for who she might be.

"Toot-a-loo, dear. I am sorry you have had to see to all of this on your own. I came as soon as I could. Howbeit, that never seems quite soon enough." Releasing her, the woman stepped back to glance down at the stern, stone effigy atop the tomb of Odel's father, then sniffed with distaste.

"Rather grim, is it not? But then he was a perfectly grim man. I never met a more cantankerous lout."

When Odel gaped at such irreverent words, the woman arched her eyebrows slightly. "Surely you do not disagree?"

"I . . . He was my father . . . And he is *dead*" was all she could come up with in answer. Lord Roswald certainly had been a cantankerous lout. But Odel would bite her own tongue off ere being disrespectful enough to say so about her own father.

"Hmm." The woman's mouth twisted at one corner. "I take it you believe that old adage about not speaking ill of the dead? Well, my dear, that is very good of you. I myself am of the firm belief that a man earns his praises or recriminations in life—and death—by his actions. And deserves every lick he earns. Your father, rest his soul, earned all the recrimination a body can spew. Why, what he did to your mother alone was enough to keep me recriminating for a century, never mind what he did to you!"

Odel's eyes widened and brightened suddenly. "You knew my mother?"

"Knew her?" The odd little woman's smile softened. "My dear, we were best friends. As close as can be. Until your grandfather forced her to marry your father. What a tragedy *that* was." She moved to the second sarcophagus in the room as she spoke and peered sadly down at the likeness of the beautiful woman it held.

"She was lovely. Even this cold stone cannot hide that," she murmured, then glanced at Odel. "They were not suited at all, of course. Your mother was young, beautiful, and lighthearted while your father was old and bitter. He had already had and lost one family—and he was determined to subdue and hold on to Lillith and whatever children she gave him in any way he could."

The woman's gaze moved back to the stone effigy and a sigh slid from her lips. She caressed the cold marble cheek sadly. "He choked all the joy and youth out of her ere the first year of their marriage was ended. Her death when you were five was a mere formality. All the life had left her long ere that."

Odel dropped her gaze to the likeness of her mother, touched by the first real sense of grief she had felt that day. That sadness was quickly washed away by the woman's next words.

"You look much like her. Your mother, I mean. That should make things easier."

"Make what things easier?" Odel asked in confusion, but the woman didn't answer. A frown had suddenly drawn her lips down as she considered the pallor of Odel's skin and the thinness of the body obvious beneath the sack-like black gown she wore. Odel knew that while her features were the same as her lovely mother's, they were presently pinched with stress, and that there were dark smudges beneath her eyes that nearly matched the unrelenting black of the veil that shrouded her hair.

The woman moved so swiftly that Odel couldn't stop her start of surprise as the veil was suddenly snatched from her head. The action tugged loose several of the pins that had held her hair in place, sending them to the floor with a soft tinkle. Her hair slid eagerly down around her shoulders in waves of dull color.

Seeing the lifeless hair that should have shone fiery red-brown, the woman pursed her lips, concerned. "He did not choke the life from you as well, did he?"

Odel's eyes dilated at the rude question, then she blurted, "Who *are* you?"

The old lady blinked. "Who? Me? Oh, dear, did I not introduce myself? How silly of me. My goodness, no wonder you look at me as if I were mad, dear. You haven't a clue who I am. Why, I'm Tildy, child."

"Tildy?" Odel frowned over the name. Her memory nagged at her faintly.

"Your godmother."

Odel's eyes widened at that. "My godmother?"

"Aye. Aunt Matilda. But you may call me Tildy, dear. Matilda puts one in mind of large, horsy women with prominent teeth."

"Tildy," Odel murmured, obedience coming automatically to her, then she frowned as she stared incredulously at the little woman. Matilda had been her mother's cousin—a poor orphaned cousin who had been taken in and raised by Lillith's parents. The two girls had been as close as sisters. Closer. Best friends.

But Lord Roswald had not suffered his wife to have friends. It had been his opinion that all of Lillith's attention and affection should be shared only among himself and their children. He had forced her to end all contact with Matilda—or Tildy, as she preferred—shortly after their marriage. Still, that hadn't stopped her mother from naming the woman Odel's godmother.

Unfortunately, it hadn't been long after that that Matilda had taken a fall from her horse that had ended in her breaking her neck.

Eyes widening incredulously, Odel whirled on the woman. "But you are dead!"

"Am I?" Tildy asked, seeming not the least perturbed. "Where did you ever hear a thing like that?"

"Well, from . . ." Turning, Odel gestured vaguely toward the stone image of her father, then glanced back sharply when the little woman clucked beside her.

"Aye. Well, we all have our faults, don't we?"

Odel stared at Tildy uncertainly as she tried to discern exactly to which fault the woman was referring. Was Tildy implying her father had lied? That seemed the obvious answer, since her aunt now stood before her, not looking the least bit dead.

"You're named after me. Did you know that?" Tildy asked cheerfully.

Odel blinked, distracted from her thoughts. "I am? But your name is—"

"Matilda Odel," Tildy told her promptly. Her expression softened affectionately as she reached out to brush a stray strand of hair off Odel's cheek. "And I was so looking forward to being your aunt. But of course, then there was that riding accident, and—" She shrugged.

"The accident?" Odel asked with a frown.

"The one that ended my earthly life," Matilda said impatiently.

"You mean the accident *did* kill you?" Odel squeaked.

"Aye. In my prime, too," Matilda murmured tragically, then sighed and straightened her shoulders. "Alas, such is life. Anyway, I have been watching out for you all these years as a godmother should, but I couldn't interfere before. Vlaster said it wasn't—"

"Who is Vlaster?" Odel interrupted absently, her gaze shifting to the door. It wasn't that far away. If she could just distract this madwoman for a moment . . .

"Oh, he's my supervisor." Odel glanced back to see the woman peer at the floor as if in search of something. "He is around here somewhere. He probably headed straight for the keep. He dislikes the cold, you see."

"I *do* see," Odel said carefully, easing a step to the side and a little closer to the door.

"Aye." Matilda made a face. "He was none too pleased to be coming down here at this time of year, but your case has reached a rather crisis point."

"Yes," Odel agreed, taking another sidling step.

"I was able to convince him, thank goodness."

"Of what?" Odel took another step.

"Why, that your father's treatment of you had made you afraid of love. That without some serious intervention, he will have succeeded in his efforts to make you as bitter and lonely as he himself was." The woman explained herself patiently, then beamed at her. "But 'twill be all right now. I am here, specially sent to see you happy."

Odel paused and stared at the woman in shock. "Are you implying, my lady, that you are some sort of guardian angel?"

"Well." She made a face. "I am not quite an angel yet. Angels don't need canes and fairy dust."

"Canes and fairy dust?" Odel's eyes widened further.

"Aye. I am just a godmother, a fairy godmother. I need a little help performing my miracles," she admitted unhappily, then brightened. "Though if I succeed at helping fifty of my wards, I shall be graduated to angel."

"And what number am I?" Odel asked, curious despite thinking the woman quite mad.

Matilda winced, her answer coming reluctantly.

"You are my first. I have been in training up until now, you see."

"Well, that figures," Odel muttered to herself.

"Never fear, though. I graduated at the top . . . Well, close to the top of my . . . I didn't fail," Tildy ended finally. She sighed and took Odel's arm, urging her toward the door Odel had been so eager to escape through just moments before. "Never mind that. All will be well. But there is much to do."

"Much to do with what?" Odel asked warily as her "guardian" dragged open the doors. Sunlight and a crisp winter breeze immediately washed over them.

"With *you*, dear. I am here to find you a husband."

"Find me a husband?" Odel paused and stiffened at the claim. That was the last thing she had expected—and the very last thing she wanted. "I have no need of a husband."

"Of course you do, dear. Oh, my goodness, yes. One cannot procreate alone, you know. A man is needed for that chore."

Odel flushed, then paled in turn. "But I do not wish to procreate."

"Of course you do. 'Tis your duty. As the Bible says, 'Go forth and multiply' and all that. Yes, yes, it does and so you shall."

"But I am not even betrothed, I—"

"Aye, I know. Most remiss of your father. Terribly selfish, too, keeping you chained to him so.

He wanted to keep you all to himself no doubt, but we shall fix that. We will have you betrothed and married off in no time."

"But—"

"Now, I'll have no arguing from you. I know your father insisted on your staying at his side until he died, but he's gone. And it is my job to look out for you now. I do so want to attain angel status— they have wings, you know—and after you I will only have forty-nine to go." Tildy's gaze settled on her determinedly. "But I do have something of a time limit. I have till Christmas to see you happy and married."

Odel stiffened. "Which is it?"

Tildy blinked. "Which is what?"

"Which are you supposed to make me? Happy or married?" she snarled, then turned to march across the bailey. Her heart was pounding something fierce, just as it had over the years when her father had raised his voice and his hand to her. Only this time was different. She wasn't feeling fear. Instead, she was *furious*.

She had spent the last twenty-five years under her father's power being ordered about. Every wish, every desire she had ever had, had been belittled or thwarted by him. She had no intention of putting herself back under another man's thumb.

"But, my dear!" Matilda rushed after her, obviously alarmed. "Every girl wants to be married. Every girl wants a husband, children, and a home."

"I am *not* every girl," Odel snapped, then suddenly remembered that this woman was quite mad. There was nothing to fear here; she didn't need to fear losing her freedom. Not truly. The thought made her pause.

She was free. A small laugh slipped from her lips, then she picked up her pace again and began to hurry up the steps to the keep. She was free! Why, she could go inside right now and . . . and sit by the fire if she wished. Her father would not be there yelling at her to fetch him this or do that. She could, well, she could do whatever she wanted. For the most part.

"Oh, my!"

At Matilda's exclamation, Odel paused just inside the door of the keep. She did not have to think hard to figure out what had brought that gasp from her lips. Roswald Castle had done it. She felt all of her excitement of a moment ago slip away as she peered at the great hall. Her father's presence was everywhere. It pervaded the keep as if he were not truly dead at all. Odel peered about and sighed. "It is rather grim and gloomy, is it not?"

"Aye." Matilda nodded solemnly.

"Father never liked the sun much," Odel muttered unhappily as her eyes adjusted to the dim interior. "He always insisted the arrow slits be covered with leather, no matter the season, and—"

"There is only one chair in here," Matilda pointed out as if Odel had not noticed.

"Aye," Odel agreed unhappily. In the whole huge great hall, the only stick of furniture was her father's large chair by the fire. He had always insisted the tables and benches used at mealtimes be collapsed and leaned against the walls lest some "lazy loafer waste time sitting about."

"And there are not even any rushes on the floor," Matilda added with amazement.

"Father said that was just a lazy servant's invention to keep from having to scrub the floor daily."

"Scrub the floor? But these stone floors are so cold without rushes that the air is seeping right through my slippers."

"I know," Odel almost moaned the two words. "I have always wished it were otherwise." She glanced at Matilda. "If you really wished to make me happy, you could send me a wagonload of rushes, not some useless bossy husband."

"That, my dear, is a very good idea," Matilda decided grimly. Immediately, she tugged open the small pink sack that hung from her wrist. She slipped her hand inside, pulled it out a moment later, then raised the closed hand in front of her face. After muttering a couple of sentences, she opened her fingers and began to turn in a circle, blowing, as she did, on the glittering dust that rested in her palm.

Odel was busy gaping at this, her mouth hanging open like a fish, when Matilda's little spin brought them face-to-face. Finding herself in the center of a small cloud of the glittering substance,

Odel gasped in surprise, then quickly closed her eyes and mouth, and tried to step back out of the way. She was too late. She had already breathed in a good deal of the dust, and it sent her into a fit of coughing and sneezing.

"Oh, dear!" Matilda was at her side and thumping her back at once. "I am sorry, my dear. I had no intention of blowing it in your face. I am sorry."

"What are you doing?" Odel choked out, straightening slowly as her sneezes and coughs subsided.

"Aye. Well, I did mention that where angels could perform miracles without it, I need it to—"

"Oh, my God!"

"What is it?" Matilda asked, then turned to survey the room at which the girl was now gaping. "Oh." She grimaced uncertainly. "Too much, do you think? Perhaps I should have used a little less fairy dust, hmmm?"

"Fairy dust?" Odel repeated faintly, her eyes sliding over the room in shock. The floor was now covered with a clean carpet of rushes, and the walls were so white that their brightness almost hurt the eyes. As well, several huge tapestries now adorned them. Odel had never before seen such beautiful, rich weaves and she marveled at them briefly before taking in the rest of the room.

The lone chair that had sat by the fire was no more, yet the room was full of furnishings. Several large carved chairs sat grouped around the fire, huge soft cushions on each, making them look remarkably comfortable. The trestle tables and benches that had been collapsed and leaning against the wall were now set up, long white cloths covering the tables' rough surfaces. Two dainty pillows on the center of the bench of the uppermost table denoted where she and Matilda should sit.

"My God," Odel breathed, then whirled on Tildy accusingly. "You *do* have magic!"

Matilda sighed. "Aye, dear. Did I not say so? I told you I have fairy dust to help—Oh! There you are, Vlaster." Bending, she picked up a cat that slid through the open door behind them.

"Vlaster?" Odel echoed, then her eyebrows rose as she recalled Tildy's earlier mention of the name. "Your superior is a cat?"

"At the moment, yes."

"At the moment?" Odel repeated. She started to turn away in dismissal, only to pause as her gaze took in the room again. Moaning, she closed her eyes and swayed slightly. "This cannot be happening."

"Are you feeling faint?" Tildy asked with alarm, letting the cat drop to the floor to put a supporting arm around her. "Just breathe deeply. Breathe."

Odel obediently took a couple of deep breaths, relieved when some of the tightness in her chest eased. The buzzing that had been filling her ears began to fade.

"Better?" Matilda asked solicitously. Odel nodded.

"Aye, but—"

"But?"

"You have to put this back the way it was."

Matilda frowned. "Do you not like it? I could—"

She shook her head, her eyes opening and scanning the room. "I like it, but what will the servants think? They will know something is amiss."

"Oh, ta-ra," Matilda laughed and waved her cane in a vague circle. "There! They shall all now believe that my servants did it."

"You have servants?"

Matilda stilled and frowned at that, then peered down at the cat she had set down. "Vlaster?"

In the blink of an eye, the cat was gone. In its place stood a man. Tall and thin, dressed in a frock and brais of black, he wiggled a black mustache at her, then ran one hand through his hair as black as the cat's fur had been.

"Oh, no no no." Odel began to back slowly away, her head shaking.

"Aye. It is perfect," Matilda said gaily. "My dear, meet my manservant, Vlaster. Vlaster, my goddaughter, Odel."

"Manservant?" There was a touch of irritation in the man's voice, but Odel was too busy shaking her head to notice.

"Nay," Odel repeated faintly and Matilda hesitated, frowning.

"Aye, I suppose he alone could not have achieved all this, could he?" Turning, she marched to the door, peered out into the bailey, glanced around briefly, then stilled suddenly and smiled in satisfaction. Putting her hand to her mouth, she began making the most god-awful quacking sounds.

"What are you doing now?" Odel hissed, hurrying to her side. "You sound like a—" Her eyes widened, and she stepped back from the door abruptly. Six of the brown female ducks that had been penned by the stables, came waddling through the keep door. "—duck," she finished in amazement, then frowned and closed her eyes, waving her hand impatiently in front of her face as Tildy unleashed another cloud of glittering dust.

Despite having seen some wholly inexplicable events in the past few moments, Odel was not at all prepared to find six women of varying ages and sizes suddenly standing where the ducks had been but a moment before. Each of them was wearing a gown the same dull gray-brown as the ducks' feathers. The ducks were no longer in sight.

"Oh," Odel groaned. Her hand went to her forehead in horror as her own thoughts rolled around in her head.

"Mayhap you should lay down, my dear. You appear to have gone quite white."

"Nay, nay. I . . ." Odel forced her hands down and her eyes open, but the moment her gaze took in the new room, the furniture, the six maids, and the tall, dark Vlaster, she closed her eyes again. "Aye, mayhap I should."

"Aye, I think so," Matilda said gently. The older woman took Odel's arm to urge her toward the stairs to the upper floor. "A nice little nap will do you the world of good. I will wake you when it is time to sup. No doubt you have been sitting up by your father's bedside since he fell ill, and are exceedingly weary. A little nap, then a nice meal, will set everything right."

"Aye," Odel grasped eagerly at that explanation of the odd things happening in her home; she was hallucinating. "I am just over-tired. A little nap, then something to eat and everything will be back to normal."

"Well, I hope not," Matilda muttered a little wryly. She opened the door to Odel's room for her.

"How did you know which room was mine?" Odel asked curiously, but as she entered, she had a sneaking suspicion. At what she saw, she quickly turned her back to the room.

"What is it?" Matilda asked with alarm, peering past her. Understanding crossed Tildy's face as the woman took in the large comfy-looking bed, the cushioned chairs by the fire, and the lush rose-colored curtains that hung above the bed. The chamber looked warm and cozy. It had *not* looked like that when she had left it this morning. Roswald had been too mean and cheap to see to his daughter's comfort.

"Hmmm," Tildy said with a shrug. "I did use quite a bit of dust . . . but this just saves me from having to tend to it now. Are you not happy with your new room?"

Eyes still squeezed firmly shut, Odel merely began to chant under her breath. "This is not happening, this cannot be happening."

"There, there," Matilda murmured, turning Odel back around and steering her toward the bed. "A nice nap is just what you need."

"This is *not* happening," Odel said under her breath, collapsing onto the bed when Matilda pushed her against it. "This cannot be happening."

Chapter Two

$\mathcal{J}$t was happening all right.

Odel stared around the redecorated great hall and shook her head for at least the hundredth time since Matilda had arrived. She had taken her nap, but things had not changed back to normal—and it had been a day and a night. The walls were still a smooth bright white, decorated with colorful tapestries; the floor rustled with rushes; and furniture filled every corner of the room. More than that, now the furniture was full of people. There were the usual servants at the nooning meal, the soldiers, and so on, but now the keep also had several guests. At least two dozen men lined either side of the head table. There had been half a dozen of them at sup last night—all young, wealthy, and single lords who had arrived while she slept. Another twenty had arrived since then, riding gaily into Roswald as if by invitation.

Matilda called them suitors; Odel called them pains in the arse. She had no intention of getting married. Worse, she felt extremely uncomfortable under their obvious flattery. Even the lovely new gowns they praised—she had woken up to find her chests overflowing—had not eased her discomfort. Odel was not used to the presence of others. She had spent so long restricted to the company of her father and his servants, she had no idea what to say to these preening visitors—handsome though they might be.

"Are you all right? You look flushed," Matilda leaned close to murmur.

Shifting where she sat, Odel sighed unhappily. "I am just a bit warm." It was true. Frowning slightly, she glanced toward the doors leading outside and announced, "In fact, I think I shall go for a short walk once the meal is over."

"What a lovely idea," Tildy said cheerfully, which immediately made Odel suspicious. She didn't have long to wait before her suspicions were borne out. Matilda added, "I am sure that Lord Brownell or Lord Trenton would love to join you."

"Do please stop trying to push those men on me, Tildy. I have no interest in them," Odel said wearily.

Matilda's face fell like that of a child who has been refused a treat. Odel felt guilt pinch at her and she sighed, but she did not retract her words. She really had no interest in marrying. The sooner Tildy accepted that, the better.

"THERE IS ROSWALD up ahead, my lord."

Michel blinked the snowflakes out of his eyes and glanced up at Eadsele's words. His gaze narrowed on the castle rising out of the stand of trees ahead. Yes, Roswald would suffice. The mounts were tiring and he needed to find a place to rest them. It was an unexpected occurrence, seeing as it was only past midday and they had only set out for the last leg of their journey home several hours before, but the horses were definitely blowing and Michel wasn't the sort who would run his animals into the ground. They would stop here until morning.

"Aye. So it is, Eadsele," Michel agreed, vaguely amused by the boy's excitement. No doubt he was getting sick of traveling after these last two weeks trudging through the snowy landscape of England. Michel really should have collected the lad in early autumn, but had been kept busy at Suthtun, the impoverished estate he had inherited this summer. He'd had little time to think much about his new squire, let alone chase down to southern England to collect him. If Eadsele's father hadn't been a friend and asked him to train the boy as a favor—

"Do you think they will have room for us?"

"I do not see why not. I have never met Lord Roswald, but I have heard that he does not entertain much." Michel frowned to himself as he tried to recall what else he had heard.

His neighbor was wealthy, he had known that, but even if he hadn't, he would have realized it rather quickly as they rode through Roswald's main gates a moment later. Prosperity showed in the round rosy cheeks of the children, and their pets. Poorer castles and their attending villages often could not afford pets, or had ragged hungry-looking animals—not the shiny-coated, muscular beasts at play in the courtyard.

A hollow sound drew his attention to the keep's main stairs as the cloaked figure of a woman exited the great hall. As she closed the door behind her, she turned. Her face was hidden by a fur-lined hood, but a scarlet gown peeked out from under her cloak with each step she took. She briskly descended the snow-laden steps.

Was this Lord Roswald's wife, his daughter, or merely a guest? Michel wondered as his horse came to a halt at the foot of the steps. Realizing he would have to ask to find out, he dismounted, moving inadvertently into her path.

"Excuse me, my lady," Michel began politely. He found his words waved away impatiently as the woman did her best to move around him.

"Just leave your horse with the servants and go on in," she instructed without even a glance. "Vlaster will show you to your room."

"Ah," Michel turned as she hurried past him, his confusion plain on his face if she had bothered to look. "Are you—"

"Aye, my lord. I am Lady Roswald. And I will surely be pleased to make your acquaintance later. In the meantime, Vlaster will see to your comfort."

"Thank you, but I think you may have mistaken me for someone else. I am—"

"I know, my lord," she interrupted again. At last, heaving a sigh, she stopped and whirled to face him. The impatient twist to her lips was all he could see beneath her cloak's hood as she spoke. "There are twenty more just like you inside. And no doubt, just like them, you are eager to inform me that you are the wealthiest, most handsome man for three counties. You find me beyond beautiful and exceedingly charming and want to vow you would willingly die a horrid and painful death if only I would smile in your general direction." Her words were a weary recitation.

Michel blinked, then shook his head, a wry smile plucking at his lips. "Well, if you are comparing me to the village swineherd, I suppose I am all of those things. But I really had no plans to die today—not even for one of your undoubtedly beautiful smiles."

The woman stood still for a moment, then reached up to pull back her hood and peer at him. He suspected, by the way her eyes widened, that it was the first real look she had taken at him. Just as this was his first real glimpse of her.

Her hair was a deep brown, shot through with strands of fiery red. Her skin was pale and smooth, her nose straight, her eyes a pretty blue, and her lips were not too full, nor thin. She *was* pleasant to look on, but not so lovely that a man would die for a mere smile—at least not this man.

Michel had too much to do and too little time

to be bothered with the needs and demands of a woman. He would leave off having to burden himself with one until he had Suthtun up to snuff. Then, he supposed, he would have to take a wife to make an heir, but he really wasn't looking forward to the chore. In his experience, wives were more trouble than they were worth. His own mother had practically sent her husband, his father, to the grave with her demands for rich fabrics and glorious jewels. The man had died in battle, one of many battles he had hired himself out for in an effort to appease her. Nay. There would be no spoiled, demanding wife for him.

STARTLED OUT OF her annoyance by his nonchalance, Odel lifted her hood off to peer at the man. Now she stared at him with some amazement. When she had first come outside, she had thought him yet another of the suitors Matilda had invited. They had, after all, been arriving one after the other all day.

Fair-haired men, dark-haired men, tall men, and not-so-tall men, they had paraded into Roswald like baby peacocks. Every single one of them was single, exceedingly handsome, and at least comfortably wealthy.

This man, though, he was different. He was tall and strong, like the others, but his dark, longish hair framed features too harsh to be considered handsome. Her gaze slid over the rest of him, noting that while his clothes were clean and of good quality, they had obviously seen better days. He clearly wasn't wealthy like the others. Still, the glint of amusement in his eyes made him somehow charming to look at. Forcing a polite smile, she said, "I am sorry, my lord. Obviously I have made an error. Who did you say you were?"

"The new Lord Suthtun."

"Oh." She recognized the name and a feeling of solemnity overtook her. "I was sorry to hear of your uncle's passing. He used to visit my father on occasion. He was a very nice man."

"Then you are Lord Roswald's daughter?"

"Aye."

He nodded briefly. "Aye, well, I am traveling home from collecting Eadsele here." He gestured to the young lad now dismounting behind him. "I realize 'tis only a couple more hours home to Suthtun and I dislike putting you out, but the horses are tired and I do not like to overtax them in such weather. Do you think your father would mind if we stopped for the night?"

"My father died several days ago," Odel told him distractedly, glancing over at the castle doors. Were there any rooms left? She suspected there were not. Truly the castle was full to its turrets with prancing dandies and—

"I am sorry." The man's words interrupted her thoughts, but when Odel glanced at him questioningly, he added, "For your loss."

"Oh, aye. Thank you." She looked away, still not comfortable with her own lack of grief at the loss of the man who for most of her life had treated her no better than a servant. Spying one of the stable boys waiting patiently a few steps away, she waved him forward. "Tend to his lordship's horses, please, Tommy." She gave the instructions, then gestured for Lord Suthtun to follow her up the stairs to the castle.

Odel didn't turn to see if he followed; she didn't have to, she could hear his footfalls behind her on the steps. This was no tippy-toed dandy who moved as silent as a cat. Nay, his steps were solid and heavy behind her as she led him into the castle.

The noise and heat in the great hall rolled over them in a wave as they entered it, and that reminded Odel of her hope to escape, however briefly, from her suitors. Grimacing at the cacophony of laughing and jesting male voices she had been trying to flee only moments before, Odel sighed and peered about for Matilda or Vlaster. It only took her a moment to find them. In a room full of colorfully dressed men as tall and solid as trees, Matilda's short rounded figure, encased in another god-awful pink creation, stood out like a plump pink mouse in a room full of large and healthy gray rats. Of course, Vlaster wasn't far behind. His tall impossibly thin and dour black form was never far away.

Odel was about to raise her arm to catch her aunt's attention, when suddenly the woman was bustling toward them, Vlaster following her like a tall, dark shadow.

"There you are, my dear," Tildy cried brightly as she reached them. "I had begun to wonder where you had gotten to. I should have known that one of your handsome suitors had—" Her words died, her mouth opening soundlessly as she turned to peer at the man standing beside Odel. "Oh." Her gaze slid over his less-than-handsome face and worn clothes, her smile wilting like a rose cut from its stem. "Who are you?"

"This is Lord Suthtun, Aunt Matilda," Odel announced, glaring at the older woman for her rudeness.

"Suthtun?" Matilda's nose twitched, her forehead wrinkling with concentration. "Suthtun. I don't recall sending a missive to you, my lord," she announced unhappily, then turned to Vlaster. "Did I, Vlaster?"

"I do not recall one, madam," the man murmured, a dour look on his face.

"Nay, neither do I. Suthtun. Suth-tun."

"He is a neighbor to the north," Odel said through her teeth. "And quite welcome here."

"To the north?" Matilda questioned with a definite lack of enthusiasm, then she sighed and nodded. "Oh, yes. Suthtun; that poor little holding of that friend of your father's." Her face puckered up again with open displeasure. Apparently Tildy had set her sights on wealthier game. Embarrassed by her godmother's openly rude behavior, Odel hurried to intervene.

"He is traveling home from court and sought shelter here," she explained quickly. "I assured him that would be fine."

"Oh. Aye, well of course, it behooves us to help a neighbor, does it not?" she said, but didn't look pleased at the prospect. In fact, she sounded decidedly annoyed. She turned to Vlaster to ask, "Do we have a room for his lordship? Or shall he have to sleep on the floor?"

"Aunt Tildy!" Odel gasped, giving Lord Suthtun an apologetic look.

"Do not be offended on my account, my lady," the nobleman murmured with the same good humor he had shown earlier. "I am an unexpected guest and would be pleased for even a spot on the great hall floor by the fire—if it is available."

Odel blinked at the man, amazed at his claim. Surely, had any of the other lords been asked to consider such a spot, they would have been wroth at the insult. They had all required a room from what she had seen, likely to house all their various clothing and finery. This man, however, appeared to travel light, a small sack dangling from his relaxed hand his only baggage. He also lacked the attendants the other noblemen seemed helpless without. Lord Suthtun had only a young lad with him—his squire, she supposed.

"I am sure that will not be necessary, my lord,"

Odel murmured, turning to her aunt. "Surely Lord Beasley and his cousin, Lord Cheshire, could room together for one night."

"Oh, nay," Matilda exclaimed at once with horror. "Lord Beasley has more gold than the king—and Lord Cheshire is quite the most handsome of your suitors. They are both most important men; I cannot think they will thank you for the insult."

Odel grimaced at that. Most handsome and wealthy they might be, but Lord Beasley was vain and Lord Cheshire was arrogant. Doubling them up could only help the two men's dispositions. "They shall survive the insult, I am sure," she said with a wry smile. "My neighbor is in need of a bed for the night."

"Aye," Matilda agreed reluctantly. "I suppose with the ague coming on his squire, his lordship could indeed use a bed. Very well, I shall see what I can do to smooth this over with the lords Beasley and Cheshire."

"Thank you," Odel muttered. She was grateful for her godmother's acquiescence, but confused by her words. Her gaze had moved to the boy in question. Much to her surprise, the lad did seem quite pale. He was also trembling as if with a chill. She had not noticed that outside. In fact, she thought she recalled him looking quite robust.

"Eadsele, are you not well?" Lord Suthtun asked the boy now, looking as startled as Odel by the boy's sickly state. Pressing the back of his hand to his squire's forehead, Lord Suthtun scowled. "You're on fire. How long have you not been feeling well?"

"I don't know, my lord. I was cold while we were traveling, but thought it was just the weather," he answered miserably, swaying where he stood. Lord Suthtun reached out and caught the lad's arm to steady him.

"Hmph." Matilda turned away with purpose. "You'd best put the boy to bed before he falls down. I shall send servants up to move Lord Cheshire's things."

"If you would follow me, my lord," Odel said. Suthtun lifted the boy into his arms and followed as she led him to Lord Cheshire's room, somehow managing to wave away any eager lords who might have slowed their progress.

"I shall have one of the servants arrange a pallet for the boy," she said as she let him into what had—until a few moments ago—been Lord Cheshire's chamber.

"Nay. Have them arrange one large enough for me." Crossing the room, he set the boy gently on the bed and pulled the furs up to cover him.

Odel was still for a moment as she watched him care for the squire. The man seemed extremely kind; his voice was soft and reassuring, his hands gentle. Her own father had never shown her such tenderness. Her thoughts were disturbed a moment later as the door opened behind her and servants began to file into the room. Within moments Lord Cheshire's things had been removed, and water and a clean cloth had been supplied. Lord Suthtun bathed the lad's head.

"Is he your son?" The tenderness the man showed was exquisite, and the question burst from Odel's lips before she had even realized it had come to mind. But Lord Suthtun didn't seem upset. He hardly seemed to notice, so busy was he with his caretaking.

"Nay, he is my squire, the son of an old friend placed in my care to train and raise."

His answer seemed to suggest that he would tend as kindly to anyone under his charge, and Odel pondered that. This man was an enigma. His clothes were old but well tended; he had claimed to stop for the night simply for the good of his horses; and now he showed dutiful care and even affection for a squire. He did indeed appear to tend well to what was his. What would her life have been like had her father been more like this man? she wondered.

"Might I prevail upon you for some mead, and perhaps some broth for the boy?" he asked suddenly.

Shifting, Odel nodded. Then, realizing that he could not see her nod, she murmured, "I shall have some brought up at once. And for the pallet to be arranged. Would you care for your supper to be brought here as well, or shall you join the table?"

His gaze slid to the window, then he glanced toward her. "I would not wish to trouble the servants any more than I have to. I imagine I can manage joining the table."

"Then, I shall have one of the servants come and sit with Eadsele when 'tis time for the meal." Odel slid from the room to see to these things.

Downstairs, she had barely stepped off the landing before she found herself surrounded by suitors. It was as if they had been lying in wait for her return. Compliments, offers to escort her on walks, to play music for her, recite poetry to her, all smothered her like a cloying blanket as she tried to make her way to the kitchens. By the time she broke loose and escaped the great hall, she was thoroughly annoyed. She nearly trampled Matilda as she tried to enter the steaming kitchens.

"Oh, there you are, my dear," her godmother said, then paused to look at her more closely. "Oh, my, you do look vexed. Is Lord Suthtun's squire worse?"

"Nay, I just—" She gestured vaguely over her shoulder, then shook her head. "Never mind. I came to arrange for some broth and mead to be taken up for the boy."

"I already arranged that," Matilda assured her.

"Oh, good. Well, then, Lord Suthtun asked that a pallet be prepared for him. He wishes the boy to have his bed while he is ill."

Matilda's eyes narrowed, her eyebrows arching

in displeasure. "Do you mean to say Lord Suthtun forced Lord Cheshire from his bed for a squire?"

Odel frowned at the woman's expression. "*He* did not force anyone. *I* suggested we put Lord Cheshire with Lord Beasley. Besides, I think it is terribly chivalrous of him to give up his bed for a sick child."

"If you say so," Matilda agreed irritably. "But I assure you Lord Beasley is smarter than to give up a warm, soft bed for a boy."

"Well, whether that is smarter is debatable," Odel snapped, then sighed as the kitchen door swung open to reveal one of her many suitors.

Smiling as he spotted her, the man let the door swing closed and hurried forward.

Chapter Three

"Would that be Lord Cheshire?"

Odel glanced up from her food to follow Lord Suthtun's gesture. He had taken a seat at the place she had saved him just as the meal was being carried out. Throughout the supper they had discussed the uncommonly cold weather they were having this winter, his squire's fever—which was still high—and various and sundry topics of less importance. Odel nodded and answered his question. "Aye, it is. How did you know?"

"Because he is glaring daggers at me," Michel murmured with that ever-present amusement. "I think he is distressed at my pinching his bed."

"It wasn't really his bed to begin with," Odel pointed out dryly, her gaze moving over the man in question to his cousin, Lord Beasley. The two men sat side by side and neither of them looked pleased. Lord Cheshire looked especially resentful as he glared at Lord Suthtun. In truth, both men had already made their displeasure with the new arrangements known to Odel. When she had stood firm on the arrangements despite their complaints,

they had settled into some unsubtle pouting. Odel
didn't know whether to be amused or put out by
their behavior, but it was obvious they both felt as
her aunt had predicted; they were much too important to be forced to double up.

They had even been making noises about leaving. She guessed she was supposed to be overcome
with dismay at the threat, but the only feeling she
could work up was a vague relief. Really, having
all these men fluttering around was quite wearing.
Having a couple of them leave would hardly put
her out.

"So?" The drawn-out word drew Odel's curious
gaze and Lord Suthtun grinned. "Which one do
you favor?"

Odel stared at him blankly for a moment, then
felt herself flush. Apparently he had determined
that the lords all gracing her table were suitors. Of
course, she remembered, Matilda had said something about suitors when he and his squire had first
arrived.

"Actually, I am not interested in any of them,"
she said at last, grimacing when his eyebrows
arched in disbelief. "Having them here was my . . .
Aunt's idea. I have no desire to marry."

"Ever?" he asked.

"Ever," Odel assured him firmly, then scowled
at his expression. "You find that difficult to believe?"

"Well, aye, I guess I do. Most women wish to

have a husband to supply all the riches and jewels they need to be happy."

Odel's mouth tightened at that. "I desire no man to supply riches and wealth. I have more than I need." More than she was even used to or comfortable with at the moment, she thought a bit unhappily. While it was nice that the keep was not as mean and cold as it had been, Matilda had rather overdone it.

Suddenly realizing that Lord Suthtun had been silent quite awhile, she turned to see him examining her as if trying to decide if he should believe her. She supposed he must have decided to take her word, because he next asked quietly, "Then what of a husband to provide children?"

Odel swallowed. She had never really even considered the possibility of children. She had given up on them a long time ago, when she had realized that her father had no intention of letting her marry and leave him. Now the possibility rose before her and she actually found herself tempted for a moment. Then she recalled that she would have to marry to have them—and that a man would likely make her children's lives as miserable as her own had been. "I would like to have children," she admitted quietly. "But, I fear, the price of a husband seems overly steep to me."

Lord Suthtun considered her briefly, then murmured, "Lord Roswald must have been even more of a tyrant than I had heard."

Odel peered down at her plate uncomfortably, then changed the subject. "Inheriting Suthtun must have come as something of a surprise."

He was silent for a minute, then followed her lead. "Aye. My uncle was still relatively young, and even had he not been, his son should have inherited. The fact that they both died within days of each other from a cold was a great surprise to all. How did your father die?"

"His heart gave out. In his sleep," she explained, then forced a smile for the servants who suddenly appeared before them. There were four in all, carting a suckling pig.

"Shall I?" Lord Suthtun murmured, withdrawing a small jeweled dagger from his waist and gesturing toward the platter.

"Thank you, yes." Odel watched as he sliced off some of the juicy white meat and moved it to her plate—a silver one no less, more of Matilda's magic. Many castles, she'd heard, had a silver plate and goblet for their lord on special occasions, but Roswald had never been one of them. Odel's father had been too cheap. Now everyone at the high table was eating off a silver plate and drinking from a silver goblet. Father would be rolling over in his sarcophagus, she thought with some enjoyment.

A small sound from her right made her realize that a small mountain of meat now sat on her plate. He was reaching to put more on, but looking quite perplexed. Obviously, he had been waiting for her to say "enough." Her father would have given her the thinnest, toughest serving he could manage, and that would have been that. She was not used to her wants being observed. Flushing with embarrassment, she murmured, "Thank you," and was relieved when he nodded and turned his attention to filling his own plate.

It wasn't until he set the dagger on the table between them that Odel noticed its beautiful carved hilt. "Oh, my, how lovely," she commented, picking it up. "Wherever did you get this?"

"It was a gift from the king." He peered at his food as he answered, looking particularly embarrassed. Which only managed to make Odel more curious.

"What was the gift in honor of?"

Suthtun shrugged slightly. "I assisted him in an endeavor," he answered vaguely, then changed the subject. "Did your father never arrange a marriage?"

It was Odel's turn to look uncomfortable. "Nay."

"And your mother?"

"She died when I was quite young."

They were both silent for a moment, then her guest asked, "Is your Aunt Matilda the only family you have left?"

Odel nodded. "And you? Were your uncle and cousin your only family?"

He shook his head. "The former Lord Suthtun was my mother's brother. My mother and my two sisters are both at Suthtun now, no doubt preparing for Christmas."

"Your father?"

"He died when I was young."

"Your sisters are younger than you, then."

He raised his eyebrows. "Aye. How did you know?"

"Well, you did not mention any husbands, so I just assumed."

He nodded. "Yes, my sisters are both quite a bit younger. There was another sister and a brother between us, but they didn't survive past childhood."

Odel murmured some suitable sounds at that, then asked, "And ere inheriting the title and estate of Suthtun, what—"

"I was a mercenary," he answered, apparently unperturbed by the question. And quite successful at it, Odel guessed, now understanding where his expensive clothes came from. As a mercenary without land or title to eat up his funds, he had been free to spend his earnings on such things. Now a lord of an impoverished estate, he spent his money more carefully.

Suddenly, all he had said began to ring bells in her mind. The knife was in honor of a favor he had done the king. He had been a mercenary prior to inheriting Suthtun. His name was Michel—a French name, and not all that common in England. In truth, she knew of only two men with that name: the man seated beside her and a mercenary who had saved King Edward II from a suspected witch in Coventry.

She recalled her father having spoken of it with a laugh; he had been sympathetic to no one, not even his liege. The "witch," John of Wiltham, had been arrested for attempting to poison the king with a potion. Accusations of black magic had quickly followed. Wiltham had been held in Coventry to stand trial, but when the king had gone to question the man personally, Wiltham had attacked him, trying to kill him with his bare hands.

It was said he would have succeeded, had a mercenary accompanying Edward not stepped in and killed him. The king had reputedly given this mercenary—named Michel—his own jeweled knife in thanks. She recalled her father's jealous dismissal of the whole incident.

Odel's gaze dropped to the knife on the table, her stomach rolling over. "You are Michel the witch-killer."

Michel grimaced, then shook his head. "I have killed hundreds of men, yet I kill one accused of witchcraft and suddenly I am Michel the witch-killer."

Odel relaxed somewhat at that, and even managed a smile. That was true; he had only killed one witch—and that had been one trying to kill the king. He was not exactly a witch hunter. "You have nothing against them then?" she said in a joking manner, but her gaze slid to where Matilda sat observing the guests.

"Well, I would as soon kill one as look at them," he admitted, drawing Odel's face back around in alarm. "But I am not interested in hunting them down. Witches are a nasty bunch. Sneaky, too. Killing with potions and elixirs rather than facing a man in fair battle. Aye. They are a nasty lot."

The knight turned his attention to his meal then, unaware that Odel was now trembling with fear. Her poor aunt! Tildy might call herself a fairy godmother, but anyone seeing her cast dust in the air and mutter over it would surely call her a witch. And Michel would not need to hunt to find her. Dear Lord, if he saw her pull one of her stunts he would—

"Well, I had best go check on my squire," Michel announced suddenly, getting to his feet. Pausing, he turned to take Odel's hand and bow over it. "Thank you for the lovely meal, my lady."

Odel nodded, then watched him leave the table. He crossed the room and jogged lightly up the steps.

"Oh, my, that is a lovely dagger, isn't it?"

Turning, Odel glanced at Matilda, then down at the dagger she was gesturing to. Lord Suthtun had forgotten his blade. "It was a gift from the king . . . for killing a witch!"

Tildy's eyebrows rose, but rather than appear worried, she merely said, "Well that makes sense.

The man obviously couldn't afford to purchase it himself."

"Wealth is not everything, Matilda," Odel said irritably, picking up the dagger and wiping it on a crust of bread.

"Well, it may not be everything, but it certainly helps to make a body happy," Matilda answered promptly.

Odel clucked in disgust. "Oh, aye, it certainly did that for my father." She gave her aunt a pointed look, then rose.

"Where are you going?" Matilda shifted around in her seat to peer after her as Odel started away.

"I am going to return Lord Suthtun's blade and check on his squire."

She hurried away, and was at the top of the stairs before she realized anyone had followed. But just as she turned toward the room Lord Suthtun had been given, a hand on her arm made her stop and turn. The man behind her made Odel's stomach lurch.

"Lord Cheshire." She tried for a smile, but knew it was a bit stiff. She really wasn't in the mood to hear any more of his complaints about rooming with his cousin. "Is there something I can do for you?"

"Aye." He hesitated briefly, then lifted his chin. "I am a very handsome hu—man, am I not?"

Odel managed to restrain a grimace. Sighing, she nodded solemnly. "Aye, my lord." It was the truth. Lord Cheshire *was* quite the most handsome man she had ever laid eyes on. His hair was a pale brown that flowed in waves down to his shoulder. His eyes were as black as Vlaster's jacket. His face and figure were perfection itself; she was being honest when she said, "You *are* very handsome." Then she continued with, "Now, if you would excuse me?"

Odel started to turn away to continue on to Lord Suthtun's room, but Cheshire grabbed her hand, drawing her to a halt. "Nay."

"*Nay?*" She peered at him narrowly as she tried to free her hand from his.

"First we must settle this. I am the most handsome man here. Would you not agree?"

Sighing, she nodded impatiently. "Aye, my lord. In fact, you are the most handsome man I have ever seen."

"Well, then, why do you avoid me? Do you not know how fortunate you would be to have me to husband? Why do you resist falling in love with me?"

Odel's mouth dropped open at the forward question. "I . . ."

"I would be a good husband to you. I would let you eat all the juiciest morsels. I would give you five or six babies. I *would* make you happy."

Eyes wide, Odel heard a high, almost squeaking sound slip past her lips. She quickly closed her mouth, then shook her head in the hopes of clearing it so that something useful might come to mind to say. She was still struggling when he suddenly swept her into his arms. Passionately, he breathed, "We would do well together. You *will* love me." Then his mouth descended on hers.

Odel wasn't very experienced when it came to kisses—well, all right, this was her first—but if this wet, mushy experience was what they were all like, she decided, she could do quite nicely without them. Her decision never to marry had not been a mistake. She began to struggle in Lord Cheshire's grasp.

"Unhand her!"

That voice was rather like the crack of doom, Odel thought faintly before Lord Cheshire finally released her. Steadying herself with a hand on the wall, she turned to peer up the hall. Aunt Matilda was barreling toward them. Who would have thought such a deep authoritative voice could have issued forth from her plump, usually cherubic countenance? Although she didn't look very cherubic at the moment. She looked furious. And, oddly enough, Tildy in a fury was quite an intimidating sight.

Odel almost felt sorry for Lord Cheshire. The man was suddenly looking terrified. Almost, but not quite, she decided, using the back of her hand to wipe away his slobbery kiss.

"How dare you overstep yourself so!" Matilda raged, coming to a halt before them, her eyes spitting fire.

"I . . ." The young nobleman looked away, anywhere but at the woman confronting him, then suddenly drew himself up and spoke. "She wanted me to. She loves me. She wants to be my wife."

"Poppycock!" Tildy snapped, not even bothering to look at Odel for confirmation. "You cannot fool me. I can see right through your lies. You thought if you forced yourself on Odel I would have to agree to a marriage. Then you would be set up here for the rest of your miserable days."

Lord Cheshire shrank slightly under her wilting glare, then whined, "Well, so what if I did?"

Matilda's eyes narrowed to angry slits. She flicked her cane at him once, set it down with a snap, then smiled with satisfaction. "That is so what!"

Odel turned in bewilderment to peer at Lord Cheshire, but he was no longer there. A scuffling sound drew her gaze downward then. Her mouth dropping open, she gaped in horror at the rat now sitting where Lord Cheshire had been but a moment before. "Aunt Matilda!"

"What?" Tildy asked innocently, her gaze shifting curiously past Odel. The squeak of a door opening sounded behind her.

Odel whirled, her horrified gaze landing on Lord Suthtun as he stuck his head out into the hall. Peering down the dim hallway toward them, he arched an eyebrow in a silent question.

"Is anything amiss? I thought I heard—"

"Nay," Odel assured him quickly, rushing down

the hall to urge him back into his room. It wasn't until she noticed the way his eyes had widened that she glanced down to see that she still held his dagger. No wonder he was backing away so quickly. "I—Here." She turned the weapon around and held it out to him, explaining, "I just wanted to return this . . . and Aunt Matilda followed to have a discussion with me. All is well."

"Are you sure?" he asked, accepting the weapon.

"I am positive. Everything is fine. Really. Fine." She nearly choked on the lie, vaguely aware her voice was unnaturally high and squeaky sounding. She grabbed the door and pulled it closed, adding a slightly frantic, "Sleep well."

After she shut the door in his face, Odel whirled and hurried back to Matilda. "You undo that right now!" she hissed fiercely, glaring at her godmother and pointing furiously downward.

"Undo what right now?" Tildy asked with bewilderment.

"Undo what?" Odel cried in amazement. "Do you not realize that Lord Suthtun would as soon kill a witch as look at her?"

Matilda looked unperturbed. "And so he should. But I am not a witch."

"Yes, but—" Odel began, then shook her head. This was no time to explain. Trying for patience, she ground out, "Turn Lord Cheshire back into . . ." Her voice died as she glanced down and realized she was pointing at nothing. The rat that had been Lord Cheshire was gone. A frown of dismay replaced her anger. "Where did he go?"

Matilda shrugged. "No doubt he just skittered off somewhere. Rats tend to do that." Never fear though, Vlaster shall find—Oh! There. You see! Vlaster has already found him."

Following the woman's gesture, Odel peered toward the stairs. She paled at once, her eyes dilating with horror. Her aunt's "servant" stood at the top of the stairs, holding the rat by the tail as if he were about to swallow it. "Vlaster!"

Pausing, the liveried servant closed his mouth, straightened his head, and turned to look at her in silence.

Odel was at his side at once. Snatching the squirming rat from him, she held it out in front of her and turned back toward Matilda with a determined expression. But she had only taken a couple of steps when the door to Lord Suthtun's room opened again and his head popped out once more. Obviously he had heard her shriek. Dropping her hand, she moved the rat behind her back and tried for an innocent expression.

"Aye, my lord?" she murmured, the calm image she was trying to project ruined somewhat by the way her voice rose at the end. She gave a sudden jerk as Lord Cheshire broke free of her hold, and was now scrabbling up the back of her gown. Biting her lip, she tried not to squirm as his little clawed feet scrambled over her rump and started up her spine. If he bit her, she was going to step on the little bugg—

"I thought I heard a shriek," Lord Suthtun explained quietly.

"Oh. Aye." Odel almost moaned the words as the rat crawled under her long hair and made its way to the nape of her neck. She felt its cold nose against her flesh, and she had to bite her lips to keep from shrieking again. *It is only Lord Cheshire*, she reminded herself. *It is only Lord Cheshire. Oh, God!*

"Oh, 'twas nothing, my lord." Matilda stepped in to reassure him. "Odel just thought she saw a rat."

"Ah." The man's gaze shifted from Matilda to Odel, then widened. "It would seem she did see one."

Odel closed her eyes with a groan. She had felt Lord Cheshire move to her right shoulder. No doubt the little beast was now peering from her hair. Putting her hands out before him as the rat started to climb down her front, Odel offered him a platform to stand on as she lied. "Nay. Not *this* rat. This rat is . . . er . . . a pet. I thought I spotted another *rat*!!" She shrieked, whirling away as, instead of moving onto the hand she had lifted, Lord Cheshire took a nosedive down the front of her gown. He was now nestled between her breasts, and apparently quite happy from the way he'd quit squirming.

Pulling her gown away from her chest, Odel dug

her other hand in to retrieve the wayward suitor. Matilda was there at once, her cane raised as if to zap her, or the rat, or both. Releasing her gown, Odel immediately snatched the cane with her now free hand, grabbed ahold of the rat with the other, and ripped it out of her top.

"Are you quite all right?" Lord Suthtun was at her side now as well.

Taking a moment to glower in warning at Tildy, Odel handed the rat to her, then turned to Lord Suthtun. "I am fine, my lord," she assured him, her voice unnaturally brittle. "Just a little trouble. All taken care of now," she assured him, frowning as she realized that Matilda, Vlaster, and Cheshire were now disappearing down the stairs. "I—umm—I really have to get back to my—er—guests, my lord." She began backing toward the stairs. "Is there anything you need, then . . ."

"Michel. And no, thank you."

"Good night, then, Michel." With a grimace, she whirled and set off after her aunt.

MATILDA AND VLASTER were nowhere to be seen when Odel reached the bottom of the steps. Muttering under her breath, she waved away the men who immediately began moving in her direction. Perhaps Matilda and Vlaster were in the kitchens. She had nearly reached the door to the steamy room when a cold rush of air swept through the great hall, rustling the rushes. Pausing, she turned to see Matilda entering with Vlaster on her heels. Odel promptly changed direction and rushed toward them.

"Where have you been? Where is Lord Cheshire? What have you done now?" Her words came out in a frenzy as she reached the pair.

Matilda patted her arm soothingly. "Nothing, dear. He went . . . er . . . home."

"Home?"

"Aye. He left."

"How?"

Matilda scowled. "What do you mean, 'how'? He—"

"Did you turn him back or not?" Odel hissed. "You did not leave him a rat, did you?"

"Oh." Her aunt gave a little laugh. "Well, no. You needn't worry about that, my dear. Lord Cheshire left here just as he came. Now, why don't you go for a nice little walk with Lord Beasley? He mentioned earlier that—"

"I do not *wish* to take a walk with Lord Beasley. I do not wish to walk with *anyone*," Odel interrupted wearily, her shoulders slumping as the tension left her body. "I do, however, wish you would give up on my marrying one of these men. I really have no desire for a husband, Tildy!"

Face softening with sympathy, Matilda reached out to briefly clasp Odel's hand. "I know, my dear. But then if you did, I would not be needed here, would I?"

Odel opened her mouth to try to convince the older woman to give up her quest and let her be, but instead closed it and shook her head in defeat. She did not have the energy to argue with the woman. She had been doing so for the last two days without result.

"You look tired. Why do you not go to bed? I shall see to your guests."

"They are not my guests. *You* invited them here, and . . ." Odel began impatiently, then shook her head and turned away. "Oh, what is the use? You do not listen to me, anyway. I am going to bed."

Chapter Four

"You should go below and eat."

Michel let the fur drape fall back to cover the window and turned to find Eadsele sitting up in bed. The boy was still pale, but he looked a bit more alert than he had for the past week. "Are you feeling better?"

Grimacing, his squire shook his head apologetically. "I am sorry, my lord. I am never sick. Really."

Leaving the window, Michel moved back to sit on the side of the bed. "Do not apologize. It is hardly your fault that you are ill."

"Aye. But 'tis only a week until Christmas, and I know you must be eager to return home."

"Do not worry about me. I am enjoying the rest." He meant to assure the boy, but didn't sound very convincing even to himself.

Not wishing to overburden Lady Roswald's maids when she already had so many guests, Michel had insisted on nursing the boy himself. He had spent the last week stuck here in this room, trying to bathe down Eadsele's temperature when it was high, covering him with furs when he had the chills, and urging bowl after bowl of broth down the boy's sore throat. To a man used to days filled with activity, this was becoming unbearable. And yet, the nights had almost made the week pass quickly.

A smile curved Michel's lips as he recalled the last several nights. While he had insisted on staying with Eadsele during the day, the Lady Odel had convinced him to let a maid take over his nighttime vigil so that he could spend his evenings below— and also get some rest. Since the first night, he had joined the table for supper, then fallen into the habit of chatting and playing chess with Odel.

Odel. He smiled slightly now as he thought of the way her eyes sparkled when she laughed. He'd found himself regaling her with all the funny little stories he could recall. He also liked the way she blushed when he complimented her, so he found himself slipping them in, in order that he could enjoy the pink flush that covered her cheeks.

Aye, Odel had helped to keep him from going mad this last week and he could hardly believe that the company of a woman affected him so. But he had come to know her quite well this last week, and what he had learned was that not all women were the greedy grasping creatures his mother had always seemed.

At least, Odel wasn't. She never seemed to take advantage of the servants around her as his mother did, ordering them to do this or that, and even, he suspected, making up things just to play the grand lady. Odel did most everything for herself.

Murmuring that the servants were busy with their own tasks, she would fetch the beverages while they played chess each night. She even often threw logs on the fire and built it up herself rather than asking a servant. Odel also hadn't worn a single jewel to adorn her gown this last week, though he was sure she must have many such items.

Aye, she was different from his mother, and Michel liked her all the more for that. He could hardly believe his luck. With a keep full of wealthy, handsome men, he was surprised she gave him any time at all. But not only did she give him attention, she paid little if any attention to the rest of the guests.

"You would do better did you not spend all of your time in here with me, my lord," Eadsele suggested, interrupting his thoughts.

His gaze focusing on the pale boy in the bed, Michel shrugged and smiled.

"Someone has to stay with you."

"The maid who sits with me while you eat offered to sit with me during the day—should you wish to enjoy the holiday diversions Lady Roswald is supplying."

Eadsele's voice seemed almost eager. Michel was pleased to see in the boy's face the barest trace of color, too. His new squire had been an apple-cheeked lad when he had collected him, and had remained so through most of their journey. It had only been upon their arrival here that he had become so deathly pale, when he had been stricken by this illness. His pallid complexion since had been most worrisome. Now, the faintest flush of pink again touched his skin.

"Lady Roswald is beautiful, do you not think, my lord?" At the sly words, Michel's eyes narrowed on the boy. Lady Roswald had visited Eadsele's sick room once or twice a day, sometimes staying to play a game with them to cheer the lad. She was very kind. And she was also beautiful, though he had not thought so at first. Hers was a loveliness that grew on you. Still, there was something about the boy's tone of voice that made Michel suspect his motives.

"Why do I get the feeling you would be eager to see me go?" he asked abruptly.

The flush in the boy's cheeks stained his face a bright red, and Michel's eyes widened slightly. He recalled the way the boy had brightened every night when the maid, Maggie, arrived, and suddenly he understood. The boy had a crush on the little serving wench.

Michel didn't know why he had not picked up on the fact sooner, or why it so surprised him now. Eadsele was already fourteen.

"So tell me about this maid," Michel murmured, his lips twitching when Eadsele flushed even darker.

"The maid? She tells me about the feasts and

the celebrations," he said as if it were of no consequence. At the sound of activity in the bailey below, the boy gave a relieved look and glanced toward the covered window. "What is that? Do you think they are going on a hunt?"

Standing, Michel moved back to the window and peered out at the snow-covered bailey. "Nay. 'Tis just a wagonload of flour."

"Hmm." Eadsele shifted restlessly. "From what Maggie says, there has been a grand feast every night."

"Aye," Michel murmured, still looking down on the bailey.

"I would think they should need to go hunting soon then, should they not? The larders should be running low by now. It has been a week since we arrived and there has been no hunting done at all."

Michel nodded at that, his mind suddenly fixing on the suggestion. He was tired of being caged indoors with Eadsele, but up until now he had felt it was his place to look after the boy. After all, the lad was his charge. But it seemed Eadsele had a more attractive nursemaid in mind. And now the squire had given him a good idea. He would enjoy a nice brisk ride right about now, and hunting game to make up for what he and Eadsele were eating was the perfect excuse. That would give him a chance to get outside without feeling he was neglecting his duties or overburdening the Roswald servants.

"You are right," he announced, letting the fur drape again fall into place to block out the bailey below. "A nice stag or boar should—" What he suspected was a trace of triumph in Eadsele's eyes made him pause. He got the distinct impression he had been manipulated. Still, he decided, it didn't matter. He wished to get out and about anyway. If Eadsele wished to gaze upon the little serving wench, let him.

"Good morning, my lady."

Odel felt a shot of alarm run through her on finding Lord Suthtun seating himself next to her at the table. During the week since his arrival at Roswald, Michel had never once come below to break his fast.

Which was a relief to her of course, she assured herself. After all, it lowered the risk of his coming upon Matilda and her magical moments. She hadn't worried about that with the Roswald servants. Matilda had assigned the duck maids to serve in the great hall, which left the real maids to tend to the bedchambers and kitchens, safely away from the likelihood of seeing anything unusual. Odel also hadn't had to worry about the men-at-arms witnessing anything. It turned out that they were all quite disgusted with the preening ways of the lords lounging about Roswald Hall, and did their best to avoid them. Her men still came into the hall for meals, but were quick about it and left as soon as they were finished.

It was only Lord Suthtun Odel had to worry about. His decision to nurse his sick squire had been quite convenient if he were to stay at Roswald. It left her with only the evenings to worry that her odd aunt might suddenly pull out some fairy dust, or wave her cane in front of, or even worse at, him.

Odel had done her best to keep him away from the woman. She sat between them at the dinner table, always keeping up a lively chatter so that he would have no reason to address the strange godmother. Then, once the meal was finished, she had taken to playing chess with him each night by the fire.

The best thing about that was Odel had found Michel a worthy opponent. For every game she won, he won one as well. They were most evenly matched. Actually, she had enjoyed talking and playing with the man since his arrival, and she was suddenly aware that she would miss those companionable evenings when he left. Which was perhaps why the idea that the boy might be improving was presently upsetting her. Once Eadsele was better, there would be no excuse for Lord Suthtun to remain. And while she knew she should be relieved that his departure would vastly simplify her life, at the moment she was more concerned with the loss of a man who was quickly becoming a friend. Her first friend.

"Is Eadsele all better, my lord?" she asked, putting aside her own confused feelings for a moment.

"Nay, I fear not."

Odel felt relief rush through her and tried to stamp it down. She should be feeling disappointment. If she had any sense she would feel disappointed. Every minute he remained was risky. It appeared, however, that her good sense had abandoned her. "I am sure he will recover soon."

"Aye," Lord Suthtun agreed, then cleared his throat. "Actually, Eadsele mentioned something I had not thought of."

"Oh?"

Michel nodded. "He mentioned that no one had gone on a hunt since we had arrived and I wondered—"

"Oh, what a marvelous idea!" Matilda crooned suddenly from behind them.

Odel whirled to peer over her shoulder. She hadn't heard the woman approach. Managing a smile, she then glanced back at Michel. "Aye, my lord. You are very considerate, but that is not necessary. We have plenty of meat."

"No, we don't. In fact"—lifting her cane, Tildy swung it quickly toward the door to the kitchens, then set it down with a satisfied thump—"we are fresh out. I was going to suggest a hunt myself."

"Matilda," Odel growled, glaring at the woman in warning, but her godmother blithely ignored her. Instead, she beamed briefly at Lord Suthtun, then turned her gaze over the whole of the room.

"Everyone! Yoohoo!" She clapped her hands to gain the attention of the others in the room.

Her suitors, Odel sighed inwardly at the thought. She was going mad with their ridiculous compliments, their sessions of preening in efforts to gain her attention, and their long, drawn-out dissertations on how handsome, wealthy, or clever they were. She had never known that noblemen could be so vapid; but then, Father had never really let her socialize. Gazing at her guests, she was almost grateful. Added to that, she was starting to find her appetite affected by their presence at the table. Odel had come to notice that they all had the oddest way of eating. First of all, they ate constantly— all day long from what she could tell. But it was the way that they ate that disturbed her most. They each brought their food up to their mouths with both hands, keeping their backs straight, heads up, and eyes alert as if watching for some thief who might steal it. It was the oddest thing she had ever seen, made stranger by the fact that they *all* seemed to do it. Only Lord Suthtun did not. Odel had mentioned it to Tildy, but the woman had laughed and claimed that those manners were all the rage at court these days. To Odel, it was creepy. It reminded her of something she couldn't quite place.

All of this had managed to make Odel extremely grateful that Lord Suthtun came below for the evening meals. It gave her an excuse to escape the other men. And his habit of staying below for an hour or so afterward allowed her to stay away from them.

Nervous of what Matilda might do, Odel had urged him into a game of chess before the fire the second night after his arrival and every night since. She had used the claim that she was chilly as an excuse to rearrange the seats. Placing her own chair with its back to the fire had forced him to sit with his back to the great hall at large. His being unable to see what was going on in the rest of the room had allowed her to relax.

Odel had actually enjoyed their games. Michel was a witty man and charming even, something she had not expected in a warrior. And he had not minded her beating him at chess; he even seemed mildly pleased by it. Which was very different than she was used to. Odel's father had always claimed she cheated and knocked the board to the floor when she won against him. But Lord Suthtun merely cast her an admiring glance and complimented her strategy, a reaction Odel shared when the knight himself won. She had woken up today looking forward to the evening ahead.

Now, she felt the beginnings of panic creeping up on her again. A whole day in the presence of Tildy and her magic. If Tildy should turn one of the men into a rat or perform some other magical act in front of Lord Suthtun . . . well, she doubted he would see a difference between a fairy godmother and a witch. Feeling helpless, she listened to Tildy outline her plan for a big hunting party. A feeling of doom was dropping around her shoulders even as she did.

"THERE!"

Odel glanced at Michel at his excited whisper. She had been busy looking over her shoulder at Tildy and the others. Her godmother rode on a small plump mare that Odel was sure did not belong to the Roswald stables, following several hundred yards behind Lord Suthtun and Odel. The other lords rode in a group behind her.

Matilda was as stiff and tense on the animal as could be; she looked about as pleased to be on a horse again as Odel was to be on this hunt. Briefly, recalling that her godmother had died in a fall from her mount, Odel almost felt pity for her. Then her gaze fell on the pack of suitors bouncing around in their saddles behind her and Odel had felt all pity die. Good heavens! Not a one of them could ride. What sort of lords could not ride a horse?

"Do you see it?"

Turning away from the group trailing behind them, Odel followed Michel's pointing finger. Their horses slowed. A huge wild boar was rooting in the bushes ahead. Drawing her mount to a complete stop, she reached instinctively for her bow, feeling excitement and fear begin to course through her. Wild swine had become rarer the last couple of years; to chance upon one now was quite lucky. The thought made her pause and glance back toward Tildy, her eyes narrowed. Any good fortune was suspect.

Expecting to see the others hanging back, Odel's eyes widened as she saw that Tildy and the men hadn't yet slowed. They were riding up at full speed, apparently unaware that she and Michel had come upon game—and dangerous game at that. Her hand jerking on her reins, Odel instinctively shouted out a warning.

A curse from Lord Suthtun was followed quickly by an angry squeal. Odel whirled back to see what had happened. She realized at once that her shout must have startled Michel just as he had taken aim. An arrow now quivered in the boar's hindquarters, and she was quite sure that he wouldn't have aimed *there*. But there was little time to think of much more than that. Michel had feathered the beast's posterior, and the boar wasn't at all pleased.

"Oh, dear," she murmured, then tightened her fingers on her reins in alarm. Michel shouted a warning as the boar charged.

The next few minutes became a swirl of chaos. Like a pack of dogs on the scent of blood, the suitors who had flanked Odel's aunt now charged onto the scene. They swarmed around Odel and Michel, crowding them so much that there was no way to swerve or retreat as the boar came at them, squealing madly. The horses, smarter than their riders, began to whinny and snort, rearing back in terror. Odel managed to keep her seat, but the lords—lousy riders all—went tumbling to the ground. Their shouts were added to the chaos as they rolled and darted about, trying to avoid the feet of the horses off of which they had fallen.

Given so many new targets, the boar suddenly stopped, apparently unsure who to attack first. After a brief hesitation, it headed after the nearest man. Shrieking, the lord in question charged for the nearest tree, the boar hot on his heels.

Had she not been busy trying to stay in the saddle, Odel would have marveled at the man's agility as he scrambled up that tree. He was quickly followed by his friends, one after the other, as the boar charged each.

It would have been the perfect opportunity for Odel or Michel to shoot another arrow into the boar, but neither could get a clear shot from their bucking steeds. Seated sidesaddle as she was, and with her horse dancing on its hind legs, Odel began to fear she could even stay mounted. Feeling herself begin to slide toward the ground, she desperately tightened her hold on the reins. Then, realizing that she was doomed to fall, she let go and concentrated on landing on her feet.

Now *she* was a target for the boar. But, unlike the others, Odel knew she couldn't scramble up a tree—especially not as she was dressed. Not wasting any time, the moment her feet hit the snowy ground, Odel grabbed up her skirts and began to run. Behind her she heard Michel shout, the boar snort, and Tildy's high-pitched yell, but she didn't take the chance of looking back. She had no time. Boars with their vicious tusks were deadly—especially when injured and angry. She charged into the woods at full tilt, wishing that skirts weren't so hard to run in, wishing that the ground were not so slippery with winter snow, and wishing above all that she had stayed home.

Chapter Five

One minute Odel was running for her life and the next her legs were pumping uselessly in the air; she had been caught around the waist and lifted off the ground. Michel now held her, and she hung down the side of his horse. Apparently he had regained control of his mount enough to rescue her. Odel had barely grasped that when something tugged at her skirts. Peering down, she cried out in horror. The boar was less than a heartbeat behind her, and one of the beast's tusks had caught in the hem of her skirts. She felt her stomach roil, but Michel tugged his reins to the side, swerving away from the boar and ripping her skirts free.

Looking back, Odel saw the beast turn to charge after them, but Michel put on more speed, urging his mount to a gallop. It quickly widened the distance between them leaving the snarling animal behind in the brush.

Several moments after the boar had dropped out of sight, Michel let his mount slow then come to a halt. Using both hands, he lifted Odel and drew her around before him on the saddle. Seating her sideways, he frowned. "Are you all right?"

"Yes," she breathed, managing a weak smile. "But that was close."

"Aye." He didn't smile—in fact, he looked quite grim. He glanced back over his shoulder. There was no sign of the boar now. "You would think those idiots would know better than to charge in like that."

Odel heartily agreed, but merely murmured, "Thank you—for saving me."

Turning his attention back to her, Michel's expression softened in a small smile. "It was my pleasure," he assured her. His voice was husky, and he raised one hand to brush a strand of hair off her cheek.

Odel covered his hand with her own, but glanced shyly downward. But not for long. Michel immediately tilted her head back up, his lips coming down to cover hers.

At first, Odel froze under the gentle caress of his lips. Other than Lord Cheshire's slobbery attempt to drown her, she had never been kissed. And where Lord Cheshire's mushy ministrations had made her want to wretch, this man's kiss was heavenly. It was strong, warm, and demanding. Masterful.

It seemed so natural as he urged her lips apart for an open-mouth kiss, that Odel didn't think a thing of it. She merely slid her arms around his neck and held on as he invaded her. Her toes curled in her slippers and little moans sounded in her throat, shocking her, but she found herself terribly disappointed when at last he broke away.

Sighing, Odel opened her eyes slowly. She peered up at him, but he was sitting stiff in his saddle, his head up and alert as he peered over her shoulder. Still, it took a moment before the roaring his kisses had caused in her ears subsided enough for her to hear what had drawn his attention. Something was moving through the woods toward them. Odel leaned to the side to peer over his shoulder just as Tildy came crashing into the clearing on her ungainly little mare.

"*There* you are! Well, thank goodness you are all right." Matilda drew her mount to a halt and peered at the two of them. Displeasure tightened her lips as she noted the way Odel rested on the saddle before Suthtun, her arms around his neck; the way his own held her about the waist. Surely she was annoyed that one of the suitors she had supplied was not in Michel's place.

"The boar was brought down, and a couple of the others even managed to fell a stag. They also bagged a couple of pheasants, so we shall have a fine feast tonight." Tildy pronounced this abruptly, then turned to head back.

"What? How is that possible?" Michel asked. "We just left the clearing."

Odel closed her eyes. She knew how it was possible. Tildy's magic, that was how.

"Well, some of us were busy while you two were mucking about," Matilda snapped.

"We were not mucking about," Odel said at once, coloring. "I was running for my life and Lord Suthtun saved me."

"Hmmph." Matilda's lips tightened further. "And I suppose it was luck where he brought his horse to a halt?"

Michel and Odel shared a perplexed look, then peered about in bewilderment. There was nothing but leafless trees and snow. Then Odel glanced upward, and a small gasp slid from her lips. *Mistletoe.* The upper branches of the trees sheltering them were laced liberally with the vine. She hadn't noticed it until now. And judging from Lord Suthtun's expression, neither had he.

"Your horse ran for home before anyone could stop him, my dear," Matilda announced, drawing their attention back to her. "You shall have to ride back with me."

Odel turned her dubious gaze to the mare her aunt rode. It was extremely small, and really rather round—like the woman who rode it. Odel had her doubts as to whether the animal could manage both of them. Apparently Lord Suthtun did as well. His arm tightened around her waist. "There is no need for that, my lady. She can ride back with me."

Matilda gave a snort of displeasure, then without another word she turned her horse and trotted off, leaving them staring after her.

"Well," Odel said uncomfortably, avoiding his eyes. "It would seem the hunt is over."

"Aye," Michel said. He peered down at her silently for a moment, then glanced up at the mistletoe overhead. "It would seem you owe me a kiss."

"Oh?" Odel glanced up as well. "I thought you already took one."

"That was for saving your life. This one would be for the mistletoe."

Odel blushed prettily, then leaned up to press a quick kiss to his lips. "How is that?" she asked a bit breathlessly. She settled back on the saddle.

"That was very nice," he said solemnly. "But there is an awful lot of mistletoe."

Feeling heat and excitement pool in her belly, Odel nodded just as solemnly. "Aye, there is, my lord."

With a smile he bent to kiss her. It was not the sweet, swift rubbing of lips she had just given him, but another of the long, hot, toe-curling variety. And this time, Odel's reaction was more violent. She was helpless; arching into him, her body responded of its own accord. Her tongue slid out to join his, her fingers curling almost painfully in his hair, and she shuddered. Surely, this was a Pandora's box, this reaction that burst to life within her, begging to be opened.

She wanted more, and that was frightening. It was a hunger she had never before experienced, that swelled within her.

The years under her tyrannical father had convinced Odel that marriage and children were not for her. She'd had no wish for a husband who might be as cold and dictatorial as her own father had been. But that had left her feeling lonely and empty. Until now. Now the emptiness was being filled, the loneliness abolished. And, she realized in some far-off part of her mind, it wasn't just the kiss that made her desire him so. It was the chats and chess by the fire, the soft laughter over dinner, his warm arms that had saved her from the boar. This passion that was licking at her insides had begun some time ago. She was beginning to care for this man, and couldn't lie to herself about it. She had wanted him from the first moment she'd seen him.

His presence at Roswald was a dangerous thing; she had known that from the start. If he saw Matilda up to her tricks, there would be trouble. But had Odel approached Tildy about using some of her fairy dust to cure the boy? Nay. Had she suggested he continue home and leave the boy to be nursed? She might have sent Eadsele home with one of her men-at-arms when he was recovered, but nay. Had she encouraged the man to stay above stairs for the evening meal to reduce the risk of danger? Nay. In fact, it was she who had suggested he might enjoy a break; it was she who had insisted he join them.

Why? Because Odel had enjoyed his presence at dinner, and their shared evenings. Too much to send him away. She had spent the last few days wandering about the keep waiting impatiently for supper to arrive. She had alternated between thinking up excuses to visit him and Eadsele in their room, and thinking up witty things she might say, stories she had heard that might amuse him.

Odel *liked* this man. She enjoyed his company. She found him handsome when he laughed. And now, she realized with a sense of foreboding as he slowly drew away to peer down at her, she hungered for his kisses and touch like a flower craves sunlight. Odel wanted to pull his head back for another meshing of mouths. She wanted to cleave to him. She wanted to strip off his clothing and feel his naked body against hers. To Odel, all of that was more dangerous than his discovery of Matilda's magic could ever be.

Dear God, she wondered with dread, how had she let this happen?

"You are so incredibly beautiful."

Odel blinked at his soft words and felt her fears momentarily dissipate. Did he truly believe that she was beautiful? For most of the last twenty-five years she had been a shadow, her face pale, her limp hair pulled tightly back off her face, her expression as unhappy as she had been. But in the week after her father's death, since Matilda's arrival, Odel had felt herself bloom. Her face had regained some color. Her hair now held a healthy shine and even a slight wave. And in the week since Lord Suthtun had arrived, she had even begun to smile.

"You are beautiful, too," she whispered shyly.

Much to her amazement, he immediately threw back his head and laughed.

"Nay, my lady. I am an old warhorse. Battle scarred and—"

"You are not old, my lord," Odel interrupted abruptly. "Why, you cannot be more than thirty."

"Thirty-one," he corrected gently, brushing a tress off her face. "But I used to feel much older."

"Used to?" Unconsciously she tipped her face, encouraging him to stroke her face as if she were a kitten.

"I find that being around you makes me feel like a boy," he murmured huskily, then reached for the reins of his mount. Taking them in his hand, he blew a breath out. She found herself staring at those lips that had caressed hers a moment before, and he managed a crooked smile. "I suppose we had best return now."

"Aye," Odel agreed softly.

Nodding, Michel started to urge his mount forward, then turned it toward the nearest tree. Drawing it to a halt, he reached out and plucked down a sprig of mistletoe. He set it in her hair just above her ear, kissed her quickly, then plucked a berry from the small sprig, and slipped it into his pocket. "A remembrance."

Swallowing, Odel smiled weakly, then turned to look ahead as he urged his mount forward again. *Remembrance?* For when he left and her life returned to the lonely place it had been.

That thought made her so sad that Odel found herself unable to think of a single witty or amusing thing to say during the ride back to the keep. Instead, they were both silent. It wasn't until they entered the keep that either of them spoke, and then they both gasped in surprise. The hall had been transformed. Mistletoe, pine bowers, and streams of cloth and ribbon hung everywhere, and the tables were covered with white linen and preparations were under way for a feast.

"There you are!" Tildy suddenly appeared and bustled toward them.

"What is all this?" Odel asked in amazement.

"Why, 'tis for the feast," the woman exclaimed as if it should be self-explanatory. "And we are going to have wonderful entertainment. A traveling group arrived while we were out. We shall have jugglers and tumblers, and a dancing bear. It will be marvelous!"

"All of this just to celebrate today's hunt?" Odel muttered in disbelief.

"Well, not just that," her godmother exclaimed. "But Christmas is coming on rather quickly, and that is a time for joy and celebration."

"What? No Lord Suthtun this morning?"

Odel made a face at Matilda's slightly sarcastic comment and shifted to make room for her godmother on the trestle table bench beside her. It had been several days since the hunt, and there were only three more days until Christmas. Lord Suthtun was still at Roswald.

Michel had been joining her to break his fast every morning since the day of the hunt. He had still spent a good part of the day above stairs with Eadsele, but he had started to take his meals below, claiming he did not wish to burden the servants with the extra work of carting a meal up to him. But today he had not come down. Eadsele was again very sick.

Though for the past several days the boy had appeared to improve—yesterday Lord Suthtun had even brought the boy below to sit by the fire and announced that tomorrow they might risk continuing on—during the night, Eadsele's fever had suddenly shot back up. This morning he was as ill as he had been the first night. Returning home was now out of the question, of course, two-hour journey or not, and Michel had decided to remain above stairs with the boy to see if there was aught to be done.

Odel missed him already. She had grown quite used to having the man around, a fact that was just as awful for her as his absence. Her feelings for the man had only continued to grow these past days, along with her desire. There had only been a few opportunities for stolen kisses since the hunt, and after every one, Matilda had shown up, eyeing them with disapproval. She was making it more than obvious that she was truly displeased with the time Odel spent with Michel. But then, Matilda had been displeased with the man's arrival right from the first. Odel supposed that her godmother considered his presence a fly in her ointment. The goodhearted but damnably stubborn woman still wished to marry Odel off to one of the rich, handsome suitors she herself had provided.

Odel paused. Now that she realized that her feelings for Michel had reached a point where his leaving would be painful, Odel found herself wishing that Matilda had found a way to remove him. In fact, it suddenly seemed odd that the old woman hadn't.

"I am sure Lord Suthtun is a very nice man," Tildy was saying, "but he isn't nearly as handsome or wealthy as the suitors I have provided. I wish you would waste less time on him and spend more with a lord like Beasley. Or perhaps Lord Trenton, he is—"

"Explain something to me," Odel interrupted. Matilda's eyebrows rose.

"What dear?"

"Why have you not simply cured young Eadsele and seen Lord Suthtun out of here? That would have left the way clear for the others." As she made the observation, Odel stiffened as her own words sank in.

"What is it?" Tildy asked warily.

"My God," Odel breathed, then shook her head. "Nay. It cannot be."

"What?" Matilda was suddenly looking wary.

"Nothing." She forced herself to ignore the brief thought that struck her. Had Matilda not cured the boy because she did not really wish Odel to fall in love with one of her supposed suitors? Had Michel been the man Matilda was really trying to get her to fall in love with all along? After all, it was rather odd that Lord Suthtun had chosen to stop at Roswald to rest only two hours' journey from Suthtun. And it was rather odd that the boy's illness had come on so suddenly. But, no. This was all just coincidence, she assured herself. Wasn't it?

"Why did you not cure the boy?" Odel repeated.

"Oh. Well, my magic does not work on humans," Matilda assured her, but she was staring downward as she said it, reluctant to meet her gaze. Odel felt her stomach clench slightly; her godmother was lying.

"This *was* your *plan*, wasn't it?" she said quietly. Matilda's expression closed. "What?"

"You never intended that I should fall in love with one of the others," she accused. "You knew I could not fall in love with any of those vain, silly, shallow men. You gave me a castle full of them, then presented me with Lord Suthtun in the hopes that I would fall in love with him."

"Now that is just silly. Whyever would I do a thing like that?" Matilda gave a nervous laugh and Odel exhaled in angry disappointment.

"I should have realized that was what was going on sooner," she said sadly. "You were so rude to him." Odel shook her head. "But that was all just part of your plan. You were rude, so I was extra nice. Then, too, my fear that you might perform some magic trick around him meant I would spend an awful lot of time trying to keep him away from you and the others, which would constantly throw us together."

"Oh, really, my dear." Tildy gave a strained titter. "You give me far too much credit. I could never be so devious."

Tildy was a horrible liar. She wasn't very convincing at all. Odel almost wished she were. Then she could believe that Michel's interest in her was real. But like all those handsome, wealthy lords that were sniffing about her like dogs around a bitch in heat, Lord Suthtun's interest was induced. She was not foolish or vain enough to imagine that any of their attraction was real. In fact, that was part of the reason she had found their presence at Roswald so annoying. Aside from the fact that she wasn't interested in a single one of her suitors, she had suspected that their interest in her had to be a result of Matilda's magic. And yet, she had thought Suthtun was different. Tildy had seemed to dislike him so much, Odel had thought—

"Excuse me." She stood up stiffly and walked away from the table, positive her heart was breaking.

Chapter Six

"*A*re you ready?"

Odel grimaced at Matilda's question, but nodded grimly. "Aye. Is it time yet?"

"In just a moment." Matilda sounded excited. Odel was not. This was the fourth time Matilda had said, "In just a moment." Meanwhile, Odel stood waiting uncomfortably in the kitchens, trying to ignore the gaping of the cook and his staff. They had never seen her like this, she supposed. Well, they had best enjoy it, because it was doubtful they would ever see it again. She crossed her arms over her chest self-consciously. While the costume Matilda had created for her was lovely, she was positive her nipples showed through the diaphanous material.

Created. Odel rolled her eyes at that. The woman had made her strip naked in her room, then taken out a pinch of fairy dust and blown it on her. When the dust had cleared, Odel had found herself wearing this, the most amazing creation she had ever seen—a toga-like gown made up of the gauziest material ever. It was like wearing nothing

at all. Or wearing the stars. Even her skin seemed
to glimmer, likely with remnants of fairy dust. It
showed a lot of her flesh. It was indecent.

If she had realized she would be expected to wear
a costume like this, Odel would have put a halt
to the pageant Matilda had suddenly proposed. At
the time her godmother had mentioned it, Odel
had thought that arranging the skits might keep
the woman out of trouble. Little had she realized
that she was to be the feature attraction. When
Matilda had begged her to be in it, the woman
had sworn her part was a very minor role, that she
would not even have to learn lines. And the role
called for a woman, Tildy had said, and Odel was
the only suitable lady present. Her aunt had not
bothered to mention the role she was to play. Although, even had she said as much, Odel may have
still agreed, not realizing what it would entail her
wearing. Now that she knew, Odel was wishing
she had simply nixed the pageant to begin with.

"Now."

She glanced to Matilda questioningly, but the
woman was stepping aside and pulling open the
kitchen door. Six lords, also coerced into playing
roles, immediately began to move forward, pushing her out into the great hall on another of Matilda's creations: a platform on wheels, covered with
gauzy blue material somehow made to remain in
the curved shape of waves. Odel was Aphrodite,
the goddess of love, rising from the waves.

Sighing inwardly, Odel struck the pose Matilda had insisted on, clasping her hands beneath her chin and slightly arching her back. There was silence in the room as she rolled out, then Matilda's gay voice began to narrate the story of Aphrodite and Ares. Odel stayed where she was, her gaze searching the audience for Michel, but he was nowhere to be seen. Perhaps he hadn't come below, she thought sadly and sighed. She had been avoiding him. She hadn't been rude to him or anything—this was not his fault after all—but for her own self-respect and sanity she had decided to keep her distance until he left. She had been hard-put to ignore the confused glances he'd been casting her way ever since.

Matilda had just introduced Ares. Odel glanced around to see the god of war step through the keep doors at the opposite end of the great hall where he had been waiting. Out in the cold, she thought with a grimace. She almost felt sorry for Lord Beasley, the man that Matilda had assigned the role of her illicit lover. But as the figure drew nearer, Odel's eyes widened. Her jaw dropped as she took in Michel's wry smile. Dressed in a short—almost indecently so—toga and carrying a shield and sword, he mounted the steps to her foamy platform.

As Matilda narrated the tale of Aphrodite and Ares, lovers despite Aphrodite's marriage to Hephaestus, Michel's expression turned apologetic. He took her in his cold arms.

"What are you doing?" Odel stealthily whispered in his ear as they embraced. "Lord Beasley was supposed to be Ares."

"Lord Beasley was not feeling well. Your aunt asked me to step in."

"Oh." Odel glanced distractedly at Vlaster. The man rode around the platform in a small chariot-like affair led by two more of her suitors wearing horse masks. Vlaster himself wore a long gold toga and was supposed to be Helios, the god of the sun, catching them in their infidelity. Honestly, the man looked more interested in the cock in a cage that he carried than in Odel and Michel; he was looking at the bird as if it might make a tasty snack. When he rode out of the keep's front doors and out of sight, Odel shifted a little closer to Lord Suthtun. "You must have been freezing out there. You are still cold."

"While you are pleasantly warm," Michel murmured, his arms tightening around her. Matilda droned on. The older woman was relating how Helios was quick to report Aphrodite's infidelity to her husband, Hephaestus, and how the two plotted to catch the lovers in the act.

The keep doors opened again and Vlaster's chariot returned on a cold breeze. This time there was a second man with him, a rather large, muscular fellow carrying a hammer: the castle smithy. She recognized him after a startled moment and smiled wryly to herself. Who better to play Hephaestus?

"Your aunt said that when the chariot came

back I was to kiss you," Lord Suthtun murmured next to her. Odel glanced up at him with surprise.

"She did?"

"Aye. She said it was to represent Ares and Aphrodite making . . . er—"

Flushing with embarrassment, Odel silenced him by quickly pressing her lips to his. After a startled moment, Michel's kiss became real. Odel felt herself melt in his arms. Her hands crept up to clasp around his neck, her body shifting and arching into him. Without thinking, she gave in, breathing small sighs and moans of pleasure into his mouth. Then something unpleasantly cloying dropped over them and Odel and Michel froze in surprise.

"Hephaestus's net," Michel muttered. Odel suddenly remembered that she was in the midst of a pageant. Aye, of course, and Hephaestus, or the Roswald smithy, had just thrown a special net over his unfaithful wife and her lover to parade them before the Olympian gods. While Odel and Michel embraced under the net, the platform was pushed around the room.

According to Matilda's narration, when presented with the unfaithful pair, the gods merely commented on Aphrodite's beauty. Many simply claimed that they would not mind switching places with Ares. Roswald's villagers and soldiers were more than happy to act the parts of the Olympians. Even a few of Odel's suitors made ribald comments.

Feeling herself blush from her forehead to her toes, Odel herself almost felt guilty. She was more than relieved when the circuit of the room was finished and Matilda continued her narration.

The net was pulled from them. Knowing she was expected to exit, Odel waited for the platform to begin moving again, but it appeared the wheels were stuck. The men who had pushed the platform out were straining painfully to move it, but it would not budge.

Frowning, Matilda recited the part where they left again, and again the men strained at the platform, but still it did not move. When Tildy frowned, then glanced toward Michel expectantly, he hesitated, then swept Odel up in his arms. Striding from the platform, he carried her to and through the keep doors. Behind them came the sound of thunderous applause.

"Music!" Odel heard Matilda shout as the doors closed behind them.

No longer in character, Odel was terribly aware of her state of undress. It was a relief when Michel set her down on the icy castle steps.

He frowned with concern, then around at the winter night. "It is rather brisk tonight. How long were we supposed to stay out here? Your aunt did not say."

Shivering, Odel made a face. "This is long enough, I think."

"Aye," Michel agreed and turned to pull open

the door, but it did not open. He pulled again. The door remained firmly shut.

"What is it?" Odel asked with a frown, reaching past him to give the handle a tug herself. The door didn't budge.

"Is it bolted?" Michel asked with a frown.

"We hardly ever bolt the door. It should—" She shook her head with distress and tugged again, fully expecting it to open.

"Perhaps the bolt dropped into place when it closed behind us," Michel suggested. Odel continued to tug impatiently at the door, not commenting. At last she began to pound on it in the hopes that someone would notice.

"I do not think they can hear us over the music," Michel murmured after a moment. Odel paused to listen. Sure enough, the musicians were now playing a rather loud song. The audience members would never hear them.

"It is rather cold out here. Is there another door?"

Sighing, Odel began to rub her arms in an effort to warm them. She turned to peer absently around the bailey. "There is a door into the kitchens."

Nodding, Michel scooped her into his arms again and promptly started down the stairs. "Which way?" he asked as they reached the bottom step.

Gritting her teeth to keep them from chattering, Odel pointed to the right and Lord Suthtun broke into a jog. He loped quickly along the outer wall of the inner keep, then around to the back and the door leading to the kitchens. Still holding her in his arms, he reached out and pushed at the door. It was as firmly shut as the front doors. Frowning, he let Odel slide to her feet on the snowy path, then grabbed the door firmly and pulled. Nothing happened. The door remained solidly closed. Michel began pounding on it. He banged for several minutes straight, but no one came to open it. They were locked out.

Shifting from foot to foot, arms crossed over her chest, teeth chattering, Odel stood, miserably waiting.

"I do not think they can hear us here either. We should—" His voice died as he turned to peer at Odel in the moonlight. Frowning, he reached out and pulled her into his arms. "My God! You are freezing." He rubbed his hands up and down her arms, then suddenly swept her up in his arms again and began to carry her back across the snowy ground.

"W-Where are we g-going?" she chattered, clasping her arms around his neck and holding on for all she was worth. She buried her face in his hair. She had hoped that his heat might warm her, but he was cold, too. He paused several moments later and she glanced around to see him pull a door open. Wincing at the loud creak it made, she squinted in an effort to see inside the room into which he now carried her. It was dark, but not pitch dark. The dying embers of a fire in the center of the small building gave off some light. Carrying her inside, Michel set her down on a stool. Leaving her there, he hurried back to close the door, then moved to the fire to urge it back to life. Within moments he had a nice-size fire going again. He watched it for a moment, then moved to squat in front of her.

"The smithy's forge," she got out between shivers.

"Aye." Michel took her bare feet in hand and began rubbing them, frowning at her icy flesh. "You are freezing."

"You, too," she muttered, and he laughed.

"These costumes were not meant for winter wear." His cold hands moved vigorously up and down her colder calves.

Odel was silent as she watched him minister to her, amazed that he would kneel on the ground to tend to her when he himself was likely freezing. His head was bowed, his hair shining in the light from the fire, his hands moving over her flesh.

"Once I've warmed you up, I will go see if I can get them to let us in," he said, his voice sounding oddly husky. His hands moved over her knees and began to smooth up her thighs.

Without thinking, she reached out, gently touching his soft hair, then stilled when he raised his head. Flushing slightly at the way he looked at her, she let her hand drop away, but he caught it. He began to rub that now, his eyes beginning to smolder. They were both silent for a moment, then he raised her hand to his mouth.

Dragging in a ragged breath, Odel automatically began to close her hand, but Michel held it open. He pressed a kiss to the tender flesh of her palm, then to the sensitive place between her first two fingers. Odel shifted slightly where she sat, her breath catching in her chest as his tongue swiped lightly at her skin. It tickled and sent little arrows of erotic excitement quivering up her arm. She bit her lip to keep from gasping aloud.

Raising his head, Michel peered at her silently for a moment, then bent to bestow another kiss, this time to the inside of her wrist.

Odel raised her other hand to touch the side of his face, her heart swelling when he turned in to the gentle caress. But then he turned back to what he had been doing, his lips nibbling her inner arm up to the crook of her elbow. Odel caught her breath and squirmed on the stool he had set her on, but the breath escaped on a low moan as he suddenly turned his face and pressed his open mouth to the side of her breast.

Shuddering slightly, she clenched her fingers in his hair, then watched, breathless, as his mouth traveled until it found and settled on her nipple. Through the soft material of the gown—the gossamer material may as well not have been there, it was so thin and translucent—he began to suckle at her nipple. The fabric rasped against her suddenly sensitive skin, and overwhelmed by the erotic feel and sight of his actions, Odel closed her eyes on a moan.

She opened them again at once, though, when he urged her legs open. Shifting to kneel between them, he lifted his head and pulled her face down for a hot and hungry kiss. It succeeded in raising Odel's temperature faster than any amount of chafing could have.

Sliding her hands around his shoulders, Odel kissed Michel with all the passion and yearning of twenty-five loveless years. She felt his hand slide up her side, then around to one breast and she arched slightly, pressing herself into the caress with abandon. She wanted this. She wanted it *all*, and she moaned in disappointment when his lips left hers. They merely moved along her chin to her ear, though, then blazed another fiery trail down her neck.

Odel was absently aware of his hands at her back, but only vaguely until her gown pulled tight and Michel muttered in frustration against her throat. Realizing that he was trying to undo her costume, she reached to help him, undoing it quickly. Yes, she wanted this.

He tugged the gown forward, drawing it off her shoulders, and pushing it down toward her waist until her breasts were bared. Forgetting the material then, he caught the two globes in his hand and bent his mouth to each. He feasted on them with an eagerness that made Odel's insides ripple with desire; she watched him pepper her pale flesh with kisses.

Even that, though, didn't prepare her for her body's reaction when his lips suddenly closed over one swollen nipple. It was as if her stomach had dropped right out of her and the blazing smithy's fire taken its place. Gasping for breath, Odel arched backward, her hands clutching his shoulders with excitement. Suddenly, the stool she was on began to overset, and her hands scrabbled against him.

Catching her against his chest, Michel shifted her to the side, then lowered her to the straw floor. His body followed, half-covering hers, as his lips and tongue continued to tease and tug at her nipple. Feeling one of his legs slide between hers, Odel automatically spread hers slightly, then closed them around him. The brush of his leg against her bare inner thigh told her that her skirt had ridden up, but she didn't care. She wanted to feel more of him. With that intention, she grabbed at the shoulder of his toga, first tugging it loose, then using it to bring him higher.

Giving up his attention to her breasts, Michel lifted his head and shifted upward, his mouth again covering hers. Odel kissed him back, but her attention was focused on his toga and removing it. Pushing it down between them, she let her fingers trail over his chest. She paused curiously at his nipples to see if they were as sensitive as her own, then she reached around to clasp his back and pull him tight against her. She arched forward to meet him. Her hands slid down to clasp his buttocks through the cloth of his toga, then slipped under it. Odel squeezed the flesh of his behind curiously, then hesitated when a breathless laugh slipped from Michel. He broke their kiss to peer down at her.

Swallowing, Odel met his gaze uncertainly, her teeth coming out to chew her upper lip as she saw amusement mingling with the passion in his face.

"I thought I was ravishing you," he murmured in explanation. "And I was feeling guilty about it, but now I am feeling a little bit ravished myself." He gave her a wry look, then, as she started to remove her hands, he added huskily, "I like it."

Odel hesitated, then smiled. She slid her hands back downward, this time bringing one forward to slide between them. He shifted slightly, watching her face closely as he gave her the access she wanted. Odel blushed, but didn't hesitate when her hand bumped against his manhood. Covering it through the cloth of his toga, she squeezed gently, watching the fire grow in his eyes. Encouraged by that, she slid her hand beneath the toga and grasped him again, her grip firm as it closed over his naked flesh. She had to pause then because she wasn't quite sure what to do next.

Michel helped. He shifted his hips away slightly, drawing his manhood through her hand, then shifted forward again. Understanding, Odel began to caress him herself. She was rewarded with a quick hard kiss before Michel caught her hand and drew it above her head. Holding it there with one hand, he slid his other hand down over her body until he was cupping the flesh between her thighs. Odel drew in a quick shaky breath, her free hand moving instinctively to push his away, but he caught that one and pinned it above her head as well.

Holding both of her hands fast with one of his own, he returned the other to again press it between her legs. He met her gaze and held it as he began to move his hand against her, pressing the silky cloth down between her legs. Then, drawing it out of the way until she lay open to him, his fingers slid over her honeyed center. Suddenly he was caressing her in a way that made her arch and squirm, and she could hear herself gasping raggedly through her open mouth as if she were drowning.

"Not fair," she groaned at last, arching into his touch. She shook her head, her hands tugging to be free.

"What's not fair?" he murmured huskily by her ear, then nipped at the sensitive flesh there.

"You will not let me touch you," she gasped, then groaned. His caress had changed in strength and speed.

"If I let you touch me, it will be over before it has begun."

"What . . . would?" she managed to get out, her body tight as a harp's string.

"This." One finger found and dipped into her and Odel cried out, her body straining as if he had branded her. Her eyes widened incredulously as spasms of pleasure shook her body. Bending his head, Michel caught her cries in his mouth, kissing her passionately as she began to float back to earth.

Leaving that warm, fuzzy place to which he had taken her, Odel began to kiss him back. Her arms were free now, and they slid around his neck. She felt his hands on her back, then he shifted position, drawing his knees up beneath him even as he pulled her into a sitting position. Michel urged her to kneel on either side of his legs and drew her forward until they were chest to chest.

Clasping him close, Odel returned his kiss, then let her head fall back as he again began to kiss his way down her neck. She gave a slight start when she felt his hand reappear between her legs, then sighed in pleasure by his ear. Though she would have thought it impossible, he began to rebuild the fire in her. His mouth slipped over one nipple and Odel leaned back further, holding on to his shoulders. Unconsciously, she rode his hand as he caressed her. This time when her body began to spasm with pleasure, he urged her upward with one hand on her bottom, then directed her downward.

Odel's eyes widened incredulously as she felt him

enter her. He was frightfully large and she felt a bit of discomfort, but then they were joined. They stayed like that for a moment, before Michel clasped her by both buttocks and urged her to move. Odel did her best, but she wasn't sure of what she was doing. After a moment, he shifted again, easing her gently onto her back.

"Tell me if the straw is uncomfortable," he whispered in her ear. For a moment, he withdrew, but it was brief before he was sliding back into her. Closing her eyes, Odel pressed against him, her hands sliding down to curl around his buttocks and urge him on. Together, they found completion.

Chapter Seven

*A*re you warm enough?"

Smiling, Odel nodded sleepily against Michel's chest, unwilling to move from where he had placed her. They had both found satisfaction this time, and afterward Michel had rolled onto his back, taking her with him. She now lay upon his warm body, rather than the cold straw of the forge floor.

She felt his fingers in her hair and shifted, then raised her head to peer at him questioningly when he murmured, "Thank you."

"For what?" she asked in surprise.

He tugged her head up to his to kiss her before murmuring against her lips, "For my pleasure. Thank you."

Odel smiled gently when he broke the kiss. "You are very welcome, my lord. And thank you. And thank you. And thank you." She punctuated each thank-you with a kiss on his nose, chin, and chest.

Chuckling, he hugged her close, then began to run his hands through her hair. "Do you think the doors are still locked?"

"Who cares?" Grinning, Odel eased into a sitting position astride him, then added wickedly, "I could stay here forever."

"Aye." Michel reached up to catch and caress her breasts, smiling when she moaned and moved atop him. Her lower body dragged over his manhood and stirred it slowly back to wakefulness. His voice had taken on a husky, hungry quality. "But we should return soon."

Odel opened her eyes and peered down at him, shifting her body. That told him better than words could that she knew what she was doing to him. "Are you *sure* you wish to go back?"

Michel groaned at the sweet torture, then caught her by one hip. "Aye, I am sure, minx," he growled. Then his expression softened. "I would talk to your aunt. I must ask for your hand in marriage." He grinned. "Then we can do this all the time."

For a moment joy filled her face and Michel felt all was right with the world. Then, just as suddenly as it had come, it was gone, and she closed her eyes, her expression shuttered.

"Dear God, how could I have forgotten," she wondered aloud. Michel felt alarm catch at him. There was something about her words and tone of voice that made him think that the happiness he had only just grasped was about to slip away. His hand tightened on her hip in reaction, as if he could physically hold on to his happiness.

"Forgotten what? What is it?"

Her eyes popped open and she peered at him

sadly, then shook her head. "Nothing. It does not matter," she assured him. "You need not offer for me, my lord."

Michel narrowed his eyes, feeling as if he had stepped into a roomful of cutthroats and couldn't be sure which would attack him first. How was he to react to her words? Was it best to proclaim his feelings and desire to be with her, or use a more pragmatic approach? As she began to turn away, he decided the pragmatic approach would carry more weight.

"Odel," he began carefully. "There is a good chance that what we just did may bear fruit."

Her eyes widened at that, then she suddenly struggled off of him and onto her feet. Bending, she picked up her gown and began to distractedly don it. Her voice was troubled when she finally spoke. "Aye. You are right, of course. But there is no need to panic. We should wait to see if—"

Michel was on his feet beside her at once. Grabbing her arm, he spun her around to face him. "I *do not wish* to wait. I wish to marry you."

Turning her head away, she avoided his eyes and sighed. "No, you don't. It is just a fleeting . . . fancy. It will pass," she assured him. "And then you shall be grateful we did not wed."

Michel felt his insides grow cold at those soft words. "You have no desire to marry me?"

"I have no desire to marry anyone," she said carefully.

"You mean to say you made love to me with no intention of—"

Odel shifted impatiently at that, cutting him off. "You sound like this was your first time. You were hardly a virgin, my lord. Pray, do not now act the outraged innocent."

Michel blinked at her accusation, drawing himself to his fullest height when he realized she was right. He had sounded just like . . . well, good lord! He had sounded like a bloody woman! Realizing he was becoming overwrought like a woman, too, he concentrated on calming himself. He watched her dress, then tried for a reasonable tone. "My lady—"

"Odel."

"Hmm?" he asked, knocked off track.

"I do think you might call me by my name after what we have just done, my lord," she pointed out.

"Oh, aye." He grimaced slightly, then politely answered, "And you must call me Michel."

"Thank you."

She was still sounding a touch sarcastic, he noted with displeasure, but restrained his temper once more. "Odel, I do not offer marriage lightly. In fact, this is the first time I have ever proposed. I want to marry you."

"No, you don't," she repeated, sounding quite firm on the point, which only managed to annoy him more.

"Pray, do not tell me what I do and do not want."

"Fine, then I will tell you this," she snapped,

stepping forward to poke him in the chest. "I have spent the last twenty-five years of my life under the thumb of a tyrant. I had to sleep when he said to sleep, eat when and what he ordered me to eat, and even wear, say, and think what he insisted I must. But that is *over* now. My father is dead and I will never willingly put myself under another man's thumb again."

She started to whirl away then, but he caught her back, his eyes burning into her. "You look at me and tell me that you really think that I am in any way like your father. You tell me that this is not just fear speaking and I will walk out that door and leave you be. Otherwise, I will be speaking to your aunt—"

"Nay!" Odel interrupted, then looked away. "I do not believe that. You are kind and gentle and you treat even your horse better than my father ever treated me, but—" She shook her head. "But none of that really matters, my lord." Her eyes holding a sad finality that was more concerning to Michel than her ridiculous outburst of a moment ago could have ever been, she said softly, "I know you think that you love me, but what you are feeling isn't real. You will wake up someday soon and find you do not want me. This is all magic. So, pray, just consider yourself lucky that I knew better than to accept you. Let it be. I will not marry you."

On that note, she turned and fled, leaving him staring after her.

"Here is where you have been hiding."

Odel turned from her window to peer at Matilda as she entered her bedchamber. "I am not hiding."

"Oh? It is nearly time for the nooning meal and you have not yet once shown your face below. What is that if not hiding?"

Odel shrugged and turned to peer out her window again.

Last night, she had hurried straight here after leaving the smithy's hut. The front doors had opened easily under her touch when she reached them, and Odel had suddenly known that the whole episode had most likely been more of Matilda's magic. Still, she had been beyond caring at that point. Weaving her way through the celebrating people, she had hurried above stairs to her room and cried herself to sleep. This morning she had woken up with the birds, changed out of her costume, and spent her time alternating between pacing and staring blindly out the window.

"I have just come from a discussion with Lord Suthtun," Tildy announced. "He is hiding it well, but he is quite distressed. He said that he asked you to marry him and you have refused. But he doesn't understand why."

"You should have explained it to him, then," Odel said bitterly.

"I would have, but I didn't know. It wasn't until he told me that you had said what he was feeling wasn't real that I understood why you had refused him. He left right afterward to check on Eadsele, however, so I came to talk to you."

"Lucky me." She sighed wearily.

"Odel," Matilda said firmly. "I told you this earlier, my dear, but obviously you did not believe me. I have used no magic on Lord Suthtun. His proposal was sincere. His feelings are true. He loves you."

"Nay." Odel didn't even bother to face her. "You used your magic to make him love me. Do not deny it."

"Oh, child. If it were that easy, I could have simply made you love whomever I wanted you to. That would have saved me a good deal of trouble, wouldn't it?"

Odel stiffened, then turned slowly to find the older woman nodding.

"It is true. And I told you this yesterday. Why will you not believe me?"

Odel was silent for a minute, then asked, "Can you swear to me that you used no magic on Lord Suthtun? Will you vow it before God?"

Matilda hesitated, then crossed her heart. "I have used no magic on Lord Suthtun."

"You are lying," Odel said unhappily. "Your hesitation gave you away."

"Oh, for heaven's sake!" Matilda cried, then moved to sit on the bed. She sighed. "All right, I may have used a little magic to make his horses tired, and perhaps to put the suggestion in his

mind that he should stop to rest here for the night.
I may also have had a hand in Eadsele's falling ill
to keep him here—"

"You made Eadsele sick?" Odel cried in horror.

"'Tis just a fever. He will be no worse for the
wear," she muttered, looking slightly ashamed.

Odel considered that briefly, then eyed her narrowly. "And that is it? You did not 'put a suggestion'
in Lord Suthtun's mind that he should love me?"

"Nay. I vow before God himself that I have done
nothing to determine Lord Suthtun's feelings for
you." She shifted impatiently. "I cannot influence
feelings, Odel. My magic will not do that."

"But the suitors," Odel murmured in confusion,
not sure whether to believe the woman now or not.
What she said made some sense. "They were . . ."

"The suitors," Matilda muttered irritably. "Of
course."

"Aye, of course. Now you're caught." Some of
Odel's uncertainty left her, replaced by bitterness.
"I am not so foolish as to believe that they would
all be so eager to marry me without some . . . *influence.*"

"Yes, well, I can see how that would confuse
you." Matilda peered down at the floor, then
cleared her throat. "You were right that there is
something amiss with them." She paused to clear
her throat again. "They are not human."

Odel wasn't sure what she had been expecting,
but it hadn't been that. "What?"

Matilda made a face. "Do you remember when you asked me if I had turned Lord Cheshire back into a man before he left? And I said not to fear, he left as he arrived?"

Odel nodded with bewilderment.

"Well, he left as a rat," Tildy admitted. Then, just in case Odel was misunderstanding what she was saying, she added, "He also arrived as a rat. All the lords who have filled Roswald these past two weeks—except for Lord Suthtun—were originally rats."

Odel stood gaping at the woman, picturing the men in question. She was recalling the way they had scrabbled so quickly up the trees. Then she remembered the odd way they had of eating and how she had thought it reminded her of something. Now she knew. *Rats.* She could actually picture them right now—eating. And as they ate they grew ears and whiskers. They were rats. All of them rats . . . And one of them, Cheshire, had—

"Oh, God," Odel breathed, her face paling and her eyes going round.

"What is it?" Matilda asked with concern.

"One of them kissed me!" she cried. She began scrubbing at her mouth a bit frantically. "Oh, yuck! Ick! Ptooey!"

Matilda rolled her eyes, but allowed her a moment of such behavior, then grabbed her hands impatiently to still them. "As I said," she repeated grimly, forcing Odel's attention back to her. "My dust cannot affect people—at least, not their choices. God gave man free will; he would hardly supply me with dust to take that away. I can change the inside of the castle, I can turn ducks into maids, and rats into love-struck men, but I cannot make you love someone, or make that someone love you."

Odel forgot about being kissed by a rat.

"Then, Michel—"

Matilda nodded. "Lord Suthtun loves you."

For a moment, joy suffused her face, then it was immediately replaced with regret. "Oh, no! What have I done?"

"Nothing that cannot be undone," Matilda assured her. Her godmother stood up, grabbed her hand, and dragged her toward the door. "Come with me."

"Where are we going?" Odel asked as she was led from the room and up the hall.

"You are going to straighten things out," Matilda announced firmly.

"But how?" Odel cried as they reached and started down the stairs. "What can I say? I thought my aunt had cast a spell on you? He will think me mad."

"You will come up with something," Tildy assured her, then paused at the bottom of the stairs. She glanced around before satisfaction crossed her face. "Look."

Odel followed her gesture to see Michel standing in the doorway to the kitchens, talking to a servant. No doubt he was arranging for something to be taken to Eadsele.

"Go to him," Matilda urged quietly, digging a small pinch of fairy dust out of her sack. She blew it in the general direction of Lord Suthtun. All at once, the doorway he was standing in was suddenly alive with mistletoe. "Kiss him. Tell him you love him. Make things right."

Odel hesitated briefly, then swallowed, straightened, and moved determinedly forward. She arrived at his side just as he finished with the servant. The girl retreated into the kitchen and Michel turned toward the great hall, pausing when he found Odel in his path. She saw pain flash across his face, then it was gone, replaced by a smooth, emotionless facade.

"Lady Roswald," he murmured formally. "Is there something you wished?"

"Aye," Odel said huskily. "You."

At his startled expression, she pointed upward. He glanced up, spotted the mistletoe, and his mouth tightened. She knew he was about to reject her, so she refused to give him the chance. Stepping forward determinedly, she reached up on tiptoe, catching his tunic and tugging him down to her. Their lips met.

It wasn't as easy as she had hoped. He did not melt into her embrace, did not take over the kiss and give his passion rein. Instead, he remained stiff and silent. Odel tried to coax some passion from him with her lips, but found it impossible.

Tears stinging her eyes, she drew back slightly. She whispered, "I was wrong, my lord. Last night . . . I was afraid. But now I am more afraid of losing you. Please, my lord. I love you."

Catching her upper arms, Michel eyed her warily. "So you will be my wife?"

"If you are sure it is what you want," she said huskily. A smile blossomed on his lips.

"Aye, I am sure," he told her quietly. "I love you, too."

Joy filling her face, Odel started to reach up on tiptoe again to kiss him, but he lowered his head, meeting her halfway. This time the kiss was mutual.

A cat's hiss and a rustle of rushes distracted Odel and Michel briefly from their kiss. They both glanced around in amazement as a pack of perhaps twenty rats fled through the open door of the keep and out into the cold winter day. Stranger, the long, thin cat that followed seemed less to be trying to catch them and more to be herding them away. *Vlaster.* It was a moment before Odel noticed that the great hall was decidedly empty of guests.

"Where did everyone go?" Michel asked with surprise when he saw where she was looking. He glanced toward Matilda.

"Who, dear?" the woman asked innocently, not seeming to notice the panic growing on Odel's face.

"Lords Beasley and Trenton and—"

"Oh, my, well. They saw the lay of the land and retreated," Odel's aunt said sweetly. She arched an eyebrow at them. "Is there something you two wish to tell me?"

Michel hesitated and glanced down at Odel, then smiled widely. "Aye. We shall be married tomorrow," he announced. He glanced down at Odel when she nudged him in the stomach. "What?"

"Tomorrow?" she asked pointedly.

"Aye," he said, then looked uncertain. "You will marry me tomorrow, will you not, Odel? I vow I shall work very hard to make you happy. I shall tell you you are beautiful every morning, brush your hair every night, and tend to you as kindly as I do my horse and my squire."

Odel burst out laughing at the proposal, then hugged him tightly. "I could not have asked for a more romantic offer, my lord. Aye, I shall marry you."

They had barely sealed the bargain with a kiss when Matilda released a husky sigh, then began bustling toward the door. "Well, that's that then. I am off."

"What?" Odel pulled slightly away from Michel. The woman had hounded her all this time to be wed, and now she wasn't even going to be present? "But tomorrow is Christmas. And I would like you to be there when we are married. Will you not stay for the wedding?"

"Oh." Her aunt's expression gentled. "I shall be

there, you may count on that. But in the meantime, I have much to do, my dear. Forty-nine to go, you know. Besides, you should spend Christmas with Lord Suthtun's family. And marry at Castle Suthtun as well. If you leave now, you should get there in time for the feast."

"But we could not leave Michel's squire. Aunt Matilda, you—"

"His squire is much better, I understand, and more than healthy enough to make the journey." The words had barely left her mouth when Michel's squire came bounding down the stairs, the very image of a healthy young lad. One could almost imagine he had never been ill.

"Are you really all right, boy?" Michel asked with a frown. The lad spotted him and hurried to his side.

"Aye, my lord," Eadsele said, then he shook his head in bewilderment. "Only moments ago I felt weak and feverish, then as suddenly as it came on, my illness was gone. I feel right as rain."

"There you are, you see?" Matilda called, gaily ignoring Odel's annoyed glance. She waved on the servants that came trundling down the stairs with Odel's baggage; apparently the woman had made them begin packing for her. "No reason at all for you to remain here alone through the holidays. Go on to Suthtun. His mother and sisters shall adore you, I promise. Why, by this time tomorrow you shall hardly recall me."

"Oh, but—" Odel began, but whatever protest she would have given faded from her mind in a fit of sneezing. There seemed to be dust everywhere. The door closed behind Matilda and the last of her servants. Turning with confusion, Odel peered at Suthtun.

Smiling, he pressed another quick kiss to her soft lips. "Come along. She is right. My mother and sisters shall adore you as much as I do."

Odel was silent for a moment, then she smiled slowly. "But no more than I adore you."

Laughing as Suthtun grabbed her hand, she ran with him toward the door and out into a whole new world.

Read on for a sneak peek
at a brand-new historical romance
from Lynsay Sands!

Hunting for a Highlander

Coming February 2020

Chapter One

"Whinnie! Whinnnnnie!"

Geordie Buchanan opened tired eyes as that call was followed by someone trying to make the sound of a horse whinnying. For a minute, he didn't know where he was. Early morning sunlight was streaming down at an angle that managed to reach him where he lay against the trunk of a tree, one of several he could see growing in rows in front and to the side of him. Seeing them, he remembered that he'd made his bed in the orchard behind the gardens when he'd returned last night. There hadn't seemed to be much choice; after weeks away he'd arrived back in the middle of the night to find Buchanan crowded with people. The great hall had been overflowing with sleeping servants and soldiers, as had the kitchen, but it was his uncle sleeping in a chair by the fire that had told him just how full the keep was. The man only slept in a chair below when he had to give up his bed to guests. Geordie had assumed that probably meant his own bed had been given to someone too.

"Whinnie!"

Geordie scowled at the annoying voice followed by another high-pitched attempt at a horse's whinny. He obviously wasn't going to get anymore sleep today. The keep was up and children were ready to play. He'd barely had the irritated thought when a young woman appeared halfway along the row of trees and turned her back to him to peer up into the branches. Geordie was just wondering if she was the person who had been calling out and whinnying, when the sound came again from somewhere to the left and farther away.

"Whinnnnny!"

The woman muttered what sounded suspiciously like a curse, and then bent down, reached under her skirts to grab the back hem of the long gown she wore, and then pulled it forward and up to tuck the cloth through the belt around her waist.

Geordie's eyes were widening at the tantalizing amount of shapely ankle and calf she was showing when she grasped the lowest branch of the tree and began to climb quite nimbly upward. She was quick about it, but had barely disappeared into the leafy haven the branches provided when two women appeared farther down the row of trees and glanced around.

Where the first woman hadn't noticed Geordie, these two did and sneered briefly as they took in the fact that he'd obviously slept out in the gardens. They didn't lower themselves to actually comment. Instead, they turned back the way they'd come and one said with annoyance, "She must have slipped past us and returned to the keep. Come on."

Geordie watched them go before shifting his gaze back to the tree. He fully expected the woman to climb back down now, but when several moments passed without any sign of her, he rolled out of his plaid, then shifted to his knees to begin pleating it. He obviously wasn't going to get anymore sleep today. Besides, he had a sneaking suspicion that the lass was like a cat and now that she was up the tree, she couldn't make her way back down. He'd give her the length of time it took him to get properly dressed again, and then offer his assistance . . . if she hadn't fallen out by that time.

DWYN LOOKED OUT through the branches of the tree she was in, and over the rolling hills beyond the back wall of Buchanan. It was a beautiful area, she acknowledged, but not as beautiful as Innes. There she would have had a view of the ocean, not to mention a sea breeze to soothe her jangled nerves. The thought made her grimace. Before this trip, Dwyn had never met a person she didn't like. The people at Innes were always kind and friendly, at least to her. But the women she'd met since coming to Buchanan . . . Well, other than Lady Buchanan herself, there wasn't one woman she liked. The other female guests here were a bunch of catty bampots, the lot of them, and they seemed to have decided to target her with their cruel taunts for some reason. The thought made her mouth twitch unhappily. Dwyn wasn't used to people not liking her, and wasn't sure what to do about it. These women were like no one she'd ever encountered. They were bored, and had chosen to entertain themselves by picking on her.

"Good morrow, lass."

Dwyn blinked at that greeting, and then leaned forward to peer down through the branches at the man who had spoken. He'd positioned himself right below her, and Dwyn's eyes widened as her gaze slid over him. He appeared big from this angle, all shoulders, but she couldn't tell how tall he was from her position. He was handsome though, his eyes a fine pale blue, his nose straight, his mouth having a larger lower lip than upper, and his hair was long and dark, with a bit of wave to it.

"Can I help ye down, lass?"

His words startled her out of gaping at him, and Dwyn shook her head. "Nay, thank ye."

"Nay?" He looked surprised at the refusal, and then frowned around at the orchard briefly, before tipping his head back to look up at her again. "Are ye sure, lass? I'm pleased to help ye, do ye need it."

"Nay. I'm fine. Thank ye," Dwyn murmured, and followed her refusal with lifting her head to gaze out past the wall again, hoping he'd take the hint and leave.

He didn't take the hint. Dwyn realized that when the branch she was on began to tremble a bit and she glanced down to see that the man was now climbing up. Her eyes widened incredulously, and then she sat back abruptly as he swung himself up onto the branch directly in front of the one she was on. It was actually a little lower than the large branch she was sitting on, but even so, Dwyn had to tilt her head back to look up at his face.

"Good morrow," he said again, offering her a smile. "Whinnie, is it?"

Dwyn had just started to smile in response when he asked that, and the expression died before it had fully formed. "Nay. My name is Dwyn."

"Oh. My apologies. I thought they were calling Whinnie."

"They were," she said grimly, but didn't explain, and silence fell between them briefly. Dwyn did her best to pretend he wasn't there then. Actually, she was mostly pretending she wasn't there either, but was back home at Innes, walking the shores with her dogs, Angus and Barra.

"Dwyn."

She turned reluctantly to peer at him.

"Who is yer clan?"

"Innes," she murmured, turning away again. "Me father is Baron James Innes."

"Innes is on the North Sea, is it no'?" he asked with interest.

"Aye, between the river Spey and the river Lossie. 'Tis beautiful lush green land," she added with a faint smile. "Innes is really situated on a large inlet off the North Sea called Moray Firth, and between that bordering it on the north, the Spey River on the west, and Lossie River on the east, but curving down around the bottom o' Innes, 'tis nearly an island."

"It sounds lovely," he admitted.

"'Tis," she assured him. "And as Da says, having the water nearly surrounding us aids greatly with defense. A good thing, since Da's more a thinker than a warrior. Which is why we're here, o' course. For all the good 'twill do."

His eyebrows rose at that. "I do no' understand. Just why are ye here at Buchanan?"

The question brought her gaze around with surprise, and then she scowled at the man. He'd seemed mostly nice up until that point. "There is no need to be cruel, sir. I ken I've no' a chance with all the other women here being so beautiful, but ye need no' point it out quite so boldly."

He seemed confused by her words and said, "I did no' realize I was being cruel. I've no idea why any o' ye are here."

She considered that briefly and then supposed it wasn't perhaps something that Laird Buchanan would talk openly about. Still, gossip usually traveled quickly in keeps, and she was surprised that he didn't know. Dwyn wished he did, though. It was all rather embarrassing to have to explain. But it looked like she was going to have to. Dwyn drew in a deep breath to begin, and then paused when the action made her breasts rise perilously in the low-cut gown her sisters had insisted she wear. Grimacing, she pressed a hand to the tops of the round mounds to keep them down as she quickly blurted, "The other women are here hoping to catch the eye of one of the still-single Buchanan brothers and lure them into marriage."

"What?" he barked, his eyes shifting swiftly up from her breasts to her face with disbelief.

There was no mistaking his reaction as anything but shock, she decided. He truly hadn't known the purpose of the visitors presently filling the Buchanan keep. Perhaps he was one of the soldiers who usually patrolled the Buchanan lands so didn't spend much time at the keep to hear the gossip.

"Surely ye jest?" he asked now.

Dwyn smiled wryly as she shook her head. "Nay. There are at least seven beautiful women presently wandering the keep and grounds, waiting for the three still-single brothers to return to Buchanan and select a bride."

"Seven?" he asked.

"And their escorts," she added. "Of course, a new woman or two seems to arrive every day so there may be eight or nine by the nooning, or sup."

When he just sat there seeming lost in thought, Dwyn left him to it and turned to peer out at the hills again. He obviously meant her no harm, and it was nice to talk to someone who was not nattering at her to sit up straight, and stick out her chest, or alternately pointing out her faults and making fun of her. Honestly, she'd never realized women could be so cruel until this trip.

"Why would these women seek out the brothers for marriage?"

Dwyn glanced around at that question, and noted that the man appeared completely flummoxed by the news she'd imparted. Shrugging, she said, "Presumably because they're all without a betrothed and their fathers wish to make an alliance with the Buchanans." She frowned and added, "Although, I do know at least one of the women *is* betrothed. Apparently, Laird Wallace is willing to break the contract in favor of a Buchanan son, should one of them be interested."

"Why?" he asked again, this time sounding even more amazed, and she could understand his shock at this news. It was uncommon to break a betrothal. The family would lose the dower that had been promised in the contract.

"Because the Buchanans are becoming quite powerful, what with the sons each marrying so advantageously. The siblings are all very close, and each now has their own castle and warriors." She shrugged. "What man wouldn't want to be a part of that and have that kind of power at his back?"

"Hmmm." He was silent for a minute, displeasure on his face, but then glanced at her and raised his eyebrows. "And yer one o' these seven beautiful women?"

Dwyn grinned with amusement. "Hardly."

That made his eyebrows rise in question. "Then why are ye here?"

Dwyn drew in another breath that nearly dislodged her breasts from her gown and covered her chest again with irritation. Holding them down with one hand, she tugged her neckline up with the other as she reluctantly admitted, "Well, that is why me father brought me. He has no sons to pass the title down to, and me own betrothed died ere coming to claim me. Father is hoping to make a match to help protect us from our neighbors the Brodies, who want to add Innes to their holdings, but . . ." Giving up on stuffing her breasts any farther back into the gown, she let her hands drop with disgruntlement as she finished, "I fear he will be disappointed. The Buchanans are no' likely to even notice me among so many beautiful women."

"Why?" he asked, but she didn't think he was really paying attention when he asked the question. His wide eyes seemed to be transfixed on her overflowing bosom.

Smiling wryly, she said, "Because I am overlarge and very plain in looks, sir." When he continued to stare at her chest, she added dryly, "'Tis why my sisters stuffed me into this ridiculously small gown. They are hoping that the Buchanans will be too busy ogling me breasts to bother to look at me face."

He wrenched his gaze up at that, his face flushing slightly, and murmured, "My apologies, me lady. It was no' well done o' me to—"

Dwyn waved his apology away on a sigh that had her nipples peeking up over the neckline, and she muttered impatiently and returned to trying to tame her breasts and force them back into her gown. Honestly, this was going to be an embarrassing stay if her breasts kept popping out like this. Fortunately, the dress she'd worn when she'd arrived here yesterday had not been quite as tight as this one and she hadn't been spilling out at every turn. Obviously, she needed to change when she returned to the keep.

"No need to apologize," Dwyn growled now, more annoyed than embarrassed. "This was my sisters' plan, after all, and it would seem it works. Perhaps one of the brothers will be so enamored of me breasts that they won't notice me face. Men do seem to like breasts," she added thoughtfully. "I think it must reassure them that their bairns will be well fed or something."

GEORDIE RESTRAINED THE laugh that wanted to slip out at her words. It wasn't a bairn he was imagining suckling at her nipples as he looked on them. Damn, but the Good Lord had been generous with her bosom. Shaking his head, he forced his gaze back to her face and examined her features.

Dwyn Innes was not a beauty. At least not an obvious beauty. She had a nice face, a straight little nose, a mouth that was neither full and luscious, nor small and mean, but somewhere in the middle, and her eyes too were neither too small nor large. They were perhaps average, but the color was a beautiful clear blue that actually seemed to sparkle when she was amused, he'd noticed.

And then there was her hair. Dwyn had it pulled back tightly from her face and set in a bun at the back of her head that was as overlarge as her breasts, but it was a beautiful pale gold with darker highlights that he would have liked to see down and flowing around her face. Geordie imagined that now, but in his mind she wasn't wearing the gown with its plunging neckline. Instead she was naked, lying in the grass below the tree with her long hair spread out around her lush body.

Geordie shifted uncomfortably on his branch as his body responded to that imagining, his cock now waking from rest and beginning to poke up at his plaid. Leaning forward slightly, he rested his arm across his lap to hide it and then stilled as he realized the pose placed his face closer to hers, just inches away in fact. Close enough to kiss, he thought suddenly, and then reached quickly for her when she jerked back in surprise and nearly tumbled backward off her branch.

"Careful, lass," Geordie warned, his voice coming out a husky growl. Releasing her once the risk of her falling passed, he straightened and suggested, "Mayhap we'd best climb down now."

"Aye," she agreed, her face a little flushed, and then without another word, she placed one tiny slippered foot on the branch next to his leg, braced one hand on the large branch she sat on, and began to push her bottom off of it.

"Dwyn!"

That shout from below startled both of them, but Dwyn physically started and he saw the way her eyes widened in alarm as her foot slipped from the branch and she began to fall. Geordie didn't even think, but leaned down and caught her about the waist, then dragged her back up and onto his lap. They both froze then, neither seeming to even breathe as another pair of females appeared under the tree and stopped to look around the orchard with obvious exasperation. They were both tall and pretty with dark hair and appealing features that were presently somewhat vexed.

"Oh, where has she got to now?" the lass in a pale pink gown muttered with irritation.

"No doubt, hiding," the second woman, dressed in a pale blue gown, responded on a sigh. "Ye ken how shy she is."

"Aye, well, she must work past that, Aileen, if she ever wishes to marry. Hiding is no' going to get her a husband."

"Oh, let her have some peace, Una," the lass named Aileen said wearily. "The single Buchanan brothers are no' here at the moment anyway, and we have harassed her enough what with taking in her gowns until she can hardly breathe, and constantly pinching her cheeks trying to give her some color. Besides, that bitch Lady Catriona and her friend Lady Sasha have both been tormenting our sister horribly. I do no' blame her for wanting a moment to herself."

"Aye," the lass named Una agreed grimly, and then growled, "They are calling her horse face now, did ye hear?"

"What?" Aileen said with dismay.

"Aye, and they have taken to taunting her by calling her Whinnie instead o' Dwyn too."

"I thought I heard them call her Whinnie, but then decided I just misheard and they were saying Dwynnie."

"Nay," Una assured her. "And they follow it up with whinnying sounds too. I'd like to scratch their nasty eyes out for picking at her."

"They are like she-wolves scenting the weakest in the herd, separating them, and then attacking," Aileen said sadly. "I wish Dwyn would fight back."

"She is too nice for that," Una said, somehow making nice sound quite disgusting. "And do no' even bother suggesting it to her. She'd just make us feel bad for being angry at them and say they were obviously unhappy to act so and needed our sympathy."

"Aye," Aileen agreed with a faint smile, following when Una moved away from the tree. "I swear she'd have sympathy for the devil did she meet him."

"Probably offer him tea," Una muttered as they disappeared from view and their voices began to grow fainter.

DWYN REMAINED COMPLETELY still at first as the voices faded away. She'd barely dared breathe once her sisters had appeared beneath them, but now that they were leaving, she realized she couldn't move anyway. Her back was pressed tight to the chest of her savior, the arm around her waist like a band of steel under her breasts, holding her in place . . . and pushing her breasts up out of her top again, she realized with dismay. There was more than a little nipple now on display in the oversmall gown, although Dwyn didn't think that had been the man's intent. She didn't even think he realized what was happening. Did he?

Dwyn turned her head and tipped it so that she could glance back at him. Much to her relief, his head was turned, his eyes pointed in the direction her sisters had taken as he waited to be sure they left. Just as she noted that, though, he glanced down toward her and then froze, the arm around her waist tightening briefly and sending her breasts farther out of her gown until the nipples were almost completely on display.

They both remained still for a moment. Dwyn was blushing fiercely and struggling to find something to say to ease her embarrassment, when he suddenly lowered his head and pressed his lips to hers. Dwyn stiffened in amazement as his mouth brushed over hers once, then twice. When he nipped at her lower lip, drawing on it and tugging gently, she opened for him. The moment her lips parted, he released the lower one and covered her mouth again with his. This time she felt his tongue slide out and Dwyn gasped with surprise as it snaked in to fill her mouth. That reaction melted away, replaced by a warm rush of excitement, though, as his mouth slanted over hers, his tongue thrusting and exploring.

Dwyn found herself responding, or trying to. She hadn't a clue what she was doing, and at first tried to keep her own tongue out of his way as her mouth moved under his, but he merely chased it. When his tongue rasped against her own, Dwyn moaned and stopped retreating to thrust back. Her hands came up then to clasp his arm under her breasts, her nails digging into his skin as she kissed back with all that she was worth.

This time it was him who moaned, and for a moment the kiss became most demanding and hungry. It was as if he was trying to devour her, Dwyn thought faintly and found she wasn't at all alarmed at the prospect. Tearing one hand from his arm, she reached up to slide her fingers around his neck, her body straining and twisting in his hold to press closer, and then he suddenly broke the kiss and lifted his head.

For a moment he just stared down at her, his

heated gaze sliding over her flushed face and then down over her exposed breasts. Dwyn followed his gaze, noting that the circles of dusky rose flesh had contracted and darkened around the small buds that had hardened and were now rising out of the center like flowers seeking the sun.

She'd just noted that when the man holding her abruptly shifted his hands, caught her by the waist, and turned Dwyn to set her on her branch again. The moment her bottom landed on the hard wood, he grabbed the front of her gown and tugged it up to cover her properly. He didn't let go of the cloth then though, but froze, still holding the material, the backs of his fingers warm against her nipples, which were responding most oddly to the unintentional touch.

Panting breathlessly, Dwyn stared at his dark hands against her pale flesh, and then he groaned, drawing her gaze up to see that he'd closed his eyes and appeared to be in some distress.

"I—Are ye all right?" she asked shakily, her gaze shifting from his pained expression to his fingers still inside her top and back. "Did ye hurt yerself lifting me? I know I am heavy. Did ye—" She paused, her own eyes widening slightly when his suddenly flashed open. He was looking at her like she was sweet meat and he hadn't eaten in days, Dwyn thought faintly, and then he abruptly removed his hands and was gone. She blinked at the empty branch in front of her, and then leaned forward and looked down in time to see him land lightly on his feet on the hard packed ground, snatch up a sack that lay against the trunk, and walk away.

Dwyn watched until he was out of sight and then sat back with a shaky sigh. Well, wasn't that . . . She shook her head slightly and reached up to press her fingers to her still-tingling lips. That had been . . .

"Oh, my," Dwyn breathed. She'd just had her first kiss, and it had been quite wonderful. At least, she'd thought so. She didn't think his walking off like that was a good sign though, and wondered what it meant. Perhaps she shouldn't have let him kiss her. Not that she'd had much choice, she assured herself. It had been somewhat unexpected, and her precarious position in his lap—

Oh, give over, her mind argued at once. She hadn't wanted to stop him, not once his tongue was in her mouth. Then she'd wanted him to continue to kiss her, and still did, she acknowledged with a grimace. Truly, she wished he was still there, holding her in his lap, his mouth moving on hers, his arms around her. But she wished he'd done more. She wasn't sure what, exactly, but . . . Her hands rose and closed over her breasts almost protectively. They had tingled and hardened as he'd kissed her and were oddly sensitive now, the brush of her palms over them even through the material of her gown making them tingle all the more.

Lowering her hands quickly, Dwyn turned to peer out over the land beyond the wall and tried not to think about the odd sensations now swirling through her body. Or who the man might be. And whether he might repeat the experience should they encounter each other again while she was here.